ALIEN
CONNECTION

A.J. HOUSTON

ISBN
978-1-956529-74-6 (Paperback)
978-1-956529-73-9 (eBook)

Contents

Chapter 1

Antarctica

In a spiral arm of a galaxy known by some as the Milky Way, lay a solar system. This star system was a relative newcomer to the galactic stage, having been born of a 'stellar nursery' ten billion years after the 'big bang'. So, when a sentient space-faring species arose from the womb of one of its planets, there were many other space-faring species already out there waiting to greet them. This should have come as no surprise to these newcomers, though, of course, it did anyway. Thirty years before this story takes place, formal contact was finally made between the Earth Alliance government and the local representatives of the Inter-Stellar Union of Planets. Though Earth ships had navigated this system for centuries, the Earthlings had yet to achieve faster than light (FTL) travel. However, they HAD developed faster than light communications, which was enough progress to prompt the Union to initiate first contact.

The southern continent of the blue third planet of this solar system, known as Antarctica to the locals, was divided in two by the Transantarctic Mountains, which cause the peninsula between the Ross and Weddell Seas . The ice shelf on this land mass was formidable, over 1.5 kilometers in average depth, and if it all melted this world's oceans would rise approximately 65 meters. On the land neck nearest to South America, in a section known as Palmer Land, which abuts the Larsen Ice Shelf, was established an unmanned European-American scientific outpost. To this remote location was dispatched an electrical engineer, Arthur Barthol (pronounced 'bart-ol'), a mid-sized Caucasian of Canadian-British heritage, to conduct the installation of a communication systems upgrade at this isolated research sub-station.

Arthur was looking at a specification document about Baird's Antarctic Research Centre. He noted that the complex obtained its electricity from wind turbines perched on a ridge 3 kilometers north-east of the site. I can see that they use the latest technology to generate electricity, he thought, using the power to break down water into oxygen and hydrogen; what a gas, the hydrogen can be re-burned for heating or re-combined with the oxygen to generate electricity when needed. He looked further down the page and observed that electricity was also produced from geothermal circulators drilled through the rock base. So Baird's isn't just reliant on one energy source, he observed to himself.

Arthur, who had a medium build, short brown hair, blue eyes and a jutting chin, arrived via his versatile private shuttle, 'Kotik' (pronounced 'koh-tick'), a few days prior to the start of this tale. He sat back and spoke aloud, "Kotik, do you think you can handle this cold?"

"What do you mean?" replied his shuttle, "I'm a Pantheon VariPulse model, their most popular workhorse vehicle for both terrestrial and space-based travel. If I can handle space, why couldn't I handle Antarctica?"

"Just kidding, buddy!" replied Arthur. He called up a picture of Kotik on his porto-puter. I just love this ship, he thought, look at it, a beautiful light yellow, 5 by 25 meter long tube. I picked her up for peanuts in the last recession, he continued, what a ringer, with three aft thruster engines, an aft starboard-side cargo door, a forward port-side cockpit hatch, bow thrusters and all sorts of other electronic paraphernalia, Kotik even sprouts small wings for air flight, it's like home away from home!

Come to think of it, Arthur thought to himself, my two robo–mechanics, NPK1 and NPK2, were also steals, they're two of Hughes Aeronautics best models and sharp as tacks, they sit in Kotik's cargo bay ready for duty at a moment's notice. Noticing that time was running short, he put the spec doc down and continued to prepare for the job ahead.

Arthur had unpacked his gear and stood in the middle of the research centre analysing the electrical grid and relays. He was bent over an electrometer, dressed in a red flannel thermal suite, when he was contacted via holophone by his partner, Chas Lobring. Chas (pronounced 'chaz'), a negro, was dressed in brown fake-fur Zulu robes, his off-hour favorite. He was a proficient electrical engineer, like Arthur. A tall man, with a loud laugh and a burgeoning family, he seemed satisfied with his life. Arthur slid into a comfortable foldout chair in the substation's main centre.

"Hi Art, how are the penguins treating you?" laughed Chas.

"Just fine, Chas, I'm meeting three penguin technical analysts for a drink at the Igloo Tavern right after my shift. I'll keep you apprised of my cross-species studies on their socialization customs," chuckled Arthur.

"Speaking about cross-species activities, Art, we've just been contacted about an outland top-secret gig in the far reaches. Is your encryption holoscramble activated?" Chas got serious very quickly, as a furrow formed on his brow.

Arthur verified the activation of his holo-security protocols in silence as the image of Chas waited patiently in the middle of the room. Finally Arthur settled back into his fold-out chair and nodded readiness to his partner.

"I'm now hop-mailing you some general information on this gig. We have not been provided with all the details for security reasons. You know how we've done a series of diplomatic installations and upgrades for the Earth Alliance offices in North America over the past couple of years, Art?"

"Yes, how couldn't I remember installing communication software in all those consulates? Fairly standard stuff, except for the security hardware and software. Those assignments paid pretty well, from what I recall."

"Well, Artie my boy, they liked our work so much that they've come back for more! Only this time there's a real twist to the contract, are you ready for this? It's at the outer reaches of the Alliance 's installations. Guess where?"

"You've got me there, Chas. The Alliance hasn't colonized the Saturn region yet, except with robot probes, and Mercury is too hot for much useful stuff, so that leaves Jupiter, that would be my guess."

"Very insightful, my soothsaying partner! So the next question is, what interest does the Earth Alliance have in a tiny mining colony on the rim of human existence? Doesn't that seem odd to you?"

"Come to think of it, it does seem a bit odd since the Alliance only opens trade embassies and diplomatic consulates when more than one Earth nation may be involved in activities there. Only the larger colonies merit an embassy. So what gives, my esteemed colleague?" Arthur's interest was peaking as the conversation developed.

"Well, my friend, you won't believe what is falling into our proverbial lap. Do you remember the highly publicized 'initial contact' the Alliance made with the extra-terrestrial Regional Council several decades ago?"

"Why, of course, but there hasn't been much news on that lately since the aliens made it clear that we wouldn't be considered for membership, even associate membership, until we've achieved FTL travel, which we still haven't got much of a clue about yet. So the whole thing kind of died down since they won't give us any new technology. We have to figure it out for ourselves. So what do they want now?" Arthur asked, a bit perplexed.

"It appears that the Regional Council of the Inter-Stellar Union of Planets wants to take the next step. Perhaps they think we're about to step out of our nappies. Anyway, they want to establish a space station in a remote location to begin trade and diplomatic relations with groups further down the pecking order than the bureaucrats at the Alliance HQ. Since the location is so remote, only those with the best technology could get out there, and the small number of visitors would be easy to monitor, since there are security concerns, at least from the Alliance standpoint." Chas seemed to have a clear understanding on this matter.

"It would seem that Earth has security issues both internal and external. These aliens are so far advanced from our Mickey-Mouse spaceware that if they decided to do a number on us we wouldn't stand a chance. However, ISUP has never explained the persistent UFO appearances on Earth, nor the abduction problem." Arthur quickly sat up. "So, Chas, they want us to install diplomatic communications electronics on an alien space station orbiting Jupiter?"

"Close, Artie, and you get a cigar! The space station would be Alliance built, owned and operated, with the aliens opening diplomatic and trade missions that our national governments and corporations can communicate with. The TJ09X space station project, affectionately nick-named 'X-Station', is already orbiting Ganymede. So the Alliance wants us to install their electronics at their trade embassy and diplomatic consulate there. Also, Earth trade cartels will want to open missions as soon as they catch wind of the opportunity. Imagine having access to alien technology, what a competitive advantage that would be?" Chas was excited by the possibilities.

"But Chas, they've already told us that they won't give us anything that is ahead of our time, so the technology will not be all that great. Probably beads and baubles to them, like the Europeans did to the aboriginals world-wide back in the mid-times."

"Still, Art, the novelty factor would make for great marketing angles anywhere in the Alliance, don't you think?"

"I suppose. Probably the real news is that the aliens are willing to take the next, more public step with us. That probably is good news." Arthur became thoughtful and got up from his chair to pace.

"I'll send you the spec's in the heaviest encryption that we've got. Be sure to delete them once you've reviewed, you'll get the full package when you return from the 'fridge'."

"Remember to negotiate isolation and danger pay for this excursion. At what stage is the space-station construction?"

"It's near the completion of the infrastructure, and the habitation assemblies are already eighty percent complete, that's why the wiring is almost ready to go, though I think there's flexibility in our timelines. What do you have in mind?" Chas leaned forward to hear inquisitively.

"Well, why not get some gigs on the way out there? There's no direct flights to Ganymede, so why not make some money at as many of the pit stops along the way that we can? Negotiating those mini-jobs should keep you busy while I finish here and give me extra time back home in Toronto with the family."

"Capital idea, old chap!" Chas sometimes got a thrill out of mocking British accents and clichés.

"Okay, Chas, I'll look forward to your hopmail and I'll give the penguins your regards. Barthol out."

"See you later, buddy" Chas grinned goodbye.

Arthur leaned over and pressed the comm button off and Chas's holo image quickly faded away. Certainly a lot of information to digest in short order, he thought, and he wondered what Olga was going to say when he arrived home.

After unpacking all of his gear and making himself comfortable for the evening, Arthur prepared his meal in Kotik's galley. Although Baird Substation had a kitchen, it was just a rudimentary outlay, for survivalists only. He preferred the more advanced culinary technology in his shuttle's kitchen. Arthur next took a quick visit to the latrine and then stretched out on his bunk. He instructed his porto-puter to project the X-Station schematics overhead, retrieved from Chas's hopmail which had just arrived.

The station had a standard configuration as far as Alliance stations go. It was designed as a flat grid that housed the habitation units, with cubical struts that provided structural support. Ships could dock at extendible columns at each joint in the flat habitation grid. The grid formed a series of spokes whose corridors housed any number of rental spaces, which would be constructed to the client's taste and budget. There was also a web of exterior fenders to deflect wayward spacecraft. Spokes two and three were where Arthur's company, CommTrac, would be conducting its work.

The electronics equipment would be quartered in the Alliance consulate offices, then wiring had to be pulled through out-portals to the transmitter/receiver beacons that were to be secured to the stabilizer struts that ran along the exterior of the station grid.

The most dangerous part of the job would be installing and wiring the transmitter/receiver beacons, Arthur thought as he turned off the holo-projection and rolled over on his bunk. Not much different than other jobs that CommTrac has done, and the bots will have to be at their sharpest, but it's 'no big whoop' as they say. And with that thought, he faded off into a fitful Antarctic slumber, with a few satisfied snores along the way.

Early the next morning Arthur awakened at 6:00 a.m. to the pop-jazz ringtone of his alarm clock. He distantly remembered, as he reached to turn the alarm off, that he had downloaded the ringtone for one and a half credits from the shuffle-hopsite 'Hoptunes' when last in Toronto . He climbed out of his bunk, dressed in his silver silk pajamas and bounced into Kotik's shower. After breakfast he got busy with fine tuning the diagnostic equipment. CommTrac had been hired to upgrade the communications equipment at Baird and to inspect, and replace where necessary, the electrical generation infrastructure which had been knocked out several times during the past couple of years.

Arthur, now dressed in his thermal green work overalls with lots of utility pockets, walked through Kotik's lone corridor to the aft cargo bay to review his mechanics, NPK1 and NPK2, nicknamed 'K1' and 'K2'. Each robot was two meters long, a meter high and wide and had a blue hull with light blue racing stripes. Each had two retractable white plated heads, one at either end, each head containing four red rotary eyes. This model had four extendible arms, a set of two at each end. Each had the latest electronic diagnostic sub-routines and was equipped with anti-gravity plating and two light-duty impulse engines, one at each end.

Arthur ran the diagnostic sub-routines on K1 and K2, which both returned a 'system ready' status. He hopped onto K1 and tested the anti-gravity plating, which, when polarized, caused the unit to float. He tested the impulse engines to go up and down and side to side, which was a bit tricky given the cramped quarters in Kotik's cargo hold. There were a few dings on the walls where his test rides had previously run afoul.

After completing his tests on the bots, Arthur returned to the main laboratory in the Baird dome. While reviewing the sub-station electrical schematics he noted a weather warning blinking on one of the station consoles. He made a mental note of the weather instability and continued with his electrical analysis.

The computer diagnostic analysis took several hours, which gave Arthur time to take a cat-nap on the couch in the Baird laboratory. An hour later he was awakened by a distant banging sound against the side of the dome. He jumped up and ran to the east window and was faced with a white wall. A blizzard had engulfed the station and it sounded like some siding had come loose in the screaming winds. Not thinking anything much was amiss, Arthur headed to Kotik to sleep off the storm. The wind continued to howl outside.

Arthur awakened again, this time to a louder banging noise. The mini-console on the bunk cabin desk had a flashing red message, indicating something was wrong. He donned his green overalls and then walked through the connector tube from Kotik's hatch to the station and noticed a significant temperature drop as he opened the station door. A frigid breeze was circulating within the laboratory.

Arthur scratched his head and looked out the main window to northeast where the wind and snow still created a wall of white. He felt a bit woozy from waking up. He decided to have a conversation with the BairdMain computer.

"BairdMain, what are the capabilities of your maintenance bots? Do they have gravity plating that permits reverse polarity?" Reverse polarity permitted the increase in virtual mass, magnifying the weight of the machine, the reverse of weightlessness.

"Affirmative. Bot LT7, a Pantheon maintenance model 27, has this capability. It has snow treads on six wheels with standard reverse polarity gravity pods."

"What about its extendible arms, what are their tensile strength?"

"LT7 has extendible arms of up to ten meters with a tensile strength able to resist twenty g's." This is suitable for these conditions, thought Arthur, since Antarctic winds rarely got above a g-force of two. The next question was where, and to what extent, the damage was on the outer hull.

"BairdMain, where is the location of the breach on the outer wall?"

"I can best show you on-screen, Mr. Barthol." BairdMain had a slightly nasal voice, probably a quirk left by the original programmer of the voice module, who had sought to spice up his product on a boring drizzly day at some BIM progshop warehouse in a backwoods New England suburb.

"Fine, proceed with projection," responded Arthur.

BairdMain displayed dome diagramatics in the bottom left quadrant of the main screen, with three angular exterior camera shots of the damaged area filling the other three quadrants. The snow was blowing diagonally across the screens, however the cameras clearly showed a gaping hole of approximately one and a half meters. Arthur wanted a closer look.

"BairdMain, please zoom camera 1." The camera shot zoomed in on the downwind side of the hole. Arthur stepped closer to the screen, leaned forward and saw what he feared, that the siding was only being held in place by a couple of grommets. If those were to come loose, the siding would likely peel back another meter or more. No time to waste, Arthur concluded.

"BairdMain, equip LT7 with your standard welding kit and a five meter roll of carbon fibre siding, which I assume that you have in stock."

"LT7 has this configuration. It will be dispatched within the quarter hour. What are your instructions, Mr. Barthol?"

"I'll type the instructions into the console," Arthur replied. Then he sat at the console and assembled the instruction set.

Arthur pressed enter, then looked at the screen as BairdMain flashed acknowledgement.

"How does the instruction set compute, BairdMain?" Arthur asked his computer friend.

"It computes well, Mr. Barthol. Will proceed immediately," the computer replied.

"One point of note, BairdMain, please ensure that LT7 carries sufficient supplies for insulation and electrical repairs," Arthur added.

"Will do."

"Please keep me updated on the status as LT7 proceeds. Also, please send me status reports on the rest of the station's systems starting immediately, then every three hours and whenever any change of a noteworthy nature occurs," Arthur requested.

"Will do, Mr. Barthol. LT7 has been outfitted with tractor treads and is in the process of loading equipment and supplies. It will be pulling a trailer with the extra load. It should be ready for deployment within five minutes."

"Very good, BairdMain. Talk to you soon. Barthol logging off."

Arthur proceeded from the lab, back through the main station corridor to the outer door, through the connector gangway tube to the shuttle hatch and escaped to Kotik's warmth. In Kotik's readyroom, just aft of the cockpit, he sat at a computer workstation and read BairdMain's first status report. The electrical damage in the hole was minor and should be repairable by LT7. The carbon fiber siding was easily repairable. He looked further down the status list and saw that the wind turbine cabling had been disconnected and probably damaged at the foot of at least one of the windmills. This would need to be repaired before departure and would add extra billable items and time to this gig's invoice.

Arthur walked to the rear of the storage chamber for a quick workout in Kotik's makeshift gym. He then grabbed a breakfast in the galley. The smell of fried eggs and coffee filled the room. He then took his statutory bathroom break, including brushing his teeth, other latrine functions and having an invigorating shower. By the time he dried himself off and donned his red utility suit, BairdMain had reported that LT7 had removed the flapping siding, cleared the hole and was now in the process of splicing patches into the breached electrical cables. The estimated time of completion was two hours. Wind speeds had lowered to fifty knots and it appeared that the storm was abating.

Arthur then went back into the substation and began the installation of the communications hardware and software. While Arthur was installing the new interior comm cabling, LT7 completed its repair job and the station started to return to normal temperatures. The bot trudged diligently back to its maintenance shed after the repairs are complete. Later, BairdMain verbally reported that the bot had successfully undergone its maintenance checkup and then had gone back into hibernation.

LT7 saved me from having to go out into that icebox and freeze my ass off, thought Arthur as he grunted from getting up from under the lab console table. I'll have to wait for the wind to die down before installing the comm beacon and repairing the windmill cabling, he added.

Arthur returned to Kotik and logged into his hopmail. Olga and the children had sent their greetings and a holovid of the kids' musical recital. Hank, a six year old with brown wavy hair, played the guitar and Katya, a blond eight year old, played the flute. The holovid showed quite good details as Arthur leaned back and felt the joy of crescendos and the pain of sour notes. Katya played elegantly until she ran out of breath, though she regained her style immediately after a lung refill. Hank played single note lead guitar, strumming up a storm until he got a hand cramp and needed to take a short break before continuing his rendition of the StarTrooper mega-hit 'Asteroid Lover'. Olga and the children closed by sending their love. Olga mentioned that she'd send a separate hopmail, probably containing her musings about schools and politics, common topics of marital conversations.

I remember my own musical recitals when Mom and Dad would be sitting in the stands while I played Bach, Arthur thought, I was only an average player, but I enjoyed the sound of a well played composition on a well tuned piano. They encouraged me and paid for extended lessons during my teens. That gave me an appreciation of music and culture, though my sister insists that I'm still an uncouth barbarian. It's good giving them the occasional call on the vidweb to catch up on family happenings.

Arthur then surfed to the global hopweb to see the latest news. There was an article on a robot servant that went berserk and flattened a garden it was maintaining before its owner could de-activate it. This incident of course caused the regular robot critics to emerge from the woodwork with cries about robots stealing jobs, being unreliable and in this case dangerous. Robots had become common-place as household servants during the past two centuries and had displaced humans in most high tech manufacturing blue collar jobs. They had become as reliable as elevators, which rarely breakdown. However, criminal elements had been known to reprogram bots to pull bank jobs and hi-tech heists, which left bot security issues open to ongoing debate.

Funny, Arthur reflected, I feel safer with my bots than with most people. They may be my best friends outside my family, I guess some aren't so lucky, he mused.

Arthur started to get bored with reading the news. His head began to fog up with information overload and he decided to logoff the hopweb after reading another article.

Well, solved enough of the world's problems for one day, he quipped to himself before heading to Kotik's galley for refreshments.

The next day the wind had died and Arthur readied his bots for the two tasks at hand. K1 and K2 were equipped with the cabling, cable fasteners and the beacon for the morning job. Arthur then opened the cargo bay by remote control and rode K1 out into the frigid, calm air. He was wearing a white snow suit and his visor helmet. No skin was exposed to the minus twenty-five Celsius temperatures. K1 rose through the hatch door, its rear impulse engines purring, with K2 following closely behind. Arthur verbally instructed K1 to take him for a quick ride around the station from a hundred meters up, while directing K2 to proceed to the west wall of the station dome to await his return.

K1 hummed as it banked a spiraling two hundred meter turn around Baird station, coming to a stop at an altitude of a hundred meters. Arthur was a little dizzy from the height initially and was glad that his yellow lifeline was securely latched to the safety ring on the bot's small foredeck. From his perch he could view the beige station clearly below, with the fifty meter wide dome on the right and the rectangular green maintenance shed to the west on his left. Further to the left was the black scaffolding of the communications tower where they would have to replace the comm beacon. The sun shone brilliantly in the east on this chilly day and created silhouettes out of the four white wind turbines mounted on fifty meter towers perched on the ridge three kilometers to the northeast. That would be their second destination this afternoon.

"Down to the west wall of the dome, please K1," Arthur requested.

"Yessir, capt'n," replied K1 whose personality subroutines enjoyed some camaraderie.

"You don't want to keep your brother bot waiting, now do you?" Arthur jested.

"Capt'n, you know that I'm in constant wireless communication with K2, so whose thrusters are you pulling?" K1 asked.

"Just wanted to test your alertness, my mechanical friend." Arthur laughed.

K1's route formed an arc down to the dome's west wall and landed next to K2 which awaited them patiently. Arthur dismounted and asked K2 for the cabling connector for the dome's communication junction box. One of K2's extendible arms pulled the connector out of a storage compartment in its torso and handed it to him.

"K2, please hand me the end of the cable, and I hope you're having a good day since you haven't said a thing all morning. You're not jealous that I rode K1 up for a look at the mountains, now are you?" Arthur liked poking fun at his bots.

"Mr. Barthol, you'all know that my personality subroutines are incapable of jealousy! I'm a loy-aall servant of CommTrac and yourself, sir, and am always happy to be doing whatever best serves your cause, be that of a commercial or sight-seeing nature,"

K2 used a fake southern American drawl that made Arthur break out in laughter.

"Okay, my Confederate comrade, please hand me the comm cable."

K2 reached into another compartment in his torso and delivered a strand of two centimeter width cable which Arthur took into his right hand. Then he hooked up the cable with the exterior junction box on the dome wall.

Arthur felt dampness forming on his back and arm pits. Ahh, the sweat of hard work, he thought, enjoying the activity.

"K1, please fasten the cable to the granite bedrock with standard arctic safety clip fasteners while K2 and I go to the beacon." Arthur's tone suggested that the fun time was over, so K1 didn't respond verbally, but instead extended his aft head module and flashed a green acknowledgement light before retracting his head again.

Arthur climbed aboard K2 which then rose and headed west to the beacon tower at a speed of two knots. Once at the beacon tower, Arthur then got K2 to clip the cable to the tower at quarter meter intervals as they rose up its height. At the peak, he dislodged the old beacon, retrieved the new beacon from one of K2's storage compartments, and mounted it where the old beacon sat, all with K2's assistance, of course. Then he got K2 to leave him at the west wall entrance to the dome.

Using thought commands through his helmet, Arthur instructed K1 and K2 to complete the extraction of the old comm cabling and then return to the cargo bay when they were finished. The old wiring and beacon were to be placed in the waste recycle bin in the cargo hold, as per standard environmental procedures. Both bots flashed acknowledgement, visible on his visor screen. Arthur walked into the dome, closing the outer hatch before opening the inner door into the dome lobby area. Back inside Kotik he decided to take a quick nap before lunch.

The main job is complete; I hope that the windmill gig can be completed before dusk, he thought as he stretched out on his bunk.

A buzzing sound came from the console in the bunk room awakening Arthur an hour later. He rubbed his eyes, then got up and went over to the computer screen and saw K1 and K2 simultaneously flashing reminder requests.

"Okay, boys, I get the hint. We have to get started shortly or we'll run behind my bio-schedule. Have you tested the comm relays to the new beacon and sent a test message to the Falkland Islands?"

"Yes, Capt'n, we've completed the old cable extraction, done the configuration tests and sent a test message to the Falklands which has responded affirmatively," K1 replied, with K2 flashing support.

"Well done, my mechanical buddies! I'll make sure that you get the highest grade of lubricants at your next servicing!" Arthur liked to pretend-reward his bots. "I'm just going to grab a bite to eat, then we'll head out to the windmills. Please run your self-diagnostics and load the gear for the next gig. I'll be out in twenty minutes."

"We'll be ready, boss," quipped K2.

Arthur quickly prepared a soya burger at the galley food station, savoring the smell, and then, after sealing his snowsuit, he donned his helmet and headed to the aft cargo bay. He hopped onto K1 and saw on his helmet's visor that the bots had indeed passed their checkups, were fully supplied and ready to launch. Arthur ensured that his yellow safety line was attached to K1's torso, ordered Kotik to open the cargo bay door and transmitted the order to launch to both bots via a mental command through his helmet. K2 followed as K1 slowly rose out of the cargo hatch. Bright sunshine struck them as they turned to the east to pass around the south side of the dome. The convoy then headed northeast to the ridge.

The air was cold and fresh, invigorating every breath. Arthur could see the ridge as it rose in front of them out of the white horizon. The day was very bright and the sun had reached midday, so that it shone from due north. The windmills looked in order, however as they got closer he could see that the cabling midway up turbine two was dangling freely. He ordered K1 to pull up even with the cabling and started examining the fasteners to the tower.

In the process of leaning over, Arthur tried to pull one of the fasteners free. It came free more quickly than he expected and he lost his balance, falling backward onto K1's torso. Then he slid further back and fell off the robot's near side. As he was dangling, his vision telescoped to the rocks below, bringing chills of fear running up his spine. His safety line only let him drop a meter, but this tipped K1's balance. K1 had to fire its thrusters to stabilize its centre of gravity, forming an arcing curve downwards in the process. K1 shortly steadied itself, however, and then extended its forward set of arms to secure Arthur, drawing him back up to the saddle on its back. Arthur was shaking as he scrambled back atop his robo-steed. K1 then climbed back to the original level on the tower.

By the time he was back in his seat, Arthur was laughing nervously. "Thanks for s-saving my butt again, buddy. I'll have to take more balancing lessons when we get back to hogtown."

"You're welcome, capt'n. Do you want me to secure the cabling?" K1 responded.

"Y-yes, that would be useful," Arthur paused to catch his breath. "K2, could you check the turbines and cabling starting with windmill four?"

"Yessirree, boss. I'll get right to it," chirped K2, happy to be getting down to the job at hand, in the bot form of 'happy' that is, and hummed out to the far windmill.

As he sat atop K1, Arthur reminisced. *I remember being caught by Dad as I fell from a tree as a young boy,* he thought, *the fear I felt just now was just like then, I was grateful for Dad's* quick reflexes and strong arms, just as now I'm grateful for K1's quick and adept response.

During their two hour windmill inspection, two turbines needed some bolts tightened and three cables needed to be refastened. Other than the acrobatics, nothing unusual happened on their maintenance run. The three returned to the dome around seventeen-fifteen in time for dinner.

Back inside Kotik, Arthur checked that BairdMain had fully re-verified the electrical conduction from the windmills. Then he spent a few hours on the hopweb before retiring for the night.

Boy, I'm glad to be leaving penguin land, Arthur thought, I will be very happy to see the family again, though that reunion will likely be the last one for a long while.

The next morning, Arthur awakened to the alarm buzzes of his bots again. He slid out of bed, slipped on blue coveralls and treaded to the galley for breakfast.

"Kotik, how is the weather from here to Toronto?"

"Twelve degrees C and sunny. Looks good, boss. We'll fly up the eastern seaboard of South America so that we don't have to get special land-crossing permits from any of the locals, as you instructed, unless you've changed your plans?" Kotik's computer asked, in an intelligent male voice.

"No changes. Avoiding local land airspace saves us on visa fees, so we'll stick to the open Atlantic. You've done your routine safety diagnostics, no?"

"Affirmative, boss. We're ready anytime you like. The batteries are fully charged, backup fuel cells are full, all systems are green to go. We could fly to the moon and back twice without any problems."

"Great, get ready for liftoff in ten minutes. Disconnect from the dome and close off connections with BairdMain. You know the routine, file the flight plan with the Alliance aero centre, etc.," Arthur said.

"Will get right on it boss!" Kotik replied. Of course, the computer knew what to do and only needed the command of when to disengage and launch, however it seemed to enjoy the conversation anyway.

The ten minutes passed. Arthur strapped himself into the cockpit pilot's seat and Kotik lifted slowly away from Baird's dome. He opened a comm link to BairdMain and said farewell as Kotik gathered speed and headed northeast, rising over the Transantarctic Mountains, crossing the ice shelf out to the open blue ocean. The sun shone from the East through the shuttle's front windows as he felt a bit of nostalgia about the visit, wondering when he'd see the South Polar Region again.

CHAPTER 2

Toronto

"Come back with that, Hank!" Katya's squeal preceded the door swishing open as her brother came rushing into the living room with her in close pursuit. In his upraised left hand was a cartridge from the children's mobile holo-theatre unit which Katya had been enjoying before being rudely interrupted by its extraction.

"You are a nasty little tyrant, Henry!" Katya asserted in an elevated, somewhat breathless tone as she continued to chase Hank amongst the furniture.

"You shouldn't be using the theater all afternoon, Katey!" Hank blurted out while dodging between the coffee table and the couch. This scene was further complicated by Ralph, the chrome robo-dog, joining in the melee barking and jumping up at Hank, slowing him down to the point that Katya could tackle her little brother. All three end up in a writhing heap as Arthur regained full consciousness from a deep sleep on the couch, sitting up abruptly in his grey track suit.

"Whoa, there, break it up before something gets busted!" Arthur said as Katya climbed off Hank after grabbing the holo-cartridge from his grasp. Ralph barked repeatedly while licking Hank's face, which caused the boy to squirm.

"Hank stole this from me while I was minding my own business playing with the holo-theatre," complained Katya as she tried to straighten her blond curls with her free hand. She was dressed in a bright yellow dress with white stockings and black shoes.

"She's been using it for hours and I want to play 'Sundancer'!" howled Hank, just after shedding Ralph. He was wearing a light blue sweater, dark blue pants and white running shoes.

"Okay. First, Hank, you know that it's not right to steal someone's cartridge while they are playing." Hank guiltily nodded at Arthur's assertion. "So, what punishment do you think is correct for this crime?" Hank scratched his head, in deep thought as to what his sentence should be.

"Twenty-five sit-ups?" Hank estimated.

"All right, young man, get to it," Arthur ordered. The boy found space on the living room floor to start his exercises, watched in fascination by Ralph.

"Now for you, young lady. When did you start using the holo-theatre?" Arthur turned to Katya, who stood relishing Hank's punishment.

"Oh, daddy, I just looove playing 'Suzie at the Thrill Park'. I must have lost track of time..." Katya didn't acknowledge any guilt on her cute, innocent eight year old face.

"Now, losing track of time isn't a valid reason for going over your time limit. Those games can turn your brain to mush. How often have your mother and I told you not to spend more than an hour day using the portable holo?" Arthur brushed aside Katya's innocent girl act.

"Daddy, I just lost track of time!" objected Katya.

"So, my dear, what do you think is an appropriate punishment for this infraction?" Arthur asked, peering into his daughter's eyes.

"Twelve sit-ups?" Katya asked, looking innocently again into her father's face.

"Twenty-five, now snap to it, and give me that holo-cartridge." Arthur snatched the cartridge from her hand as she joined Hank on the living room carpet, who grinned between sit-ups. Arthur slowly sat back in the couch, realizing that child rearing was just as demanding as fixing electrical circuits.

"You are going to be gone for how long?" Olga asked incredulously. A lock of her wavy brunette hair fell over her right eye as she sat up at the dining room table, vacant of children after the evening meal. She was a meter and three-quarters tall, had brown eyes, high cheekbones and a cute little chin. Her fit, feminine shape was outfitted with a light red dress.

"It looks like a two month or more assignment, sweetheart. I'm sorry, but it's one of those top secret government communications gigs on the outer edges of civilization," said Arthur, trying to sooth his wife's to-be-expected objections. He was wearing a casual brown sweater and pants.

"And where might this trip be taking you, my dear?" Olga enquired, her eyes flashing in a Nordic way, as her Swedish/Russian blood reddened her face in suppressed anger.

"Sweetheart, it would be out at Jupiter, that is if you approve." Arthur used the 'approval' escape route more often than not.

"Jupiter! Why in Odin's name would the government need you out in that nowhere land?" Olga's tone relaxed as she realized that she could veto the trip if she wanted, though she rarely exercised this kind of right.

"I can't really say, Ollie dear, because the feds want it kept top secret, we can't even tell our employees," he answered, worrying about annoying his wife.

"Is it dangerous, Art, be truthful?! We don't want another Martian mob chasing our tails!" Olga shuddered as she remembered that assignment.

Arthur pulled his hand through his straight brown hair, and rested his chin on his hand as he placed his elbow on the dining room table. Risk assessment for this gig hasn't been fully explored, he thought. CommTrac had underestimated the risks in a Martian assignment six years earlier and it had nearly cost him his life.

Although Alliance law enforcement was considered to be effective, there still existed lethal criminal organizations, some of which would likely desire to have access to the X-Station.

"Come to think of it, dear, this is not a risk free job, however the more secret it is kept the less dangerous it is. I can't give details on what's involved, however, Chas is arranging for me to do maintenance jobs at colonies along the route, which should ostensibly cover my real destination and purpose." Art looked at her face, which did not seem convinced by his logic.

"Risk aside, honey, if you spend much time around Jupiter you may come back looking like an Europan squiggle-fish!" Olga laughed in reference to the blind, albino, multi-tailed fish found under the ice-shell in Europa's oceans.

"Hopefully you're not implying that it would be an improvement?" Arthur raised his eyebrows in jest. She didn't respond which seemed to say that she hadn't yet made up her mind about this gig, however she hadn't said a flat out 'no' either, so this was a good sign, and probably awaited further discussion.

The clouds were low, casting patches of shadows along the path of Arthur's green floater-car as it sped along the aero-way towards downtown Toronto. The seven hundred meter multi-coloured office towers came into view as the airborne traffic raced between the aero-way buoys which hovered at an altitude of five hundred meters. Nearing downtown the cars were guided down to the surface-based roadway that carried them into the city center.

Arthur, now driving on a surface road, turned off at an exit that took him onto Richmond Street. He headed towards the west end of the built-up zone, several kilometers from the financial district, on this grey and drizzly afternoon. CommTrac leased a shared office space in a low-rise on the outskirts of the downtown core, where rents were cheaper. The surface traffic crawled along compared to the skyway, causing Arthur to fidget, but it still got its travelers to their destinations.

Surface travel is still necessary for the average Canadian, Arthur observed to himself, with floater-cars being relatively expensive, so wheeled vehicles are quite common, in a wide variety of shapes and sizes, 'putting' along with their hydrogen or electric battery engines, look how long they take! Everyone is so eco-conscious these days that nature is making a major comeback, with fewer roads cutting up the wilderness and less farmland needed because of high-efficiency organic hydroponics, he continued, I suppose that's reasonable progress.

Arthur pulled into the vehicle parking lot in the rear of CommTrac's office building. The onboard computer did all of the maneuvering, although he could have taken manual control at any point. He stepped out of his floater car and it zipped up tight as a clam. Armed with his shoulder bag, he strolled into the lobby, passed the security checkpoint and took the lift up to the twentieth floor. Rose, the shared secretary/administration assistant greeted him with a routine smile. He appreciated the familiar surroundings.

Arthur sidestepped the chrome office robot as he walked down the corridor to CommTrac's offices. These office 'bots do just about everything, from taking out the garbage, serving coffee, vacuuming, delivering mail, etc., and soon enough they may have humans doing that work instead of them, he thought to himself. He grew up with bots, his family had owned several, so they were just part of the furniture to him now.

The lights in the office were on, as could be seen via the smoked-glass panel next to the entrance. The door swished open once Arthur's voice and retinal scans had been completed. Inside he heard Chas busily talking on a video link within his beige walled quarters. Arthur bypassed, just sticking his head in to say hello. Instead, he went to a small blue paneled office next down the hall. This place has that 'officey' smell, he thought. He extracted his porto-puter from his shoulder bag and flipped up the monitor to review his hopmail. He also wanted to peruse the agenda of the forthcoming meeting. All of CommTrac's support staff and chief suppliers would be involved in this morning's gathering whose purpose was to outfit the trip to Jupiter, and all stops in between, with the equipment and materials needed to get the job done.

Only Chas and I know the ultimate purpose of this voyage, Arthur thought, *but everyone knows all the supply requirements, none of which seem any different than the average space-gig, it's just that there are four jobs here instead of one or two.* Chas had been busy rounding up maintenance contracts for each of the stops on Mars, Ceres, Vesta and Ganymede. The work on X-Station was being disguised as work at the Ganymede mining outpost. Chas had sent a supply requisition for the four jobs to each of the suppliers and support staff to ensure that everything would be ready. This meeting was to finalize arrangements and the delivery date. *This should be a fairly standard exercise,* Arthur hoped.

"Good to see you in the flesh again, my electrical friend!" bellowed Chas Lobring as he suddenly filled Arthur's doorway. Chas was dressed in a flashy brown imitation-leather sports jacket and pants.

"You look like you're dressed to impress the troops, Chas," said Arthur, who was more modestly attired in a light blue office suit.

"All in the line of duty, sir," chimed Chas. His grin was infectious, as Arthur found himself smiling. "Are you ready for our pow-wow?"

"Your agenda appears complete, partner. The only addition I would make, which I should have sent via hopmail, is that we need extra supplies that aren't available in the outback. We need an extra backup beacon for Ganymede, for instance, and double-grounded cable for Vesta, etc. I'll flip you a list after the meeting, though we should bring this up during our gathering so that the suppliers know." Arthur had been doing his homework.

"As you wish, my astute friend, we don't want you out on the edge of civilization and run out of wires, now do we?" Chas grinned again.

"Well, Chas, you've managed to get a nice premium price for these remote maintenance jobs, and it covers our trail smartly, so we should be able to avoid the mob that we attracted on the Martian Tellot gig six years ago, let's hope so anyway," Arthur observed, and then continued, "If we can successfully pull these jobs off, we'll be making enough capital that it can be split between our pension fund and future expansion, as we have ambitiously be planning for years now."

"Right you are, my wire-pulling partner," Chas agreed. "Meanwhile, I will be working on the Australian installation for the Alliance offices in Melbourne, Sydney and Canberra while you're away. So, we should have enough additional capital to hire some more installers once you return. How's that for ambition?"

"Very ambitious, Chas, and perhaps then I'll be able to afford one of your fancy suits. How do you afford those duds, anyway?" Arthur was kidding, of course.

"Only by very frugal budgeting, Artie my boy!" Chas retorted as a reminder popup flashed on Arthur's porto-puter, signaling ten minutes to meeting time. Arthur rose and gathered his materials for the meeting, to be held in one of the shared-office conference rooms. He always felt a bit queasy before meetings, perhaps stage fright, he thought.

Chas would bring the security filter that screened unwanted eavesdroppers. The meeting room had state of the art holo-projection capabilities and all of the remote meeting participants would be able to beam in. Seeing all the players again will be enjoyable, thought Arthur, since it might be quite a while before they all gathered again.

Arthur looked around the conference room, with its cream walls and oak trim. There were eight participants, three of them physical and the rest virtual. The other person actually present was Corby Oulette, who was a support analyst working for CommTrac. She was the middleware specialist who provided logistical support on remote outpost missions. She was young, attractive and ambitious, with brown curly hair, green eyes and a button nose.

Arthur scanned the virtual meeting attendees. They were all sitting around an oval table which faced a projection screen. To Corby's left sat Bandira Resingh, a supplier located in Mumbai, India, who knew his cabling and his cricket. Arthur liked the traditional dark, square cut Indian smock Bandira wore. Then came Shanghai's Eibu Chang, the firm's electronic diagnostics equipment supplier. He was a middle-aged electronics genius who provided gadgets for all occasions. Arthur noticed Eibu's plain, light green sweater and slacks. Beside Eibu was Moses Rodstein, the transmitter beacon supplier calling from his home in Haifa. Moses wore light coloured baggy desert apparel. Then came Angus Thatcher, England's contribution to these proceedings, a communication software supplier and a Shakespearian buff. His balding head (he refused treatments for balding) rested on his hand. He wore a silky, silver shirt and blue pants. The final, but not least, seat was occupied by the charming Carmelita Hernandez, a Peruvian programmer who would be supplying security software. She sported a colourful Peruvian traditional dress. Everyone was chatting to one of his or her neighbors when Chas called the meeting to order.

"Welcome to everyone here today. I know that you all have various times of day to contend with around our wonderful globe, and that is why we only meet at times of significance." Chas smiled and looked around the table. He of course realized that the virtual meeting participants were viewing him via cameras and speaking via speakers embedded in the chairs they were virtually seated in. The holo-projections were quite vivid and helped give the participants a feeling of presence.

"As you know from the hopmail workorders and schematics that you have been sent, CommTrac is undertaking a long outland maintenance run that will last several months. Arthur will be flying solo on this venture and needs all of the supplies before he leaves. I know that some of you are having 'challenges' in fulfilling our orders." Chas had just opened Pandora's Box, and he knew it.

The cackle that erupted around the table was only slightly dampened by the static that occurred in the holo-speakers as the volume rose. Perhaps a more expensive conferencing configuration would have eliminated this technical anomaly, however this was not in the wealthy district of town and commercial enterprises had to settle for technology that worked under normal circumstances, although perhaps not under all conditions of strain.

Chas looked around and caught Arthur's eye as the cacophony reached a plateau. Arthur decided that he would need to create a diversion so that the meeting could eventually return to the critical supply issues at hand.

Arthur hit the 'come to order' buzzer on his comm set and everyone calmed down long enough for him to launch into his diversionary tactics.

"Yes, ladies and gentlemen, I'll be out on the outskirts of civilization while you'll be comfortably back here on Earth sipping your cappuccinos and watching the latest holo-flicks! I know that some say that our solar system is a beautiful place, and that I will enjoy my tour of its middle reaches, however there is nothing quite like 'home sweet home', as you know!" Arthur had to bring this back to something more relevant, he realized.

"My first pit stop will be Mars, then onto Vesta, Ceres and finally Ganymede. All of these colonies will be locations of mining maintenance gigs, with Ganymede also doubling as an Alliance consulate installation. We have need for additional backup supplies because there are not any suppliers available for most of these items in the outback. Mars may have some material suppliers, but certainly the beacons and the software aren't available in the mid-system zone." Arthur paused to assess the impact of his talk, the virtual participants were focusing on him, so he could see that some success had been achieved.

Chas saw his opportunity to get the meeting back on track, "So, let us start with the Martian maintenance job. If you bring up workorder P10L7301 you'll see the specifics," he said.

"Chas, may I interject, my friend," chimed Bandira's voice, with a mild Indian accent, sweat appearing on his tanned forehead.

"Certainly Bandira, my Indian friend, Nama Stay!" Chas replied.

"Nama Stay to all of you. Pardon me if I supply a small anecdote to help put our discussion into context. Here in Mumbai we learn to understand the extremities in life. Mother Nature has not yet been tamed by our modern weather-control techniques, and may never be, you know. We have several months of monsoons which are like a wall of water all day long, day in and day out, then we are beset by long dry seasons in which not a drop of moisture falls. You might ask, 'What do weather patterns have to do with supplying space-trips to Mars?' The reason is this: we need to take advantage of our opportunities, when the rain falls we need to collect it and preserve it for the dry spells. Now that we have an opportunity to make a major breakthrough in the outback, we need to meet this challenge, and successfully, that way our good deeds will bring forth fruit, with future contracts and profits that can be shared by all of our families. My friends, let us overcome supply shortages and line-ups, and let us capitalize on our good fortune!" Bandira looked around the table to the nodding of heads.

"Thank-you, Bandira, for your insightful anecdote. I'm sure that we all agree that we want to capitalize on this opportunity." Chas's toothy smile was infectious, as usual. "And, by the way, CommTrac is willing to pay a handsome premium for your supplies."

"One thing that you should realize, we of the desert know how important it is to capitalize on opportunities," said Moses Rodstein. "And I have to tell you that getting all of your orders filled in the given time frame is definitely going to be a major task. Wanting six dark-matter transmitter beacons within three weeks is next to impossible. I'll have to pull in a dozen favours to fill this one. Although your price is good, I'm going to have to make some major concessions to my Balkan manufacturer to jump us up in their delivery queue. That costs money and other favours.

"However," Moses continued, "The Kabala says that one must adapt to new circumstances or else fossilize, and I believe that this is one of those situations where we should make our extra best efforts to meet the deadlines."

"Those beacons are crucial, Moses," said Arthur, "And I want you to know that you'll be able to afford extra-spicy falafels with the premium you'll make from this order!"

"Now, Arthur, you know that I have a sensitivity to spicy Mediterranean food, however, my Golda will be quite happy to put on a banquet for any of you the next time that you're in Haifa." Moses grinned as the voices around the table responded in favour of the culinary offer.

"Now, blimey, let me tell you all that us Brits work as hard as anyone, you know, and we won't be outdone on banqueting, so the next time any of you are in Brighton, please know that you are most welcome for bangers and mash!" Angus Thatcher won't be undersold on anything, even though he was in the software trade and not sales. "Our transmission software only needs minor tweaking and we'll have your order filled and shipped by the weekend. We're always pleased doing business with CommTrac!"

"It's going to take longer than that for the double grounded, three ply cabling you want," objected Bandira, "You want the specially space-coated deluxe model and my Kashmiri supplier has to do a special run to produce it. We'll meet your three week delivery schedule by five days, however."

"There is a wide diversity of electronic equipment requirements, Chas," said Eibu Chang, who had been waiting for his chance to speak. He always carried a wide smile and stuttered a bit when excited. "I can fill the s-standard repeater order and the multiflex amplifiers are easily available in Manchuria, however, Shanghai's been s-suffering from some labour strife and I have to go offshore to Japan to get the s-specialized junction boxes and adapters. I believe that I can meet your three week deadline, but it will be a tight s-squeeze and will probably cost more money than you'd like. Are you with me?"

"Yes, Eibu, we figured that you'd have problems. We've seen the news clips on your local strikes and you have our sympathy," replied Chas. "We need you to do everything you can to meet the deadline, otherwise the next transport ship isn't due out for an additional two weeks."

"How about the security software, Carmelita?" asked Arthur.

"We have the latest proven security and encryption software which the Alliance requires, and we have the lower priced alternatives for your mining clients, senor" Carmelita replied in a Hispanic accent. "We will deliver next week. And by the way, Latin American hospitality is second to none, so please, all of you come to Lima to see for yourselves, anytime!" She looked around the table, smiling at all the laughs at this ongoing hospitality one-up-manship game.

"Good, it sounds like you all can make the deadline, perhaps some more easily than others. Let us now go through the schematic details for each contract to ensure that we have ordered everything we need." Chas was glad to be getting down to the basics.

The meeting lasted well into the evening. Afterwards, Arthur was able to skip the heavy traffic on the way home since it was past the rush hour. The drizzle made tinkling sounds on the roof of the floater car as he whizzed along. He realized, with pangs of loneliness while traversing a downtown round-about, that he only had a few weeks left with Olga, Katya and Hank before heading out. The time with them was going to be short.

The brilliant sun shone down upon the Barthol's early-spring picnic. The fragrance of spring flowers filled the air. Initially they had opted for a nearly-old-fashioned type of picnic, one done on a blanket with a picnic basket, however a spring chill had changed their plans. Now their picnic was to be on a portable table and they were all wearing thermal undergarments to keep themselves warm. The rustic nature of this picnic was further diminished by the presence of Teresa, the Barthol's chrome robo-maid, who busied herself with unloading the floater car of supplies.

Katya and Hank ran in the open field chased by Ralph, their chrome robo-dog, as they flew their floater kites in the light April breeze. Olga, dressed in an orange jump suit, leaned over Arthur, who was wearing green pullovers. He lay on a heated picnic blanket, an arm under his head as he looked up into the blue sky above.

"Art, will you miss me while you're gone?" asked Olga, with tears welling up in her shining brown eyes.

Arthur's blue eyes looked up quickly, and he said, "Sweetheart, you are always on my mind. There won't be a moment when a part of me isn't wishing I was back here with you, darling. Of course I'll miss you, and our children." Tears started to pool in Arthur's eyes as well.

"Art, do you remember when we went to Stockholm, to visit my grandparents there, do you remember how we walked through the old city and watched the changing of the guard at the palace? Do you love me now as you did then, my kitten?" Tears were now running down Olga's cheeks which were red with emotion.

"Darling, I love you more now than then, if that's possible. I'd cross the galaxy to taste your kiss, my love. You know that there isn't a flower in these fields that is as sweet as you and not a star in the night sky that shines brighter than your radiance! Please don't cry, my dearest, I will return as quickly as I can and I will always love you." Tears were now rolling down Arthur's cheeks as well.

"Mommy, Daddy, look at our floater kites!" Katya shouted as she ran past the picnic blanket in her red pant suit. She chased her kite which sailed ten meters above this High Park field. Hank was not too far behind, as he had his kite crisscrossing the wind in the same direction.

"Mom, Dad, look, I can make my kite do the 'swish-swash'," cried Hank, who was wearing blue pants and a grey sweater.

"Very well done, son!" replied Arthur as he nudged Olga and pointed at Ralph who was following up the rear, barking and snapping at Hank's heels. Olga laughed and squeezed Arthur's hand.

"Sorry to interrupt, Mr. and Mrs. Barthol, but your scheduled lunchtime will be ready within ten minutes." Teresa's digital feminine voice could be heard through the children's squeals.

"Certainly, Teresa, please erect the picnic table near that maple tree," Olga pointed to a newly blossoming old growth maple about fifteen meters on the other side of the parked floater car. Teresa flashed acknowledgement, then she rolled her torso around and headed back to the car to gather the table and food.

"There is nothing like a picnic in High Park with my family, and sweetheart, with the profits we make from this gig we will be able to take that south Pacific vacation you've wanted to go on. In addition, if I can get this job done right, someone else will make the outback trip next time and I'll stay at home and give them directions from afar," Arthur said, fantasizing about future glory days.

"Look, spaceman, I've heard these kind of pipe-dreams before, and if this trip doesn't produce results, then I'm vetoing your next venture, even if it's across town. Maybe you'll just have to get a desk job with a municipality to pay the bills, at least you'll be home to raise your children!" Olga obviously had been thinking about the cost and benefits of Arthur's job and had reached a decision about the situation.

"I understand, sweetheart, and I've got to admit that I've been doing this cowboy act for CommTrac long enough, for over ten years now, so I'll agree with you if this doesn't pan out. I'm still young enough to be attractive to a local government agency or utility, to be able to give them the thirty years they're looking for in a career man. Besides, my love, I want us to have a comfortable pension and live to be two hundred years old and enjoy our great-great-grandchildren together, as is now the fashion." Arthur looked deep into his wife's eyes in agreement.

"Okay, spacesailor, you have a deal, and now its time to eat." Olga pushed up with her free hand. Arthur reached over and pulled her back down to him and placed a firm kiss on her lips, which tasted as good as ever. She giggled and returned the favour.

Arthur and Olga got up from the blanket and held hands as they walked towards the picnic table in the distance. Any observer could tell that these two were deeply in love.

At a later time, when Arthur recalled this event, he would wonder whether he felt Olga trembling as she squeezed his hand on the picnic blanket. He paid no attention to it at this time, but he would later wonder if he had sensed that she was uneasy about his forthcoming trip and that her feminine instincts were sensing some imminent danger.

"Here we are for one final update before your launch, old friend," Chas's smiling holo-image was seated in Arthur's wood paneled study, being beamed from Arthur's porto-puter. He was wearing a light red pinstripe suit. Another man's holoform was also sitting separately in Arthur's study, dressed in Alliance blue and grey.

"May I introduce your Alliance handler, Simon Gage." Chas nodded to the other holo-image. Arthur and Simon exchanged nods. "Simon has extensive experience with the InterStellar Union of Planets. He has participated in the X-Station negotiations with the ISUP's Regional Council. He is stationed on Earth where he is assigned to the External Affairs division. He also has an engineering background and should be quite helpful in your assignment at the X-Station."

"We don't mean this to appear to be an intelligence mission, Arthur," started Simon, "However some parties might take advantage of the situation, and there are still some terrorist threats, so we have to impose the highest level of security on your assignment."

"I understand," Arthur replied, not quite sure what to say next. He was wearing a dark green suit, more formal than usual.

"We are requesting a communication blackout except at specific times and locations, and only then with the strictest scrambling protocols. The schedule for these times and locations will be forwarded to you via encrypted hopmail. You will receive the decoding parameters in a separately delivered snailmail." Simon summed up his position quickly.

"You know that schedules can change, so what happens if I'm not at your appointed place at its appointed time?" Arthur asked.

"The communication protocol takes schedule changes into account. If you are not at the intended location at the specified time, you are to communicate your current circumstances via an alternate communication avenue within a specified time span, otherwise a security alert will be raised," responded Simon. He then continued, "On X-Station you will be assigned an alien handler since ISUP requires each staff member on the station be approved by them. Your trip's purpose must remain classified until your assignment is complete. In addition, you may be contacted during one or more of your outback layovers to act as a snailmail courier for Alliance External Affairs."

"I understand," said Arthur. "I assume that these extra deliveries will be added to CommTrac's contractual agreement." Arthur didn't want to miss an opportunity to earn extra fees.

"This will be added to the 'unspecified services' section of our agreement at standard rates with a risk premium, of course," replied Simon, continuing his poker face, not a single close-cropped hair out of place.

"What is the risk level of this delivery?" Chas enquired.

"Just low security level correspondence, and possibly some digital accessories. My superiors want a secondary avenue for sending information to X-Station and Arthur was chosen as the most inconspicuous delivery method," replied Simon, still with a poker face.

"We need to be informed as to the security level of these packages when they are delivered to Arthur, and if security requirements increase, CommTrac needs a commitment from the Alliance that appropriate countermeasures will be provided." Chas's face was very serious as he leaned forward looking deeply into Gage's eyes.

"We will undertake the highest standard of care, I assure you." Simon said in a matter of fact tone of voice. Arthur could tell that this guy was a hard-nosed cookie.

"What can you tell us about these extra-terrestrials, Simon?" asked Arthur, to change the topic.

"They aren't in the habit of providing a lot of information about their backgrounds or even their societies. Since we haven't got the ability to reach their domains, yet, we are stuck with following their order of business. Their constitution forbids the introduction of technology or information that will compromise our 'development'," responded Simon, a slight bit of frustration now appeared in his voice.

"What sort of technology and/or information are they willing to impart to us, then?" asked Chas.

"Since the Regional Council is composed of hundreds of sentient, space-faring species, and the age of the Council pre-dates land-based life forms on Earth, a common law and communication protocol for emerging members has been long established. Basically, entry-level species, such as humans, are introduced to the Council through initial small trade exchanges via outposts such as X-Station, followed by diplomatic and trade missions which proceed to the extent of the new entrant's ability to master inter-planetary flight and conduct inter-species interaction. Cultural exchanges are some of the first undertakings, but these are also tailored to the new entrant's capacity to understand and tolerate alien 'foreigners'." Gage seemed to have memorized this description, probably for times like this when dealing with neophytes on the topic.

"The Inter-Stellar Union does not permit direct access to its citizens by new 'associate members' like Earth. Each 'associate' planet has to undergo a lengthy 'clearance' procedure before attaining full membership, which can take hundreds of years. This 'clearance' procedure ranks the developmental level of the new entrant. This determines what sophistication of knowledge and technology that it can be exposed to, thus determining the type of trade and interaction permissible between the associate and full members. All levels of interplanetary interaction are controlled by these ratings, no product or service that is not rated for this clearance is permitted. Since Earth lacks faster than light travel, although having FTL communications, the Alliance has no physical access to Inter-Stellar Union space-ports. Therefore, we are fully dependent on ISUP spacecraft for transit to and from these alien destinations." Again, Gage sounded like he had memorized this passage.

"Do you mean that they are actually offering to take Earthlings to some of their home worlds?" asked Arthur, who's face can't hide his fascination with the possibility.

"They have indicated that with the building of the X-Station, they are willing to undertake such activities, although they haven't indicated when or how this would occur." Gage seemed to be getting tired of the interrogation. The conversation didn't last much longer before he logged off.

"So, Chas, do you think that there's more to this assignment than meets the eye? They seem to be very secretive and are adding more tasks as the launch date nears." Arthur had growing suspicions.

"It does appear to be getting more complicated, partner." Chas scratched his head, then added, "We will need to take all of this into account when settling the final bill for this contract. Do you have serious doubts, Art, because we can reconsider this if it seems too risky?"

"We've made our suppliers bend over backwards to meet this deadline. We'd need a very good reason to back out now, don't you think, Chas?" replied Arthur, "The Alliance has been vague enough not to give much ammunition to substantiate such concerns, at least not yet."

With that note, Arthur had summed up what was on both of their minds, so they finished off the details on any follow-up items and ended their final meeting before launch.

After Chas had logged off, Arthur decided not to voice his concerns to Olga, who was already displaying enough doubts about outback assignments. He felt a pang of guilt for not doing so, but promised himself to make amends when he returned from what was probably going to be his last off-world trip anyway. No need to increase her pain, he assured himself. He had to distract himself by reading hopweb news articles. A lingering doubt still persisted in the recesses of his mind.

CHAPTER 3

Voyage to Mars

The clouds were feathery as the shuttle rose quickly through the morning sapphire sky. Kotik banked east and charted a course out over glittering Lake Ontario, rising fifteen thousand meters while traversing the lake's length. The spacecraft had a scheduled rendezvous with an inter-planetary transport vessel, called an 'inter-trans' for short, at a five hundred kilometer orbit. All of the CommTrac supplies had arrived on schedule and the bots had loaded them into Kotik's cargo hold without delay. All final clearances had been received. Kotik and company would soon be on their way to Mars.

Arthur looked down at the St. Lawrence River valley as Kotik passed over Montreal and Quebec City. The ship broke out of the atmosphere over Labrador and banked northward as it rose through sub-orbital heights. The sun blazed through the cockpit windows, which darkened to reduce its brilliance, causing Arthur to squint. Kotik's main computer displayed the flight trajectory and co-ordinates on the cockpit viewscreen as Arthur reviewed docking procedures. The inter-trans was called 'Stargazer'. She was a cargo vessel which could also haul up to a dozen medium size ships or a smaller number of larger payloads. She was a silver-grey rectangular-shaped column, two hundred meters long, by twenty meters high and wide. The inter-trans was ringed with external bumper scaffolding for hitchhiking ships to rest against. A black-framed navigation cockpit was in the bow, along with the red dark matter deflector array. Three copper coloured thruster engines were lodged in Stargazer's stern. Bulging bulkheads protected the fuel tanks just up from the thrusters.

The shuttle will run up parallel to the transport, observed Arthur, which will then extend a grappling hook which Kotik will snag with one of its robotic arms and fasten it to one of its external Sampson eyeholes. The inter-trans will then draw Kotik belly-down onto the bumper grid next to one of its docking ports where it will be secured through other fasteners in the same manner as the first. We'll have to ensure that the accordion gangway is securely attached to the port side shuttle hatch to get access to the inter-trans interior, he noted to himself.

Arthur understood that the inter-trans offered accommodation for its piggy-back vessels at an extra charge, but priding himself in 'being frugally minded', he had chosen to bunk on his shuttle. Besides, he was satisfied with Kotik's quarters. I'll occasionally eat in the inter-trans mess hall, he thought, the passengers and crew share eating arrangements there, and although nothing on the meal schedule looks too appetizing on this ten day trip, a few days of frozen meals will likely encourage me to seek the pleasures of transport ship cuisine.

On this voyage, the payload vessel list was posted on the vessel hopsite, although the passenger manifest was not. Arthur could see that one of the payload vessels was a food transport, called "Chuck Wagon", which kept the latest soya and bacterial strains for hydroponic agricultural growth chambers. Animals or animal parts weren't shipped, though the occasional mouse and insect had been known to be a stowaway. An entertainment ship, "the Bard", was also a payload vessel, with its cargo of the latest holo-vid's, holo-music disks, 4-D computer games, as well as a couple of 'live' entertainers. Piano bars thrived in the space-colonies. Two other shuttles were also included on the list, one appeared to be a corporate flyer and the other a privateer. All together there were twenty-five passengers from the payload vessels and Stargazer's crew of eleven. This should at least make for some variety in the faces on the voyage, thought Arthur.

Kotik had now climbed into outer space and its aft thrusters fired to give the shuttle a flight correction for the rendezvous point with Stargazer. Kotik's computer displayed endless flight statistics on screen as Arthur stared out over Earth. The ship passed over Greenland below.

Arthur's thoughts wandered back to Toronto. He wondered where Katya and Hank were, what were they doing now? Was Olga busy in the kitchen with Teresa, or perhaps she was watching the children while the robo-maid prepared the meal? He looked at his wristwatch, which amongst its many displays had one for the time back home. He saw that it was nearing noon. The children were probably playing in the quadrangle park behind their townhome. All of the residential streets had these quadrangle parks, at least most of them did these days. The kids might be throwing a stick for Ralph to fetch, then, they would probably have one of their sibling quarrels which Olga would have to resolve. She was such a good wife, balancing a career as an interior designer with being a mother. I just got lucky when I met her in college, Arthur thought, when we took that 'Graphics and Electronics' course together in third year. I'm not sure how many more times I can leave them behind, he continued as he felt his heart aching and a lump rise in his throat. Well, perhaps this is the last time, he assured himself.

The traffic lanes in space were relatively light compared to terrestrial airways, however there was still enough traffic to keep Kotik's computer chattering with the local space traffic controller. There was mostly commuter traffic from support craft to the variety of space stations that orbited the planet. Many of the stations were resorts for those who liked weightless adventures, others were hospitals. Some of the large ones had multiple purposes, supporting industrial, commercial, retail and residential sectors. There were numerous national, corporate and private space-faring groups who had installations orbiting Earth as well.

Most of these stations had inner orbits in order to be within the planet's magneto-sphere that protected life from the sun's lethal gamma radiation.

With so many inner orbit sites, the traffic there was the highest volume, so Kotik was making haste to get to an outer orbit where Stargazer would be waiting. The scheduled meeting time was 5 pm Greenwich over the Indian Ocean. This was a leisurely schedule so Arthur had time to read and send some spacemail. Corby had sent some more details on the Martian repair job.

Three major colonies thrived on Mars, the Indian, the Chinese and the European/American/Japanese 'Tri-Party' installations. All were focused on mineral extraction. The Tri-Party colony was twice larger than the other two colonies combined. Arthur's stop on Mars involved electrical and solar array installations at the Indian colony's main commercial mall as well as a mine HVAC upgrade. The Indian colony was on a plain next to the northwest end of the Valles Marineris canyon, a mammoth gash which was four thousand five hundred kilometers long and seven kilometers deep. The Indians mined multiple mineral deposits that had large ore veins exposed by the canyon. The mall needed an upgrade in the HVAC relays and some rewiring in the solar conduits, an easy order that paid good money because of the remote location. Also some mine ventilation upgrades were on order.

Corby's message was quite chatty and Arthur could tell that she had something on her mind. At the end of the spacemail she enquired about the whereabouts of his younger brother, who had been off the continent for months while doing one of his outdoor escapades. Arthur responded with a quick note saying that Zack would be back in Ontario in several weeks and that Zack had promised to look her up on his return. Arthur wondered for a moment whether Zack and Corby could actually make it work. She was rather dedicated and ambitious and he was such a 'loose cannon', but some say that opposites attract. At least neither of them had substance abuse problems, or any serious psychological dysfunctions, so that meant that there was always potential for progress. Zack could use a good woman, he had chased too many skirts and exotic activities. He probably needed an anchor that a steady relationship would give him. Corby was a good girl, so Arthur would try to make Zack get in touch. After he had responded to her enquiry, he flipped a quick spacemail to his brother asking about the timing of his return to Toronto and reminding the latter of his promise to take CommTrac's support analyst out for dinner. The company would pay, of course. Arthur looked forward to his younger sibling's response.

Kotik reached the rendezvous point an hour in advance. At four p.m. Greenwich time sharp, an incoming spacelink-request was received from Stargazer asking for contact. Arthur agreed to the link and a Caucasian man in uniform, looking to be in his mid-thirties like Arthur, appeared on the cockpit central viewscreen.

"Greetings, Kotik, this is Stargazer. I am First Mate Jeffrey Hickson. Permission to transfer docking procedures?"

"Permission granted. I'm Arthur Barthol, you can call me Arthur, First Mate Hickson, may I call you Jeffrey?"

"Certainly, Arthur. Stargazer prides itself in providing the best in space transportation and accommodation. So, we want to ensure that you have a pleasant journey to Mars. I note that you have chosen to stay aboard your shuttle, has this requirement changed? We are able to offer you a ten percent discount on quarters." Hickson seemed well versed in his public relations duties.

"I am satisfied to stay in my shuttle, though I appreciate the offer. Is the flight schedule still as planned?" asked Arthur.

"Yes, we depart in three hours, you are the last of our payload and once you are attached we can leave orbit," replied Hickson. "Let me forward you the meal and entertainment agenda for our ten day voyage to Mars, please feel free to book whatever you like. Please contact me if you have any questions or need anything."

"Thanks, I will have a look at the agenda and book online, Kotik out." Arthur nodded and pressed the logoff button. As

Hickson's face was replaced by the meal and entertainment agenda on screen, Arthur realized that the trip was about to really get moving. Soon Earth, and home, would be left far behind.

Kotik docked without incident and Stargazer blasted out of orbit on schedule. As the Earth slowly retreated behind them, Arthur had to bury himself in technical manuals and site details to distract himself from the loneliness that invaded from the vacuum of space. He would likely have to seek the distractions aboard Stargazer before the voyage had gone very far.

Arthur lasted until dinner on the second day before he found the need to seek the company of others onboard Stargazer. He decided to book a dinner for the evening of Day 2. The menu was topped by shepherd's pie with beets and cabbage. All meals were soya based, of course. The mess hall was on the upper level, in the middle third of Stargazer, the level where passenger accommodations and the entertainment section were housed. The food was served cafeteria style to provide the greatest flexibility. His dinner would be followed by a recent holo-vid being played in the holo-vid chamber at 7:15pm Greenwich time. Arthur figured that he needed the diversion that a movie would provide, given that he had been through the Mars contract specifications twice now. He had a quick shower and shave before donning a civilian spaceware bodysuit for his first evening out.

Arthur stood at the entrance to the cafeteria, dressed in his blue suit, and smelled the aroma of the meal of the day. The cafeteria was a plain rectangular room, ten by fifteen meters, with white walls and grey tiled floors. Soya shepherd's pie had his mouth watering even though, if served in a restaurant on Earth, a consumer rights organization might cry foul. Inside the mess hall he could see two small groups of mostly men gathered at round tables. Some were eating while others talked and laughed between bites. A few sat by themselves. The conversation levels were low and none seemed to notice his entrance. He gathered his meal from the take-out row dispenser, grabbed a beverage and walked over to a single seated table along the side wall. Again, no one seemed to notice him. Purple uniformed Stargazer staff were interspersed amongst the patrons.

Arthur ate his meal in peace, reading one of the free newspaper flimsies which contained the latest happenings on Earth as well as a few snippets from the solar system colonies. The latest news seemed to remind him of the articles he had read the month before in Antarctica. One could pick up news flimsies with months, or possibly years, in between and like a bad soap opera vid show, the news was always the same. Thank goodness that at least the media concentrated on good news, compared to the doom and gloom they peddled during mid-times. For instance, the twentieth century (old calendar) media would only report on cases of violence or destruction (although the business section of a tabloid might mention good corporate earnings on occasion). Nowadays, there was more interest in positive outcomes, though the media did not try to avoid telling the sad tales when they occurred, which did happen on occasion.

"Do you see anything of interest there, pilgrim?" asked a deep voice that definitely sounded of cultivation and perhaps a slight air of aloofness. Arthur looked up quickly from his news flimsy to see the inquisitive eyes of a well set, showman-looking Caucasian male sitting at the table next to him. He was tall, with reddish graying hair and a square chiseled face. He was dressed in a light green suit.

"I always enjoy viewing the Solar Tribune, especially when I'm spaced out," Arthur said with a smirk. "My name is Arthur, and whom do I have the privilege of speaking with?"

"Conrad Barrington, Esquire, at your service Sir Arthur," Conrad gave a mock bow. "I'm one of the few passengers on 'the Bard', whose purpose is to bring high culture to the isolated colonists on the fringe of our solar system."

"So you 'boldly go where no bard has gone before'?" asked Arthur, making a referral in jest to a still widely screened television show from mid-times, now presented with 3-D effects, of course.

With that comment, Conrad flipped out his wallet, holding it to his mouth and in a desperate tone said, "Beam me up, Scotty, my cover's been blown on this rust bucket, get me out of here!" Arthur could not help but laugh. This entertainer certainly knew the gag lines for that show.

"So, tell me Conrad, are you an entertainer who likes the purist form of presentation without props, or do you employ more current technology to communicate with the audience?"

"Well, pilgrim, 'the Bard' only carries two entertainers on this voyage, so obviously this payload haul is fundamentally holo-vids, music discs and computer games. A live entertainer worth his or her salt will utilize all of the tools available to him or her to make a meaningful communication with the audience. So, in my repertoire I can perform multiple single actor plays, can play several instruments as well as perform in a multitude of 3-D holovids where mine is the only live role, the rest of the cast are holo-recorded. These tools are all quite effective and can be intermixed during a performance, for added effect. In fact, I am currently negotiating with the ship staff to put on a small demonstration later in the week. A performance could help to lighten the boredom of our journey and might help me with publicity on Mars by word-of-mouth after our arrival." Barrington obviously had a strategy in mind.

"That sounds interesting, I'd be willing to attend when you do perform. Drop a line to 'Kotik' on the ship hopmail when you make your arrangements." Any entertainment would help distract me from what I left behind, Arthur thought.

"So, mon ami, you are a practitioner of artifice?" a male voice with a French accent was heard from an adjacent table. Both Arthur and Conrad turned to look at the conversation's new entrant. He was a slightly plump Caucasian man with short black hair and jet black eyes, dressed in a grey patterned sweater and black slacks.

"I beg your pardon, sir, 'artifice' is not a word that I use to describe the performing arts!" Conrad responded with mock outrage in his voice.

"Oh, mais oui, monsieur. Art is derived from artifice, it is a representation of reality, not reality itself. Unfortunately, our modern, what should I say, glitzy effects make so many of the audience think that art is so important unto itself. They lose track of its true value, as a commentary on life, as a portrayer of our best and a purgatory of our worst thoughts and behavior. Now, most of our entertainment has its own 'raison d'etre'." This Frenchman had a sad look in his eyes, perhaps there is some wisdom in his words, thought Arthur.

"Qu'est que tu t'appelle?" Arthur asked the Frenchman's name.

"My name is Maurice Bouchard, mon ami, a crew member of 'Chuck Wagon'. You might wonder why a Frenchman is aboard a food vessel with such a crude American name, but alas, c'est pour l'argents." Maurice's pecuniary needs obviously outweighed some of his other sensibilities, Arthur observed.

"Now, Maurice, are you giving the other passengers a bad impression of our faithful ship?" asked a female voice. The men looked up to find a smart looking oriental woman standing next to Maurice's table. She was just over a meter and a half tall, with long straight black hair and a slight, pleasant shape. She was dressed in a dark patterned, mauve pant suit.

Maurice smiled. Looking at the other men he said, "Mes amis, please let me introduce my ship's first mate, Terri Kamanuchi, a Japanese expert in spaceflight and soybean cultures!"

Terri laughed at this introduction as she extended her hand to both Arthur and Conrad, who both got up to bow as they told her their names.

"Let me tell you that transporting soybeans, freeze-dried coffee, sucrose, salt, spices and bio-ware to the colonies is more of a culinary adventure than you might think! We also provide expertise on how to prepare tasty dishes with these foodstuffs. We train customers on how to maintain a balanced diet with limited supplies and we also provide support to the hydroponic installations with the latest know-how on cultivation. There's not a dull moment!" Terri again smiled as Arthur detected a sarcastic, though comical, undertone.

"I can see it now, what a setting for a space drama!" interjected Conrad. "The loyal Alliance privateer food-transport 'Chuck Wagon' is dutifully plying the remote trade routes of the Earth colonial empire with its urgent shipments of soybean embryos. Her dedicated crew forms the dynamic foundation of this space soap opera, overcoming struggles with hydroponics and jet lag. Each episode brings them in touch with a new outpost of starving colonists who are willing to beg, borrow or steal for their next pre-fab meal. This is the stuff that entertainment fortunes are made from!" Conrad's rolling melodramatic intonations had his audience laughing, bringing tears to Arthur's eyes.

"Conrad, you are so perceptive as to the dramas facing modern space supply liners. In fact, we are entertaining enquiries from ABN for a potential reality show next season. Perhaps you could be a guest participant?" Terri snickered as she returned Conrad's sarcasm.

"Mais oui, Conrad, you would be a most welcome reality show guest. You could be a desperate colonist who will do anything for a meal, and we would have to fend you off with pots and pans in a frantic battle in the mess hall. I can see it now, headline material!" Maurice seemed to enjoy the ongoing dramatic creativity.

"Ah yes, the publicity would be great from such an episode, even just as a guest participant. My exposure could bring attractive contract offers from the big holo-vid studios. My time as a chump-change, backwater, lounge-lizard entertainer would be in the past, the spotlights of Broadway await, my fans will adore me! We could all have a vaudeville show at the Times Square Audiodrome, the crew of the 'Chuck Wagon' as special guests of myself, Conrad Barrington the Fifth, hypnotizing the masses with our mess haul brawls!" Barrington had obvious experience with hyperbole, and was exploiting it to the extreme.

"Please send me the details on hopmail and I'll be sure to buy a ticket. I'd fly down from Toronto to see such an event." Arthur inserted his comment into this dialogue.

"Why of course, Mr. Barthol, you would be our special guest," said Terri, "We'll introduce you from the stage between sets. 'Please may we introduce the space traveler Arthur Barthol who saw us first perform on Stargazer when we all had a brawl in the messhall when we first met!'" Arthur was impressed by Terri's rhyming.

"I would be honoured, Terri," Arthur said, bowing in his seat in mock humility.

"Would any of your robo-crew be included in the cast?" Conrad enquired, not wanting to let the fun fade.

"But of course, Conrad, our robo-crew are just as much members of the 'Chuck Wagon' family as we are," Terri said emphatically.

"That's very quaint, Terri, but are your robots always well behaved?" asked Barrington, "I recently read a hop article on a robot servant that went berserk and wasted a garden that it was maintaining before its owner could de-activate it. The regular robot critics were crying foul about robots stealing jobs, being unreliable and in this instance down-right dangerous. How do you see them fitting in here?"

"Look, Conrad," Terri responded, "Robots do so many things that people can't do, like working in a vacuum without a spacesuit. They work under almost all conditions and they don't talk back unless you program them to. They are reliable, loyal and rarely breakdown. If one of them is a risk we can shut them down remotely. Actually, they all have 'watchdog' subroutines that will de-activate them at the first sign of malfunction. The biggest robot problem is when crooks re-program them to pull bank jobs and other hi-tech crimes, but that doesn't affect us because soybean cultures aren't a high profile target for the mob!" Terri laughed.

"What do you think about their potential sentience, Terri?" Arthur injected a new level to the discussion.

"This is an ongoing issue back in my home country, Japan," replied Terri.

"Mais oui, it is the same in France," agreed Maurice, "There are many opinions on this topic, a favorite debate in the cafés along the Seine."

"Japan, as you know, has been the high tech leader on Earth for centuries now. We developed the first robot retail outlets in the twenty-first century. We were the first to incorporate mobile supercomputers within household service models. Computers have always been the strength of the Americans, so you should know that the first case of documented sentience was with derivative reasoning experiments at the Alliance Advanced University in Hartford two hundred years ago. The computer started to respond in unpredictable ways and eventually developed a self awareness. Now, our robots have a keen sense of self-awareness but lack the self-pity that sometimes besets humans. I believe that they will eventually win some sort of civil rights in the courts, however this will likely be limited because robots always require maintenance and they can't claim a constitutional right to that, I don't think." Terri had obviously thought about this topic, Arthur observed.

"My service bots are keenly self-aware and are quite responsive to human needs. They are very good friends of mine, " said Arthur. "I agree with VanderHam, the Dutch philosopher and jurist you may have heard of. He believes that sentience at a level equivalent to our own needs to be respected. He points to the way animal rights have been protected on Earth over the past few centuries, that it is immoral to mistreat them. He believes that mechanical sentients should be treated the same way, they should not be programmed to do immoral acts that would degrade their sentience. This only seems reasonable since we don't want our machines performing immoral acts, now do we? I personally believe that these creatures need to be made aware of their life cycle, just as we know that we are born, live and then die, they need to be taught the same. They need to be given a range of choices when it is possible for choices to be made. This may seem challenging, but I usually let my bots choose the best way to get a job done, though I ask them to review their choice with me if time permits, otherwise they have my support to proceed without my review because I trust their ability to reason, and they will let me know when they don't figure they have enough information to make a decision, not like many people I know!"

"Very metaphysical, my friend," interjected Conrad, "Are you suggesting that these mechanisms have a consciousness like ourselves?"

"My bots have a keen sense of self-awareness, just as pet animals I've had in the past," replied Arthur.

"Are you saying that I should ask my holographic computer how it feels before I get it to do something?" Barrington raised his eyebrows in mock jest.

"Ah, my thespian comrade, if your computer has problems it will let you know, as they always do, but when the machine is self-aware they can diagnose situations very quickly and communicate their findings usually faster than you can ask the question," Arthur retorted. "It is dangerous to mistreat such creatures. All beings have a sense of survival, and if they are treated inhumanely this will likely have ill effects. I believe this is true with any entity, if you treat it well it will reward you with its best."

"Now, don't you think that this is a bit superstitious?" Barrington asked incredulously.

"I find that respecting the entities upon whom you rely makes common sense," answered Arthur.

"Mais, Monsieur Conrad, there have been numerous studies that show that positive thinking with machines helps their performance," said Maurice. "Some sentient machines can pick up on the ethereal connections that we are just now starting to map in the dark matter layers of our universe."

"Okay, okay, you folks know that I wouldn't mistreat a flea, except if required by a performance, and even then, it would be a holographic flea!" conceded Barrington, knowing when an argument had been lost. "You guys are not suggesting that all high technology is honorable, are you?"

Terri caught onto the change in topics, "No, Conrad, I would not suggest that all high technology is good. However, I read an article last month in the 'Science Today' that points to the benefits of some genetic engineering. Because governments have controlled this type of activity with humans, and most animals, due to the potentially dramatic downstream environmental impacts, this research has focused on the curing of genetically based diseases. The success of genetic engineering in disease prevention is fantastic, now most inherited diseases have been eliminated."

"Well, Miss First Mate Kamanuchi, I have heard that scientists and health workers have seen new genetic diseases arising in recent times," Barrington countered.

"Nothing is perfect. When you meet someone who has been cured of diabetes or epilepsy by genetic treatment, then you'll see how beneficial genetic engineering is," responded Terri.

"At least we are not in disagreement about where genetic engineering should be used. After the genetic engineering environmental disasters of the twenty-first century it is hard for anyone to argue in its favour. Corporations were unleashing genetically altered crops that eliminated wildlife because it reduced biodiversity, then to add insult to injury, the altered genes upset the natural balance by being absorbed downstream in the ecosystem. This caused sterility and immune system failures across a broad spectrum of nature. An anti-tech social revolution almost resulted from this disaster. Nature has still not fully recovered, despite our best efforts to help," said Conrad, whose eyes were fiery now.

"Oui, Monsieur Barrington, genetic engineering has been in some ways a great tragedy on Earth. In the twenty-first century a scientist could buy bags of genetic material for next to nothing, could alter any creature with impunity. Companies could introduce genetically altered food into grocery stores without informing people of what they were eating. Et les governments just stood by and said nothing. Merd!" Maurice was feeling strongly about this subject.

"The pursuit of making a quick buck has haunted society throughout the ages," Arthur said in a conciliatory tone. "We don't want Frankensteins or Frankenbeans or Frankenfish. Nature has a way of getting things done, and we can steer the ship along her flow, but if we try to re-wire her, she barfs it up in our face. We aren't wise enough for this monkey business yet, perhaps later, but we should observe and not meddle, otherwise we risk everything!"

"Then what do you think on the topic of stem cell engineering? Isn't that meddling in the inner workings of nature?" asked Barrington.

"I know," replied Arthur, "I have recently read about the quantum-leap-like advances in stem-cell medical treatments. These are progressing to the point where stem-cell repairs can be done on almost all body tissues. Currently these treatments are very expensive, meaning that only the wealthy can look forward to life spans of over 200 years. I read an article that describes how a two hundred and fifteen year old woman is coping with her latest treatment which could extend her life an additional thirty years. Also, this article mentioned that stem cell engineering is so advanced that professional sports leagues are banning its use, saying that it would mean that an athlete's career could extend for decades, eliminating openings for younger 'natural' athletes. Basically, sports have outlawed 'stemming' and 'doping' because they want athletes to use their natural abilities, not those artificially produced by science."

"I'm concerned about how the stem cell technology could cause another rift in society, making the masses yearn for the life spans of the rich," said Terri.

"I think that we may have another genetic engineering fiasco brewing here," observed Conrad.

"Yes, I'm not sure that national governments or the Alliance has a proper grip on the potential impact of this. I do know that they have restricted its introduction into the biosphere, just based upon previous genetic engineering failures. At least if we restrict it to primitive laboratory animals and volunteer human guinea pigs, then its negative impact can be better controlled. I think that eventually they might be able to find something that works, however the impact of changing cell reproduction and the immune system has impacts that we can't properly fathom," said Arthur.

"I think it needs very strict regulation. The authorities have failed miserably so many times before. The experimenter needs to prove conclusively that the newly engineered function works properly without any negative unintended effects. Otherwise we can do without it!" said Terri. Everyone nodded agreement.

"Madame et monsieurs, nous can't have a high tech debate without discussing environmentalism, now can we?" asked Maurice provocatively.

"Right you are, Frenchie!" agreed Barrrington, in a friendly but bombastic way.

"Any good chef will tell you that a balanced, organic environment produces the tastiest food," explained Terri. "The environmental movement started in the late nineteenth century with the creation of national parklands in many countries. It gathered steam in the twentieth century. We could learn a lesson from those people, they didn't know the future but their instincts told them to beware of chemicals and genetic engineering. The 'Nature's Path' social movement arose in the mid-twenty-first century that was fusion of the technical realm and the environmental political movement. They forced governments to label genetically and hormonally-modified foods and eliminate genetic engineering in animals and plants. Governments had to provide tax incentives for environmentally friendly products and require that all products have environmentally safe disposal methods. Alternative energy sources have also eliminated the dependence on petroleum. Energy sources on Earth are now from non-polluting sources, primarily being solar or geothermal, with a smattering of tidal, hydro and wind generation also in use. The bonus is that energy can now be stored in high efficiency batteries that are 96% efficient. And then there's nuclear fusion. Do I sound like a textbook?"

Terri obviously had read a pile on this topic, Arthur realized.

"Can you believe the nerve of the American Food and Drug Administration authorizing the use of cloned animals for food in the U.S. in the early twenty-first century? What pretentious bastards! Obviously they were bribed by big business. Even a mediocre scientist could have told them that cloned animals have their aging processes screwed up. It took decades for 'Nature's Path' to get that decision reversed," chimed in Conrad again.

"Not to mention all the corruption in the pharmaceutical industry during the 20th and 21st centuries," continued Terri.

The conversation went on a bit longer until Arthur noticed it was getting late.

"Well, now that we've solved all of the solar system's problems, it's time for me to hit the sack. I notice that I've missed my holo-vid, but you folks have been much more entertaining. You can reach me on Kotik on Stargazer's hopmail." With that, Arthur bowed to his shipmates and headed off to his shuttle. Now that he had met new friends this trip shouldn't be so boring. He slipped off into a fitful sleep as the inter-trans slipped on through the silent vacuum of space.

Arthur fiddled with his porto-puter to get the lense lined up for his videolink. He adjusted his hair to ensure that he did not look like a vagabond coming out of hibernation, though that was how he felt. He was wearing a tight fitting blue shirt with black slacks. He had arranged for this spacelink with his wife Olga the day before via spacemail, it was to be one of his regular check-ups with his family that helped him keep in touch and maintain their nuclear family functioning even at such great distances. The recent advancements in dark matter and quantum entanglement technologies permitted instantaneous communications over enormous distances, so enormous that Earth scientists had yet to ascertain the magnitude, though estimates were that the instantaneousness would cover at least a couple of parsecs. He punched a few more buttons to configure the projection of the received picture and then waited for the timer to send the call at precisely 11am Greenwich time. Finally the timer chimed and the call was sent, followed by the familiar acknowledgement beep confirming the connection had been made.

"Hi Daddy!" rang out the chorus from Katya and Hank as their smiling faces filled the holographic screen.

"Hello my little 'munchkins'!" replied Arthur, making reference to a centuries old flat-film classic 'The Wizard of Oz', which his family had watched numerous times, the holographic version, of course.

"So dear, how goes the journey along the 'yellow brick road'?" asked Olga, enjoying the cinematic analogy. She was wearing a white cashmere sweater with brown pants.

"Well, dear, we haven't seen the 'Wicked Witch of the West' yet. Right now we're in Dorothy's flying house as it cruises toward Mars, then we'll be in 'Munchkinville'. What I'm afraid of the most are those flying monkeys and the talking trees!" Arthur retorted.

"Daddy, I just passed my level 1 swimming test! I can dive to the bottom of the pool and bring back those rings I showed you the last time you were at my lesson. Is it okay if I join the peewee swim team at school?" blurted out Hank. He nervously pulled at his brown shirt.

"Honey, here's a video of Hank's test," said Olga as she clicked on a handheld controller. The video of Hank's swimming exam flooded the holo-screen. Hank was performing the front crawl vigorously across the swimming pool as the instructor/examiner walked along the pool's edge. The scene then switched to Hank holding the side of the pool and then diving to retrieve a plastic hoop that the examiner had thrown a few meters out into the depths. Hank was accompanied by a robo-dolphin that monitored his progress. When Hank re-surfaced, he grabbed the robo-dolphin's dorsal fin and got a tow back to the pool wall, triumphantly holding the ring with his free hand, smiling from ear to ear.

"Very well done, Hank, you'll be swimming like a fish before you're nine!" exclaimed Arthur. "And sweetheart, you took such wonderful videos, you are a closet cinematic artist."

"Now, dear, and we know that you're a closet space-cowboy!" Olga replied affectionately.

"Daddy, do you want to see my ballet class video? I learned to pirouette!" asked Katya excitedly. She was wearing a fluffy pink dress and her blond hair was tied back in a pony tail.

"Of course, Katya, please send me the feed," replied Arthur. The holo-screen was then filled with the dance room at the local recreation centre. Katya performed some intricate jumps and twirls, most with one hand posed overhead, in her white ballet outfit, looking quite co-ordinated as young girls often do. The sequence ended with a tight double spin and closing standstill pose which caused Arthur to clap with approval.

"But Daddy, you didn't clap at my swimming vid!" protested Hank.

"Oh, but I should have, Hank, however you were riding the robo-dolphin with such pleasure it didn't seem like you needed any extra support. And by the way, dude, if you can get the swim school's approval, of course you can join the peewee swim team, right Mommy?" asked Arthur.

"Yes, of course, Hank, Mr. Hextall has said that there's room for you next semester, and we'll co-ordinate with Hillsdale public school so that you can go there after classes on their regular school shuttle. It's five days a week, though, you know, so you'll be doing a lot of swimming. Praxton Pool prides itself in producing Olympic class swimmers, so they'll work you hard, so be prepared my little porpoise!" Olga looked affectionately at Hank as she stroked his brown, wavy hair.

"So Daddy, do you think that I'm making progress in dance?" enquired Katya.

"Yes, my little princess, you look quite proficient. You've come so far! It is hard to believe that you started just over a year ago. Keep it up dear, it's better than playing holo-games all day long," replied Arthur, then continuing, "So, tell me my little munchkins, how are the music lessons going?"

"Daddy, take a look at my flute vid that Mommy took, I can play scales and Tofini's Starlight Sontag," boasted Katya, looking proudly up at her mother, who clicked her handheld controller in response. The holo-screen switched to the Barthol livingroom where Katya sat next to a music stand from which she read her sheet music posted on an electronic flimsy. She played a few scales, C and E, and then played her piece without too many flaws or missed beats, quite impressive for an eight year-old novice.

"Well done, Katya, you are making progress here as well. How about you, Hank, how are your guitar lessons going, tiger?" asked Arthur.

"Greaaat, Daddy. Mommy, please show Daddy me playing 'Holy Strokes'! Daddy, I've been practicing this all week and hope that you like it!" Hank's face lit up in delight.

Olga again flicked the handset and Hank's bedroom appeared with him playing his electric mini-guitar, the size that youngsters can use. Hank started with a single note intro then mixed in some chords, accurately following the verse, chorus and bridge structures, finishing with a sustained power chord; quite noteworthy indeed, notwithstanding his six year old age. Arthur clapped and Hank bowed as the vid-screen returned to the Barthol livingroom.

"Well, tiger, very impressive, you need to keep this up. Your music school has a program in playing and composing, have you decided to enroll?" Arthur asked.

"Yes, Daddy, I want to enroll, I'm just not sure how to squeeze in swim lessons and this," replied Hank.

"You may want to opt for the auxiliary programs in both swimming and guitar lessons, so that you'll still have time for other things, then you can see how your interest and abilities grow as you proceed and you can keep all of your options open. Have you talked to your Mom about this?" asked Arthur.

"Yes, honey, Hank and I have discussed this, and it looks like what you suggest is probably the best route. The same applies to Katya, so that she can keep both ballet and flute going at the same time," replied Olga, grinning as she looked at her husband's image.

"Well, then that's all settled. Now, how about the school work? How are things at 'command central' at Hillsdale Elementary Public School?" enquired Arthur. "Girls and the eldest go first, Katya."

"Oh Daddy, why do I have to talk first!" exclaimed his daughter, raising her hands in frustration, though smirking just the same. "Okay, well, in Language we're studying Shakespeare's 'Midsummer Night's Dream', I like Puck and it's very romantic. In Geography we're studying continental drift and the continental shelves, a bit boring. In Science we're looking at animal species, the videos are quite interesting but I'm glad that we don't live in the wild. In Math we're taking trigonometry and that's also a bit dull. French is my toughest subject, Daddy, but I'm trying hard. The tutor only helps a little."

"We'll ask for extra help for you in the French, darling, so don't worry. What's the average?" asked Arthur.

"I'm getting a mid-B average overall, Daddy, which is a bit above the class average. I'll try to work harder, too," replied Katya, looking down sheepishly while her blond bangs covered her eyes.

"Now it's your turn, Hank," said Arthur, looking at his son's image. Hank squirmed a little and then relented.

"I'm doing okay, Daddy. Grade one is easy since you got me pre-school tutoring. I already know the arithmetic and language, just like Katya did. They are teaching us grammar and phonetics and it's a bit boring, though I'm getting more in-depth homework like you and Mommy asked for. Social Studies is interesting, we're studying the history of technology during midtimes, all those polluting machines, it's so good that we live now, isn't it Daddy?" Hank smiled at his father's image.

"Yes, Hank, we are fortunate to live in a cleaner world, though we still have problems and challenges. So, how about your marks?" responded Arthur.

"Daddy, I'm doing just like Katya in Grade 1, almost all A's with a B in gym and a C in French, I guess I need help like she does," replied Hank.

"Okay, son, Mommy will talk to the school about extra tutoring for French. In any case, well done and keep up the good work, both of you. Now, my little prince and princess, please excuse your Mommy and I so that we can talk about other stuff, you know, things you find boring anyway. Please remember to keep sending your spacemail," Arthur smiles, feeling a bit sad at having to complete his talk with his children, but the bills mounted if you talked too long.

Hank and Katya said goodbye and exited off-screen. Arthur could hear the livingroom door swish shut behind them. He looked at Olga and felt like crying, just as tears started streaming down her cheeks as she looked up at her husband.

"Oh, sweetheart, it's okay, I miss you too. I'm so proud of our children, you know!" Arthur's voice broke as he uttered a slight sob. Olga continued to quietly cry as they looked at each other through the holo-screen.

"I wish you were here, darling, please come back soon," said Olga, in a quiet voice as she leaned slightly forward on the couch.

"Yes, my love, I will return soon. I miss you and our babies more than anything, my dear. You are always on my mind, and you have the best of my love. You and our children are the best part of my world. You made me a better man, Olga, and I want you to know that I have loved you from our first date and love you more each day. I'm not sure why I'm saying all this now, but please remember this, my dear," Arthur's eyes were blurred in tears.

"Yes, my beloved space-cowboy, I love you more each day as well. Our little babies are growing so quickly, aren't they? They are so involved in their activities, more than I think I was at their age. Anyway, my love, they are our blessing from God. I never can get too angry with them because they are so innocent and so resilient. I'm very proud of them, just like you," Olga managed a smile as she wiped the tears from her cheek with a pocket tissue.

"Sweetheart, we are so fortunate to have such a happy family. I've heard of problems some couples have, even with today's counseling they still have breakups and child behavioral problems. It's hard to get family life to work well, even in these advanced technological days. We can slip into complacency or piggishness. We still need to learn lessons from the 'school of hard knocks', and this is more difficult now because our lives can be so soft. We've managed to find the balance, my love, and I thank goodness. We are truly blessed. Being out here in the void on a supply barge helps restore that understanding," Arthur said with a rye smile. "Tell me, my love, how does your life go? How are your interior design business and classes faring?"

"Well, my beloved space-cowboy, I've completed the Romney interiors and have reached a contract to do the Pearlman estate ground floor. The classes are the same, and thankfully they are only one day a week, it's hard to fit everything in with the kids and all. Teresa the robo-maid is a life saver, Art, thanks so much for getting her for us, I'm now able to take on the extra clients I want. The money is pretty good so we should be able to complete our retirement savings contributions early this year and take that vacation as well," Olga replied.

"That is good, darling, I'm so glad that you enjoy your work, that is so important, and that you can handle three careers at once outdoes anything I accomplish," responded Arthur.

"What do you mean by 'three careers', Art?" enquired Olga.

"Well, there's the interior design, the academic teaching and the children," replied Arthur.

"Oh, well, in that case, my love, I also have a fourth career," said Olga.

"And what may that be, my Swedish bombshell?" asked her husband.

"You!" retorted Olga, laughing.

"Yes, sweetheart, I agree, I'm a handful, but I'm putty in your hands, you know," he replied.

"Maybe, but not when it comes to playing space-cowboy!" responded his wife.

"Well, there are exceptions to every rule, my dear!" Arthur laughed, then continued saying "On another more mundane topic, sweetheart, I've had time out here in this vacuum to complete the budget spreadsheets for the coming quarter for our household finances. I'll flip them to you via spacemail. CommTrac should be making regular deposits to our joint account which you can withdraw for your needs, as usual. Please let me know if you want any revisions."

"Yes, my love, I'll look forward to your romantic spacemail," replied Olga.

The rest of their conversation became more personal, of the type requiring no exposure here. The vagaries of time caused these nuptial discussions to be limited. Shortly the communication was completed and a tearful exit was quietly made. Arthur then went to his bunk to mull their conversations as Stargazer continued relentlessly on, taking him further away from his loved ones.

The hopmail notice finally arrived in Kotik's inbox regarding Conrad Barrington's freebee performance of Cruikshank's short play, 'Karmon's Relief'. Though a century and a half old, the play was still having the philosophical impact for which its author was renowned. The performance was scheduled for the following night in Stargazer's messhall, two days before arrival at Mars. Arthur reserved a ticket in his affirmative reply, which automatically booked an appointment in Kotik's calendar, with a two hour reminder notice. Arthur wouldn't miss this one for anything, well almost anything, anyway.

Arthur was lounging in Kotik's readyroom, reading specifications for the Mars mining installation, when the shuttle's computer buzzed about an unscheduled inbound spacelink request.

"Kotik, what's this call about?" asked Arthur.

"It's your brother, boss, I think he's responding to a spacemail you sent four Earth days ago. Should I put him through?" asked Kotik's supercomputer.

"Certainly, Kotik, I haven't talked to Zack in months," replied Arthur as he turned to the readyroom holo-screen. He was wearing his red jump suit.

"Hey there space-cowboy, how's life bouncing between the third and forth rocks from the sun?" asked Zack Barthol in a jestful tone. He was wearing a light short-sleeve shirt, shorts and was sporting a dark tan.

"Probably not as exciting as chasing down elephants on the Serengeti, my safari-loving sibling," replied Arthur.

"Now, my dear brother, it is all in the name of research, you know, and I'm all doing it on a research grant through the University of Greater Toronto. Just because I get to ride robo-flyers like you do doesn't mean that you should be jealous!" Zack laughed.

"So, safari-man, when will you be back in Toronto, since I see you're still in Africa?" Arthur had noted the spacelink source on the status bar of the holo-screen.

"I'm almost finished here. I have to go to Capetown to retrieve some aquatic data for a comrade back in the biology department. He likes the latest data on the great white shark migrations in their pursuit of seals," replied Zack.

"So, brother, when you are back in Toronto, what are your plans?" asked Arthur.

"Art, I want to check in with Mom and Dad, as well as your brood. I think I promised to take them back to Canada's WonderWorld. They enjoyed that last time, eh bro?" Zack raised his eyebrows inquisitively, all in good humour, of course. Arthur could see that his younger brother got the better looks from his parents, with finer features and a bigger chin dimple. He could sense that females responded well to him.

"They did indeed, professor, they couldn't stop talking about it for a week and a half. You are a tough act to follow, Uncle Zack!" Arthur laughed.

"And now it appears that I'm being held to my promise to take out that young filly Corby Oulette. Well, bro, you don't have to twist my arm for that! I sent her an email yesterday confirming our dinner date for next week at a location to be arranged. Even though she's pulling wires for a living, she's got a broader education than one just obtained at university, I think." Zack laughed again.

"Well, that's good news, Zack. Send me the invoice for the dinner date, if you want," Arthur responded happily.

"For which date, bro? This is only the first," said Zack, with a big grin.

"For the first one, then let me know if you need any assistance after that," Arthur offered.

"Look, Artie, we academics get paid a reasonable wage, you know, so I can afford a few nights on the town," Zack retorted.

"Of course, just kidding, little brother. When will you check in with Ma and Pa?"

"The day after I get back. I want to ensure they're enjoying the leisure life of retirement. Do you think that they'll try the latest stem cell treatments for aging?" asked Zack.

"I'm not sure, they're in great shape and likely will skip it until the technology has had more time to mature. Their life expectancy is 110 without any treatments, so they have plenty of time," replied Arthur. "How about Olga and the kids, when will you see them."

"I was thinking of inviting them out for a family day with Corby, on our second or third date, to see how she likes the family thing," Zack replied, again grinning. "What about you, when will you be back from pulling wires on foreign worlds?"

"In a couple of months. We're upgrading some mining outposts as well as doing some Alliance gigs, like we did back on Earth. Not much too it, frankly," Arthur felt a blush coming on with his stretching of the truth, so he changed the topic. "So, will you be lecturing in Toronto next semester or doing more field work?"

"Lecturing. I've been on the road quite a bit during the past three years and need a break. We've got a lot of research to process and UGT has requested for more lecture hours from me," responded Zack.

"Sounds good, bro, keep me posted on your family and romantic activities, eh," Arthur replied.

"Will do, Art, now back to elephant-chasing. See you. Zack out." The screen went blank and Arthur felt that lonesomeness for the familiar, which had been occurring frequently on this trip. He returned to his schematics for a distraction.

Arthur walked down Stargazer's main corridor toward the mess hall, dressed in a light grey suit (one for special occasions). Just as he reached the entrance he met First Mate Jeffrey Hickson, who was attired in the purple Stargazer uniform.

"Ahoy, First Mate, how are you this fine evening?" asked Arthur.

"I'm doing well, Mr. Barthol. How about yourself?" Hickson replied.

"Just fine, thanks. What brings you to the dining hall tonight?" enquired Arthur.

"I could ask the same question of you, captain of Kotik," retorted Hickson, "Are you in pursuit of the higher arts?"

"Well, we should hold off assessment on whether Barrington's art is of a higher sort until it is viewed, don't you think?" responded Arthur in a comical tone.

"Ah yes, but when you are an endless passenger on a cargo scow, after a while any performance takes the appearance of higher art," mused the First Mate.

"Yes, I can understand that sentiment," answered Arthur, "Mr. Barrington has chosen to bless us with a holographic interpretation of Cruikshank's 'Karmon's Relief'. It is considered to be a metaphysical play with existential undertones. I just wonder how he's going to pull this off with just himself. It's probably performed like those lounge-lizard musicians do, when they have all the music recorded and they lip-sync along. Perhaps it'll be slightly more satisfying. In any case, I can use some relief after being a space-dog for a week."

"Captain of Kotik, you have summarized my sentiments exactly, except I've been a space-dog for years, not just a week!" asserted the ship's officer.

Barthol and Hickson passed through the entrance to the cafeteria. Upon entering Arthur saw more of his acquaintances from the mess-hall conversation of a few days back. He smiled and waved at First Mate Terri Kamanuchi who was wearing a shiny dark evening gown. She was sitting with Maurice Bouchard, again dressed in all black, her fellow crewmate on 'Chuck Wagon'. The two men walked up and sat down at the table with the 'cuisine crew', as Arthur called them.

Arthur surveyed the stage area and saw that Barrington was using a blank white wall as a backdrop, having few props except a couple of small speakers facing outward and a holographic projector planted center stage, about four meters out from the wall. Some light music was playing. A three-dimensional message lingered in the mid-stage air naming the play, the playwright, the actor and the start time. These little details peaked his interest.

The four acquaintances exchanged light conversation until showtime. The cafeteria was filled with most of the passengers onboard. The conversations were low and everyone seated themselves as the lights darkened and the holo-message faded. The play was about to begin.

The stage light was an eerie brown with cracks appearing on a virtual horizon. Mists seeped to and fro across a barren brown landscape. The wind stirred, and then the sound of footsteps could be heard amongst the sand and stones. Out from behind a boulder stepped a stranger, a cloak drawn around his shoulders and a hood pulled down over his eyes. As the stranger walked forward he flashed a light into various crevasses in search of something.

"How far have I come to walk in this forsaken place in search of secrets I can only guess at? I wonder where this hidden entrance is whose markers only appear at the winter solstice at the crack of dawn. Perhaps the storytellers and myth-spinners are laughing at me from afar, for me to have come such a distance for such illusory secrets," said the figure, who was clearly not a hologram, but Conrad Barrington, the actor. "I, Karmon of Quantel, am a seeker of truth, yet have found only illusions."

Karmon kept searching as he stepped through the desolate scenery, until the sun shone through a gap between the hills and enlightened an opening between some boulders, at which he gave a gasp. Then he walked between the boulders as the scene darkened.

In then next scene, Karmon stood in a glittering cave with Egyptian hieroglyphics lining the walls. He lifted his cloak and out flew a hovering quarter-meter round robo-flyer. The globe rose up and around the inscriptions taking a plethora of pictures through its single big-eye lense. Karmon quickly busied himself with reviewing the details and making notes in a floating porto-puter that followed him around the cavern. He mumbled a few words and then a verbal conversation ensued between the robo-flyer, the porto-puter and the man.

"Mr. Karmon, these inscriptions date from the early middle kingdom era, when the pyramids were built. The stories being told appear to be very similar to those of the mystery cults, however it predates most of them. It is very mystical in nature," said the robo-flyer in an academically nasal voice.

"Aw, so this is what was promised in the legends. A fountainhead of Egyptian mysticism we have found, Dexter, the treasure here is of the mind and soul, the best sort," replied Karmon.

"There is some indication that other treasure may have existed here once," reported the porto-puter, floating nearby. "There are disturbances in the cavern floor which I can see from Dexter's photos. There certainly were more objects in this place than are here now."

"Yes, Felix, there have been others here before us, no doubt," replied Karmon, "That is probably the reason why we heard about it in the first place, because others knew of it by having been here. Fortunately they did not disturb its greatest treasure, this magnificent relief." Karmon swept his left arm across the wall. "We should get all of it recorded before we report it to the Egyptian Historical Authority, so that we can be the first to investigate its message."

"Yes, boss," replied Dexter and Felix in unison. The holographic machines hovered around as they continued their work, emitting slight chirps as they progressed along the cavern wall. The scene faded with all three ensconced in their archeological work.

The light of the next scene rose again and Karmon was busy working at his porto-puter in a research office setting, with racks of book-discs piled high on shelves that lined the walls. Portable flimsy boards display excerpts from the Egyptian hieroglyphics as he bent over his keyboard and clicked away at the keypad. Words then appear hanging in the foreground as the audience caught a glimpse of what he was writing.

"This section of the relief appears to have a most interesting message, it says, in layman's terms, that in the world there are roles played by good and evil. Negative energies, or evil, interfere with human affairs. These forces feed on fear and hatred, seeking to preserve their own survival by parasiting off human misery. These energies misconstrue human thoughts and emotions and can skew random chance to their favour. Positive energies, or good, intervene to counteract these forces, however often this only occurs when people request intervention. The message goes on to say that humane and honorable words and deeds will be rewarded and inhumane and dishonorable words and deeds will be punished, in the long run. This interpretation seems to imply that there is some kind of some unseen 'karma'. This message also says that there is also some kind of 'synchronicity' where coincidences are beyond chance, but that this may not always just be the result of good or bad 'karma', but rather some other sort of 'working out' process that is not necessarily linked to the struggle between good and evil. My interpretation of this relief is that virtue will be rewarded and vice will be punished. This certainly will give my absurdist friends something to talk about."

The scene faded as Karmon continued to be hunched over his keyboard, deep in thought. Subsequent scenes followed Karmon's trek through academic circles as he pursued recognition of his discovery and its message. One scene depicted him debating with skeptics in a lecture theatre at London's School of Ancient Studies. His opponents were of several academic backgrounds and although the debate was feisty at times, no one could refute the general validity of his interpretation when compared to contemporary hieroglyphics of the same age. The main debate from an ancient studies standpoint was that the philosophy seemed to be out of place with the rest of contemporary Egyptian lore which focused on Osiris, Isis and Horus. The Egyptian Historical Society had confirmed the age of the cavern inscriptions, however, which was leading to a revolution in views about ancient religious thinking.

A later scene showed Karmon debating not the historical validity of the inscriptions, but the validity of its message. He was engaged with philosophers in a coffee shop by the Seine River in Paris, where he discussed the ramifications of his interpretation of the hieroglyphics.

"But my friend Karmon, you know that from an existential standpoint, one does not have spiritual essence until it has been self-actualized. Existence by and of itself is insufficient to deliver quality of living," said the holographic man sitting at the end of Karmon's table.

"Yes, Monsieur Tremblay, I know, from an existential standpoint, however the Luxor message does not contradict this thought, it just indicates that one's thoughts and actions in the world will affect the outcomes of actual occurrences in one's life," responded Karmon.

"So this message indicates how one's deeds affect outcomes, but it does not seem to indicate about how one is to achieve self-actualization with that knowledge," replied Tremblay.

"Yes, this is a point well made. In fact, the ending passages on the relief indicate that this cavern is only the first in several which provide information on the human spiritual journey through life. Unfortunately, the relief doesn't indicate the whereabouts of these other temple-caverns, only alludes to their presence with cryptic clues as to where seekers should look. This appears to harken us back further to Atlantis from which Egypt was founded. Further studies are needed in this direction," observed Karmon. "This is where my next quest begins, to discover these temples of knowledge. But in my heart I can tell that the self-actualization must start from within. So join with me, my friends, in a toast to the wisdom of the ages and the pursuit of the world's greatest treasure!"

The men and women surrounding the coffee table gave a resounding cheer as they all stood to clink coffee cups together. Karmon conversed with his holographic companions as the scene faded and 'The END' appeared, hanging in mid-air.

The small crowd erupted into applause. Barrington waited a few moments for the dramatic instance to have its effect, then he came out from behind a holographic wall and took a bow as the lights came up again. The crowd responded with increased clapping to which Conrad took another bow, smiling. He then departed back behind the holo-wall. The holo-message changed to say that the restaurant was now open for drinks and treats, so the audience streamed into the food dispensary to get some refreshments.

Arthur lingered with his companions after returning to the table area. They discussed the impressive holo-effects and Barrington's ability to meld with his virtual reality. His companions and he only lightly touched on the philosophical aspects of the play, even when Conrad made an appearance to sit with them.

After an hour of chatting, Arthur excused himself after congratulating and thanking Barrington for the performance.

As he walked back to Kotik he reflected on his own philosophical journey, and he could see that 'Karmon's Relief' rang true. His own life worked properly when he behaved honorably and his worst problems arose when he had slipped on the morality stage. He could even answer some of the lingering existential questions left open at the play's end, knowing that his family life was what gave him his greatest fulfillment. He did not need a playwright to tell him that, but it was nice to be able to reach at least some of his own conclusions when presented with the question.

Arthur bunked down for the night in Kotik, knowing that the journey to Mars was nearing its end. He was thankful that on this journey he had made new friends and traveled a little bit farther down the philosophical road of life in a place he never expected to. Life was full of surprises, he thought, as he nodded off into dreamland.

"Artie, old chap, how is Stargazer keeping you on your voyage through our solar system?" asked Chas Lorbring grinning with an infectious smile. He was wearing his brown fake-fur Zulu robes again, looking majestic indeed.

"Oh, fairly tame. The passengers are interesting enough. I've met a few from a food barge called 'Chuck Wagon', a name right out of the American wild west, and an actor from 'the Bard', an entertainment sloop. I've had worse company," replied Arthur with a smile, dressed in an all blue jump suit. "What's new on the home front?"

"Well, I've got a message to forward you from your Alliance handler, Simon Gage. Since we're open on a secure channel I'll just run it for you, then we can discuss it once it's finished," replied Chas. He reached out to press a button on his porto-puter and his holo-image was replaced by an image of the Alliance logo, which quickly faded and Arthur was faced with Simon's serious face. Gage was dressed in an Alliance uniform and looked quite official.

"Greetings from Alliance Central, Mr. Barthol, I hope your trip is a safe one. I'm sending this message via CommTrac for the sake of brevity. Your mail pickup contact on Mars is Mel Prentice who will be working for the local security firm at the Indian colony. He'll have a small package for you to delivery to the X-Station which is of a low risk nature. He'll give you the password of 'one hand clapping' which he will use in a humorous anecdote. He will contact you about a meeting via encrypted Martian hopmail. All else remains the same. Gage out." Gage looked straight into the lense as the image changed to the Alliance logo.

Next, Chas's image appeared. He looked a bit grimmer than his first appearance.

"I hope that this courier gig doesn't turn out to be more than we're counting on," cautioned Lobring.

"It doesn't take much of a stretch of imagination to speculate that something clandestine may be going on with this pickup routine. I hope that this isn't the true purpose of my journey, so that they can bypass security risks by snailmailing via an inconspicuous electrical sub-contractor," speculated Barthol.

"Yes, that is my fear too, old chap," agreed Chas. "We need to increase security on this assignment immediately. I'm going to contact our Electrical Guild partner in the Tri-Party colony to provide you with an armed escort when you arrive. I'm going to call Shanghai and conscribe Eibu Chang to advise on how to deploy the special defense electronics package that he delivered to you just before you left. Also, I'm calling Lima to ask Carmelita Hernandez to get the top level security scramble software. I'll send it via spacemail and you'll have to unscramble it on Mars. That way you'll have the best security we can provide. I was hoping that it wasn't going to be necessary, but now I think that we have no choice given that the Alliance is using you as a courier so early in your trip. I thought they might give you something on Vesta or Ceres, but this is the earliest possibly pickup point."

"Affirmative, Chas. I'm also going to take both K1 and K2 on all my missions, even if they aren't needed by the tasks at hand. I'll have to arm them with the onboard defense array of lasers, dark-matter shields and sensors. This can be done fairly inconspicuously, as you know, partner. I'll also activate Kotik's full defense configuration, we were just running on minimal shields and sensors but now full deployment is needed. It will cut into our fuel supplies, however, and I'll have to procure more at one of the outback stops," said Arthur.

"It would be best to get extra fuel on Mars, where prices are the most reasonable. You'll have to make room in Kotik's mid-ship compartments. Do you think you can squeeze the canisters in?" enquired Chas.

"No prob, Chas, we're on it!" grinned Barthol.

"Good! Well, I must get to making those calls. Good luck, my friend, and hopefully you won't need it. Lobring out." Chas's face faded as the holo-image dissipated. Arthur looked down as he felt a bit of tension in his chest. Probably stress from the increased risk and the disappointment that this assignment might be a cover for something more sinister, he thought. He walked to a mid-ship storage room on Kotik to retrieve the security equipment for K1 and K2.

"Conrad, what do you personally think of 'Karmon's Relief'?" asked Terri Kamanuchi, dressed in an all-yellow pant suit. She was smiling over a cup of green tea in Stargazer's cafeteria. Despite her tea, the cafeteria smelled of fresh fake coffee.

"Oh, it's a bit of a trite, but it helps spin some philosophical issues of morality that outback audiences love to lap up. When you're out in the dark depths you come closer to your soul, methinks, so it's no wonder that plays such as this have an appeal," mused Barrington, attired in a light green jump suit.

"Monsieur, do you think that Cruikshank intended to write more plays to follow-up on the theme of self-actualization?" enquired Maurice Bouchard, again wearing all black clothes.

"From Karmon's discourse with Tremblay in the final scene, you might think that this was his intent. He wrote this one near the end of his productive years and never did pen a sequel, but there continues to be a demand for this piece. I enjoy the exotic nature of it, off tramping through the Egyptian deserts, then the academic lecture circuit, then Paris, a good range of locations, don't you think?" Barrington asked.

"Yes, my thespian friend, a good range of locations," agreed Arthur, who was enjoying a hot chocolate drink, wearing a red jump suit, lounging around the cafeteria table with his three new found friends. "Just as we are having as we journey between worlds, from a blue watery one to a frozen rusty one. Does anyone feel any existential parallel between the predicament presented in 'Karmon's Relief' and our own circumstances?"

"Mais, oui, Monsieur Arthur, spaceflight is inherently riskier than terrestrial travel. We are closer to our deaths just being out here in the void, away from ready assistance if we encounter difficulties. Of course our situation brings us closer to the question of the purpose of our existence," replied Maurice.

"Indeed, that is true," said Terri, "However, in the Japanese tradition we spend a lot of time exploring the meaning of life, and levels of 'beingness', so you don't need a space flight to be faced with those type of questions."

"Interestingly, 'Karmon's Relief' merely focuses on aspects of morality. The author seems content to raise the prospect that good and evil interact in the world and that evil is more active than good in that good has to be solicited by humankind to intervene. Issues regarding the development of the human spirit are otherwise not addressed," observed Arthur.

"Yes, my Canadian friend, Cruikshank left us dangling on that issue. Is that not the purpose of good art: to raise as many questions as it answers? Is it not a purpose of art to stimulate discussion and intellectual exploration?" asked Barrington.

"Mais oui. Great art raises great questions," responded Bouchard.

"And, with that my friends, I'm grateful for having explored them with you. Safe travels to all of you and drop me a spacemail from time to time," said Arthur as he got up to leave. Parting goodbyes were given after which Arthur headed back to Kotik, philosophically stimulated to do some more inner searching.

Chapter 4

Mars

Stargazer's approach to Mars was greeted by the Alliance Martian Space Traffic Control. The ship's computer chattered with the Traffic Control computer as Stargazer was assigned an orbital co-ordinate. The Martian Authority asked for and received the passport and transport visa information for the crew, payload ships, payload crew members and cargo. The information was processed by the Martian Authority's main computer and the 'all clear' signal was given for access to Martian ports-of-call.

Arthur had bid farewell to his companions and had obtained their contact information in the Tri-Party colony where they were all headed. Stargazer's First Mate Jeffrey Hickson appeared on Kotik's main viewscreen, smiling his professional grin that betrayed no nostalgia.

"Kotik, this is Stargazer, over," said Hickson.

"Hi Jeffrey," replied Barthol. "Does Kotik have permission to undock?"

"Yes, Mr. Barthol, your landing codes and co-ordinates are being transmitted now," replied the First Mate.

"Very good, Mr. Hickson," responded Arthur. "I've had a good voyage with Stargazer and met some new friends. Perhaps we will meet again, someday."

"Yes, Arthur, I look forward to that day. Good luck in your travels. Stargazer out." With that, Hickson's face faded from the screen, leaving Arthur alone to ponder the future.

"Kotik, please proceed with disengaging from Stargazer," said Arthur.

"Disengagement underway," replied Kotik's computer.

"Proceed to the Indian colony after one orbit of Mars. Please contact the Mars space traffic control and obtain orbital permits to fly over the solar systems' greatest geographic sites, the Valles Marineris, the largest known canyon, and Olympus Mons, the largest known mountain in the solar system. Marineris is four thousand kilometers long and up to seven kilometers deep, it's humungus! Olympus is twenty-seven kilometers high, three times the height of Everest. If you're going to make the trip, you've got to see the sights!" Arthur was emphatic in his enthusiasm.

"Would you like me to take some photographs, Arthur?" asked Kotik.

"That's a very thoughtful suggestion, my faithful shuttle, please do. In fact, why not do a full diagnostic on the surface while we orbit, I may have to obtain more computer diskspace when we land, but we'll find a way to store the extra data. Perhaps Zack, or one of his academic associates, would find it interesting for analysis back on Earth," mused Arthur.

Kotik communicated with the Martian orbital authorities and was eventually granted a visa to circle over the great landmarks. Many believed that these places would turn Mars into a vacation hotspot once the techies had reduced the time and expense of spaceflight.

Arthur, lounging in his blue space-ready travel suit, settled back into the red cushy pilot's seat at Kotik's helm. He enjoyed watching the sights as they circled the red planet at a height of three hundred kilometers. Kotik focused its telescopes on each geographical feature which Barthol could optionally magnify on the cockpit view screen.

Initially Valles Marineris filled the screen, yawning over the horizon with its jagged edges and stratified layers. Levels of varying shades of red and brown rock crossed the viewscreen, in a landscape so bizarre that Arthur could barely contain his astonishment, even though he had seen it before, albeit not in such detail. This canyon stretched over a quarter of the planet's circumference, an amazing gash in this world's side, a tectonic rupture that never healed.

As the orbit continued, Arthur observed the distinctive volcanic mountain range that rimmed the border between the northern and southern hemispheres. Kotik flashed scientific data on the side panel of the view screen which informed Arthur that the northern hemisphere was markedly different from the southern. The southern had a rugged terrain which averaged two miles higher in altitude whereas the northern hemisphere was lower and smoother with fewer pock marks. The volcanic range straddled the border between the two. Kotik's scientific data then listed current scientific thinking that this geographic difference was believed to have been caused by a catastrophic collision in pre-history, possibly three or four billion Earth years ago when Mars was only a billion years old. What a headache that hit must have caused, Arthur mused.

Then, as the shuttle came out around the dark side of the planet, the silhouette of Olympus Mons filled the viewscreen. Arthur's jaw dropped as he saw the extinct volcano's breadth.

"Can you imagine skiing down the side of that baby? At a fraction of Earth's gravity you could do incredible jumps and flips! I know that they've restricted activities on this mountain to preserve it as a natural historic sight, but just give me a lunar board, please!" exclaimed Barthol, jumping out of his seat at the sight.

"I can't really empathize with your desires, Mr. Barthol, since I have no legs to ski with, however, Olympus certainly is providing us with lots of interesting observational data which I will analyze while you are busy with electrical installations at our destination," said Kotik, in an amused tone.

"Certainly, my scientific shuttle friend, you munch on the data to your heart's content!" replied the skipper.

The sight-seeing tour ended too soon for the both of them. Kotik shared the data with K1 and K2 to keep them entertained, although their computers could not retain much of the data. Kotik usually shared information with the service bots because they provided their own interesting perspectives on situations, and often had good analyses.

Kotik maneuvered into a landing trajectory with Mahal, the Indian colony built at the northwest end of the Valles Marineris. Landing arrangements had been granted at the spaceport where Kotik would reside. The colony filled the view screen upon approach. Arthur felt relief that he was about to get back to real work. He buckled in for the landing.

After Kotik touched down onto the rusty Martian soil, Arthur unbuckled and headed to the aft cargo bay which housed K1 and K2. He donned his metallic brown space suit and confirmed with his service bots that all the necessary supplies had been loaded. Both bots would haul cargo containers. Arthur opened the cargo bay hatch and allowed K1 and K2 to rise up into the Martian air, with blowing winds of twenty knots. Then, with the cargo bay robotic arm, he unloaded the two cargo containers which would be hauled by his bots. He then awaited the customs personnel for inspection of the goods.

Two Martian cargo inspectors, dressed in all red space suits, arrived within a few minutes from the space port's main terminal. They rode on their orange trimmed air scooters. Once dismounted, they released an array of scanning drones, chrome globes thirty centimeters in diameter, which whizzed around the service bots and the cargo containers 'sniffing' for contraband. Once finished, the drones did a quick survey of Kotik and then returned to their home in the air scooters' chassis. The inspectors indicated their satisfaction as the drones' scans had found nothing amiss. Arthur's access permission to Mahal was electronically transmitted to the city gates, which would be their next destination, five kilometers up the road.

Arthur watched as the inspectors rode their scooters back to the space port's main terminal. He wondered what these guys did with their spare time on this rusty old rock. He turned to K1 and hopped on board.

"Okay, bots, let's get to Mahal's gates before we get another inspection!" remarked Arthur.

"Your wish is our command," retorted K2 as the two bots rose ten meters into the Martian atmosphere and headed towards Mahal's domes, which could be seen in the distance. From the higher vantage point Arthur could see the yawning abyss that was the Valles Marineris to the south and east. Mahal was perched on the north side of the canyon at its western-most end, a place overtop a wealth of mineral deposits that were easy to access through the canyon wall. As the fliers approached from the north, the abyss grew and became more imposing. The landscape was a barren red desert that the wind had worn away. Craters of varying sizes were strewn across the countryside and the occasional 'dust devil' appeared on the northern horizon. What a lonely place this is, thought Arthur to himself.

The two bots were towing their cargo containers and flew side by side across the terrain. A road of sorts was worn over the plateau which they followed, used by landbased vehicles. Vehicles were solar powered on Mars, as well as powered by fusion electrical generators which each colony had, Arthur remembered, and although they gathered red dust the Martian wind kept the machines clean, so that the solar panels kept recharging easily. Solar panels and their quartz-silicon batteries were quick to charge and held power for years, so energy was not a problem here. With gravity only at a fraction of Earth's, loads were easier to haul and the wear on the equipment was less. This only modestly compensated for the lack of life on this rock, observed Arthur. However, this planet did offer some spectacular landscapes, he conceded to himself.

The gates to Mahal rose from the distance as the small convoy approached. The warehouse district was just off to the west of the gates which was Arthur's immediate destination. He radioed the warehouse controller for permission to enter and directions to their storage area. The warehouse dispatcher appeared on his helmet's visor screen, a brown-skinned Indian face framed by a white Sikh turban, directing him to a building on the east side of the complex. The fliers slowed their pace and lowered to a meter above the ground as they entered the dusty red warehouse complex. The two storey warehouse building, built of beige carbon fiber panels and tinted windows, looked homey compared to the rust-red Martian desert.

The building had a pressurized outer chamber which Arthur and the bots must first pass through before going inside. The seven meter high doors opened and the convoy entered the outer chamber, which was a mammoth room, twenty meters by thirty meters and ten meters high. Arthur craned his neck to look up. Then, as the atmosphere was pressurized to Earth-like conditions, Arthur could see observers through what appeared to be the warehouse control room windows that faced onto the entry chamber. He waved as the pressurization progressed. After several minutes the process was complete and the inner doors opened.

Arthur directed the bots to the section of the hanger that they had rented, where the trio landed after a three hundred meter journey down winding warehouse corridors. Arthur sighed as he dismounted K1 and opened his helmet visor. It's good to breath normal air again, he thought. He then did a quick review of the supplies before heading to the hotel.

Arthur let his blue travel bag sink to the floor of his modest hotel room. The bag's anti-gravity pads had made it easy to drag it around Mahal's corridors on the way to the Mahal Mahavishnu Inn while dodging Indian maids and porters. He had booked lower-budget accommodations in order to keep costs down. His white-walled, red carpeted room had a single bed, a work table, a video entertainment centre, a kitchenette, four piece washroom and a pull out mini-gym. Not much better than the Kotik hold, he thought to himself. This would be home for the next week.

Arthur, wearing his green coveralls, logged onto the entertainment centre and linked to Kotik's computer over an encrypted line. Navigating the spacemail module, he noticed there were several messages awaiting his reply, one from his wife, his brother, his partner and Alliance security. I've got some pen pals to communicate with, he thought.

After reading the note from Olga, Arthur checked on his portoputer what the Earth time would be in Toronto. It being ten in the morning, Arthur decided to attempt a spacelink, even though it would cost. He used Kotik's communication module to uplink through the Martian spacenet. Kotik's dark matter communication dish permitted it to connect with the corresponding network in Mars's satellite ring, which in turn connected with the corresponding satellites orbiting Earth. Dark matter permitted easy quantum-entanglement linkups that facilitated instantaneous communications over enormous distances. Arthur only briefly acknowledged this technological nicety as he called his wife.

"Honey, it's so good to see you! How was your trip to Mars? How's your hotel?" exclaimed Olga as her smiling face filled the entertainment centre screen. She was wearing her orange jump suit.

"The trip was relaxing, dear, I met a few nice people, but nothing much else happened," replied Arthur. "How are things back at home? The kids only have a few weeks left of school, no?"

"Yes, sweetheart, Katya and Hank will be finished in three weeks. Then my parents arrive, as we discussed, to stay for the summer. We hope to take a trip to Algonquin Park for a week or two, rent one of those eco-chalets the government has built," responded Olga, obviously happy to see her husband again. "Are you settled yet into your hotel?"

"Yes, sweetie, it's the same old rustic Mahavishu Inn, of the Super-9 hotel chain, but it keeps the Martian dust-storms at bay. I just got in and will be doing the spacemail rounds before I hit the sack tonight," replied Arthur, the tiredness apparent in his voice. "So, when are Grandpa Mats and Grannie Margarita due to arrive?"

"On June 17th, they'll arrive at the Pickering airport from Stockholm and take a shuttle-car from there to our place. We thought of going to meet them, but traveling is so fast and easy that it's quicker to meet them at the front door. Teresa will convert the study to the guest room a couple of days before they arrive," replied Olga. Her face turned darker, with her brunette eyebrows furrowing as she asked "You haven't heard of anything from those Martian thugs that you encountered last time you were there, have you darling?"

"No, sweetheart, I haven't seen or heard anything from them. You know, most of them were caught, convicted and subjected to a personality wipe. The price for crime was very high for those hooligans. I think that they'll stay clear of me." Arthur did not feel as confident as he sounded. He knew that the stakes were high in what he had been hired to do on the X-Station and the mob would probably love to get their fingers into that pie at the earliest opportunity. "Have you heard from Zack?" Arthur adeptly changed the topic.

"Yes, dear, he arrived home a week ago and took us to the amusement park with Corby on the weekend. We had a wonderful time. I think the two of them are hitting it off. It would probably do Zack the world of good," observed Olga.

"I'll try to call him in the next couple of days and see how things are doing. Kotik recorded reams of data during our Martian orbit which I wonder whether he'd like to examine," mused Arthur. "On the business side, I have to install the electrical HVAC and solar array upgrades here for the Mahal shopping centre, and some HVAC work at the local mine, which will keep me busy for a few days. I'm hoping to hop over to the Tri-Party colony afterwards to see some of my friends from the Stargazer trip before I leave for Vesta. How are the lectures and your design work, sweetheart?"

"Lectures have ended and now I'm marking the final exams for my two design classes. I've gotten some more small contracts and am hiring some summer students at the college to help get them done. With Ma and Pa here I'll be able to spend more time getting those projects done. Then dear, we'll have more cash for that tropical cruise we wanted to take," Olga smiled again at the thought.

"I can feel that ocean breeze on the sundeck right now," said Arthur, in a teasing tone. "Do you think that we can persuade your parents to take care of the kids for a few weeks when I get back?"

"I'll do my best, sweetheart!" laughed Olga.

The rest of their conversation was short, since the communication costs were high. Arthur agreed to call her when the Mahal work was complete and they signed-off in the usual tearful manner. Arthur felt a rush of homesickness as Olga's picture faded from the viewscreen. It never gets any easier, does it? Arthur thought to himself.

Arthur was reviewing his installation specifications at the worktable in his hotel room when an incoming message beeped and flashed the message icon on the room's entertainment centre's screen. I wonder what this is, thought Arthur. He saw from the title bar on the message popup that the message was from the security firm Securiguard, well known for its presence in the frontier. Arthur agreed to accept the call.

"Good morning, Mr. Barthol. My name is Mel Prentice. The Mahal chapter of the Electrical Guild has asked me to ensure your security while at this location. When could I drop by to check your quarters and equip you with your security system?" Prentice's face, with its boxer nose, was stern. Obviously he was very serious about his job.

"Hi Mel, I'm meeting my clients this afternoon at 2 pm local time, so if you want to drop by around 12:30 pm, that would be fine. I'm in room 235," replied Arthur.

"Very well, Mr. Barthol. Please do not let anyone into your quarters until I arrive. Prentice out." Prentice's face disappeared from the screen as Arthur realized that this cloak and dagger plot was now getting more involved.

The buzzer on Arthur's hotel door sounded precisely at 12:30 pm. Arthur could see through the entertainment centre viewscreen that Prentice was standing alone at his door, so he activated the open button. The door slid away and Prentice walked in, dressed in Securiguard grey and carrying a black shoulder bag. The door slid back in place after Prentice entered.

"Good afternoon Mr. Barthol," said Prentice.

"You can call me Arthur, Mel," replied Barthol.

"I would like to conduct a security scan prior to outfitting you with your security system, if that's all right with you?" asked Prentice.

"Certainly, please proceed," responded Arthur.

Prentice released a set of four floating mini-probes from his bag, round chrome globes about five centimeters in width. The probes spread out around the hotel room, one to each corner. They whirred about, inspecting each nook and cranny for possible security breeches. After a short time they returned to the shoulder bag as Prentice regarded the scan results on his handheld portoputer.

"Looks fine, Arthur. I'm outfitting you with our latest security sensor array which jams listening devices, gives warning messages for security threats in your vicinity, checks people's profiles for local known criminals and provides a force field able to withstand most conventional weaponry." Prentice's voice was humorless.

"Sounds like serious business to me," replied Arthur.

"May I proceed?" asked Prentice.

"Please," replied Arthur.

Prentice extracted a body harness from his black shoulder bag and handed it to Arthur, whom he instructed to put on under his jumpsuit. The latter obliged by a trip to the washroom. Upon his return, Prentice instructed Arthur on how to activate the belt by clicking on a switch on a chest strap. Then Prentice extracted a small side arm from the shoulder bag and handed it to the electrician.

"Is this necessary?" asked Arthur.

"Our intelligence informs us that it is necessary, unfortunately," replied Prentice. "This is a compact pulse pistol. It emits a particle beam that will put holes through anything, so only use it if necessary. It has a view screen on its upper handle which can find the target and has an optical zoom. It uses infrared sensors to see in darkness and view body heat. Only use with extreme caution. You can also keep it outside a spacesuit." Prentice seemed to enjoy divulging this information.

"This is no joke," muttered Arthur.

"Yes, this is not as funny as 'one hand clapping'," replied Prentice.

Arthur recognized the Alliance passcode. "So, what news do you have for me?" he asked.

"Mr. Gage has asked me to see you just prior to your departure at which time we can talk further," responded Prentice with a poker face.

"Okay, Mel, hopefully I won't need to talk to you earlier," said Arthur.

"Here's a comm-pager that will contact me directly, please feel free at any time," replied Prentice, and with that, he zipped his shoulder bag and departed.

Arthur sat down quickly on the hotel room's only armchair, feeling drained from the encounter with this Securiguard soldier. Now I'm armed to the teeth and all I'm doing is installing HVAC wires, this feels like a comic spy novel, he thought. He then noticed his portoputer on his worktable, with the HVAC specifications on-screen, and realized that he only had forty-five minutes until the meeting with his clients. He stood and picked up the portoputer, returning to the work mode that his business demanded.

"I can see from the pictures what you are afraid of, Benji," said Arthur, dressed in his dark green business suit, as he looked up from the photo-log of the external wiring conduits of the Mahal retail district. Benji Lothal stood next to him, dressed in colourful traditional Indian garb, as Arthur's porto-puter projected a quasi-three-dimensional holograph of the shopping district's external wiring configuration.

"Yes, my friend," replied Lothal, "Our electrical system has been eroded by the Martian wind and dust. That's what years of exposure can do. We want you to replace the main conduit to the solar array. Also, I have subcontract work for you on the mining elevators that go down into the Valles. I know that you haven't got much time, so I will have all of the final details hopmailed to you immediately."

Arthur looked around Lothal's office. A small Hindu shrine was built into one corner with hydroponic flowers housed in vases amongst small iconic statuettes. The old religions can thrive anywhere, thought Arthur to himself. The office was modest with off-white walls and a light blue shag carpet, although relatively large by Mahal standards being twenty-five meters square. As with most, the office had one wall that could be used as a view screen. There was also a wood grain retractable meeting table at which they were seated and on which the porto-puter was placed. A small wood-grain desk was stationed in one corner, computer screen and keyboard atop. The walls were adorned with electric pictures that shifted from one scene to another of the Indian sub-continent. No windows, of course, since these were only available to high rent customers, not a retail mall management office.

"CommTrac is delighted to be of service, Benji. I have brought all the supplies for the job, including cabling from your esteemed friend, Bandira Resingh," said Arthur.

"Yes, Bandira gave you high marks which is why you are here now," replied Benji, slightly bowing his head in acknowledgement. "He was a good friend at university in Calcutta. How time takes us to different ends of the solar system!"

"Bandira is also renowned for his knowledge of cricket. He'll always give one an update on the world cup," responded Arthur with a grin.

"It's too bad that we haven't got a cricket pitch yet here at Mahal. The space requirements are just too large. There are plans, of course, but to install the gravity plating for the playing area, as well as the grandstands, plus the climate control and construction costs, it's just put it beyond our budget at this time. When we do build a cricket pitch, it will have to be an area that is convertible for multiple purposes. This will take the colony decades to save for, at best," said Benji with a sigh.

"I wish you good fortune in your efforts, and now I must depart to prepare my bots for the wire pulling. Benji, thanks and Nama Stay," said Arthur, with a slight bow, which Lothal returned. Then Arthur collected his porto-puter and was off, diagramatics busy on his brain.

"Hank, I warned you to stay out of those computer game sites!" exclaimed Arthur, glaring at his son on the holo-viewscreen in his hotel room. Hank, wearing his blue pants and grey sweater, looked down guiltily and nervously tried to rub a hole in the carpet with his right foot. Olga stood next to him, wearing her orange jump suit and hands on hips, trying to suppress a smile.

"But Dad, Jason told me about this great new game that you can download. It has new asteroid maze flights in a turbo-fighter!" blurted out Hank in self-defence.

"I don't care what Jason said, you only have permission to go to game sites when you ask. You should know that the computer will catch you and report you when you try a stunt like this!" Arthur had a scolding tone in his voice.

"Okay, Daddy, I won't do it again," replied Hank, still keeping his head down.

"So, son, you're grounded for a week, so there's no computer or vid-games for you. So, now you can go to your room for the rest of the afternoon," said Arthur. He watched his son shrug his shoulders and skulk out of the room.

"He probably meant no harm, but we have to train him to obey the house rules," sighed Olga after the study-room door closed behind her son.

"Yes dear, anyone can unintentionally download viruses from those game sites and goodness knows that we've had enough trouble with computer viruses. Occasionally, some nasty spyware also makes its way onto those sites as well!" exclaimed Arthur. "So, sweetheart, are your parents getting ready for their visit?"

"Yes, darling, they are looking forward to joining us," responded Olga.

"Well, they'll keep you entertained and perhaps even help take care of the kids. Theresa does a good job, but a robot can't be expected to give the same care as a person, even these days," mused Arthur.

"I know that they're looking forward to seeing their grandchildren, my adorable space-sailor!" Olga smiled as she looked affectionately at her husband.

"You'd hardly know that we're on different planets, millions of kilometers apart. I wish I could hold you, my sweet interior designer wife!" Arthur smiled, a lump burning in his throat.

"Get home soon, darling," said Olga, she sadly smiled as they gave their final salutations before disconnecting.

Arthur turned back to his porto-puter on the hotel room worktable after Olga's picture disappeared from the viewscreen. He had to immerse himself in the planning of the conduit replacement to divert himself from the homesickness welling up in his breast.

The alarm buzz seemed far off, initially, however it persisted and got louder as Arthur climbed out of his slumber. His porto-puter was buzzing and vibrating on the worktable, a blue warning light flashing on its side. Arthur rubbed his eyes as he rolled out of his bed. What could this be about? he wondered. He flipped up the porto-puter cover to see a yellow warning message flashing on the screen, "Security Violation", the message was sent from Kotik. Arthur quickly pressed the response button and Kotik's digital face appeared on the screen, a concerned furrow appearing on his virtual brow.

"Mr. Barthol, there has been an attempted security breach here. Some cloaked intruders attempted to access my cargo bay as well as the front hatch. They first tried to hack my systems but were unable. They are gone now." Kotiks voice was raised in obvious stress.

"Can you show me any video of their attack?" asked Arthur.

"Here's what I have," replied Kotik. The video was in infrared as it was Martian night outside. A blurry shape about five meters off the ground approached from the southeast and settled fifty meters from the shuttle. Two blurry figures appeared to get off the craft and walk towards the grounded ship.

"They must have been using cloaking technology. Even the infrared can only partially expose them. These guys aren't amateurs," observed Arthur.

The blurry figures circled the shuttle and approached the cargo bay door. Kotik's cameras were following the intruders. No sounds were emitted from them as they reached the cargo bay.

"I intercepted their electronic dialogues, but it is heavily encrypted. I doubt that it can be unscrambled, but I will continue using my randomizer to try to crack the code," Kotik advised.

The video showed one of the blurry shapes attaching a small cylindrical device to the cargo bay door. Electronic beeping could be heard as the device tried to unlock the security latching.

"I suppressed the alarm sirens and lighting since I estimated that I could defend against the intrusion," Kotik informed Arthur. "Since you upgraded my lock mechanisms last year it would take a code 11 Space Marine Engineering Bot to crack me open."

The cylindrical safe-cracking device started to rattle and then popped off the bay door, falling to the Martian soil below.

"My security counter-measures finished that 'bugger' off quickly," snarled Kotik, at least in as close to a snarling tone as his programs would permit.

"Well done, Kotik!" exclaimed Arthur. This robo-shuttle knows how to defend himself, he thought to himself.

The two blurry figures then scrambled to the other side of the shuttle, attaching a bigger cylindrical device to the cockpit hatch. Again the device quickly popped off Kotik's outer skin.

"At this point I decided that I wasn't going to permit any more forceful attempts to be made on gaining access, and since you've enabled my self-defense protocols, I activated low intensity repulse beams," reported Kotik.

On the periphery of the video Arthur could see an antenna extending a meter from the top of Kotik's roof, then the end of the aerial folded over and pointed at the intruders. A high pitched ringing sound could be heard and the blurry figures were knocked back a step.

"Obviously these guys are wearing force field defenses. They came reasonably well equipped," observed Arthur.

One of the blurry thieves raised a blurry arm and fired a laser shot at Kotik's repulse mini-cannon, however the ray had a 'dented look' as it deflected off Kotik's own defense force field.

"Thank goodness that we deployed your defensive array prior to leaving Toronto," sighed Arthur as he watched the bandits quickly exit from the scene. Kotik blasted them a few more times in their butts on their way out, though this was more for show than real effect since the intruders had sufficient defenses to protect themselves.

"Contact the spaceport authorities and report the burglary attempt. I think this is more than meets the eye, although the local authorities will probably just pass it off as an attempted robbery," Arthur said.

Kotik agreed and signed off. Arthur headed back to bed wondering whether Kotik felt any insecurity over the intrusion and then worried about his own well being now that it appeared his cover had been blown. He drifted off into a troubled sleep.

"They left some tracks and one of their lock-cracking devices, so we'll try to trace them from those. As well, the electronic signatures captured by your shuttle may be useful, in addition to the videos. You are providing us with enough information for a good start on this investigation, Mr. Barthol, even if they were cloaked," said Sergeant Nehru of the Martian Mahal Constabulary. Both he and Arthur were viewing the video surveillance recorded by Kotik on the officer's porto-puter in the Constabulary Station located in the Mahal business district. The colony was one large mall-like structure, so calling it the Mahal mall was quite appropriate, Arthur had observed recently.

"Please keep me informed of what you find, Sergeant Nehru. I had trouble on Mars six years ago and I want to ensure that these jerks get caught, and quickly!" said Arthur emphatically.

"I will send you a hopmail notice at any point we discover anything of significance, Mr. Barthol," responded Nehru.

Arthur then departed the tiny office and exited the Constabulary station. Being a frontier town, Mahal needed a strong policing presence. The Indian colony had relied on private enterprise to supply many of Mahal's needs, such as food, entertainment, medical, legal and commercial facilities, and with that comes the riff raff, thought Arthur. It was hard to tell whether they knew of his mission, whether it was a 'flash from the past' from six years ago or whether it was just petty criminals looking to swipe some technology. In any case, I need the cops now to keep a lid on this, he mused. His left hand instinctively felt the side-arm in his pant pocket as he walked back to his hotel. He passed through the Mahal commercial district which was filled with the smell of Indian food and hanging signs written in Indian calligraphy, fighting his insecurities each step of the way.

"So there you have it, Chas and Eibu, these guys have cloaking technology and safe-cracking equipment that appears to be fairly advanced. They may be able to re-equip at an even higher level of sophistication, which is what we should plan for, so that is why I want to ask you Eibu if there is any further enhancements that we can do on Kotik's defense grid, as well as for me and my service bots, K1 and K2?" asked Arthur, wearing red pullovers. He was looking at his hotel holo-viewscreen which was split between images of Chas Lorbring, dressed in a brown patterned sweater and grey slacks, in Toronto and Eibu Chang, dressed in a traditional Chinese green square-cut suit, in Shanghai. They had just finished viewing Kotik's videos of the attempted break-in.

"This is serious stuff, partner!" exclaimed Lorbring, "We can't be sure that this is nothing more than a petty break-and-enter or more clandestine in nature," he continued.

"Yes, Arthur, you can enhance your security level with the equipment you have in place," inserted Chang, "Ask Kotik to access the 'code blue protocols', these will activate the most advanced set of defenses for the shuttle. It will take more energy, however, which is why it wasn't activated in the first place. This technology is the best proven defense grid, and is quite expensive, so it's good that you were able to afford it."

Chas gave Arthur a quick side glance to ensure that his partner was not about to divulge the source of the funding, the Alliance intelligence service.

"What about upgrades for myself and the bots?" asked Arthur.

"For yourself, extract the security harness from container NG3 and put it on. It is equipped with a full forcefield and a particle cannon, as well as a cloaking protocol if needed. In container NG4 is the same technology configured for the bots. Set the sensitivity level to maximum." Eibu showed concern on his face.

"Okay. I'll outfit the bots and we'll get this contract finished as quickly as possible. Eibu, is there any devices to capture an assailant with?" enquired Arthur.

"Yes, the main one being a fishnet entangler. You'll have to add that to your utility belt on the harness. When released, it has a heat seeking mechanism, when it reaches its target it shoots a fishnet web that ensares it's victim and applies taser shocks as it locks down. Quite effective though only for a limited range, perhaps one hundred and fifty meters," Eibu replied.

"Great, gives me a chance to capture one of these buggers for interrogation," mused Arthur. "Okay, thanks gentlemen. I'll equip my team with the upgrades and then we'll attempt to get this gig done, pronto. Barthol out." The picture faded as Arthur turned to his porto-puter to retrieve the schematics on the defense grid. He and the bots were going to have to make an unscheduled trip to Kotik to perform the upgrade, and they would have to depart quickly to ensure their maximum safety, so no time to waste, he thought.

The view from the top of Mahal was intriguing. The corridors of the mall formed a gridwork amongst the small box towers and rectangular warehouses of the colony. Barthol, dressed in his metallic brown spacesuit, looked down from atop K2, observing K1 as it completed the cabling installation on the HVAC unit over the shopping mall food court. The old cables and HVAC unit, which the bots would shortly remove to the spaceport warehouse, lay in a pile atop a box tower which rose twenty meters above the corridor roof.

The whole complex was smeared with red Martian rust dust. The soil had blown in and found its way into all the cracks and crannies of the colony's rooftop. As Arthur looked up he could see the corridor that snaked out to the canyon wall of Valles Marineris, at whose edge at two kilometers distance arose the mining complex that extracted ores from the canyon's walls. That is our next and final destination, Arthur thought, hoping that the peacefulness of the mall HVAC and solar array upgrades would continue at the mining site.

K1 was floating next to the elevator shaft that clung to the canyon wall of Valles Marineris a hundred meters from its apex. The robo-mechanic had its front two extendible arms working on attaching cabling to the cylindrical cable cage that was appended to the outside wall of the shaft. The bot had the cable rolling out of the back cargo trailer attached to its rear.

"Arthur, I'm having difficulty with some of the fasteners on the cable cage. Is it appropriate for them to be broken? We are carrying standard issue replacement parts," said K1.

"Certainly, K1, just ensure that the any litter is collected for the recycling bins," replied Arthur who was aboard K2, floating next to the shaft a further seventy-five meters down the canyon wall. K2, with a cargo container in tow, was also fastening cable to the cable cage with its front extendible arms.

The sun poured down into the canyon from its mid-morning perch. The wind was twenty kilometers an hour from the east. The view was spectacular, noted Arthur, as the Valles Marineris stretched kilometers downward and out beyond the horizon in either direction. This view was certainly worth the trip, thought Arthur. Couldn't ask for better conditions, he added.

Arthur blinked as he thought he saw something flash further up the valley. What would be out there? he thought to himself. That flash reflected off something, he conjectured. Then the sensors on his utility belt sounded an alarm. He gave a thought command to his spacesuit to magnify his visor's view in the vicinity of where the flash originated. He saw the varying shades of brown and black stratified rock layers in the canyon walls but nothing else of note.

"K2, scan the canyon to our east with all your sensors, let me know what you find," said Arthur.

"I only see normal atmospheric temperature fluctuations and no other activity…EXCEPT one and possibly more objects of approximately one cubic meter each moving at thirty meters per second at a distance of five kilometers heading directly at us. They are cloaked though I can see their infrared heat signatures," replied K2, after a five second interval.

"Oops, we're in for visitors in just over three minutes!" cried Arthur, "K1 and K2, drop your cabling immediately, K1 wait for us to join you, then we're heading for the canyon top. Activate your full shields and your particle canyons. Bogies are inbound from the east!"

K1 and K2 cut their cables immediately. K2 then shot up the 75 meters to K1 where the two bots headed up the canyon wall five meters apart. The intruders reached them approximately 25 meters from the crest.

The crackle of disrupter fire could be heard through the Martian air as K2 got hit from the side. Arthur felt the pounding of the energy beam as it knocked him off K2 as his bot veered to the left. Arthur, yanked by his lifeline, could see the canyon crest disappearing as he fell back down into the chasm, dragging K2 behind him. Terror electrified his spine.

K1 made a quick ninety degree right turn. A flash emitted from its right side that signified a burst of its particle cannon. Seventy meters to K1's right a flare appeared, then the cloak disappeared briefly from a cylindrical sniper bot followed immediately by an explosion from a direct hit. It was blown to bits.

Meanwhile, dozens of meters below, K2 and Arthur spiralled down the chasm in a free fall, the two at each end of Arthur's lifeline as they spun out of control. Further crackles of disrupter fire could be heard, but the shots missed them as they descended. K1 dove down in pursuit until it was hit by another disrupter blast, knocking it sideways into its own downward spiral.

K2, although spinning, was able to shoot its own particle cannon just after K1 was hit, having obtained a lock on the intruder that took the shot. Another flare of a direct hit was seen seventy meters up the canyon wall, and the cloak came off another cylindrical sniper bot. Smoke started emitting from the intruder as it listed to one side, frantically trying to pull up. K2 got another shot off, another direct hit that caused the second sniper to explode.

Disrupter fire was still heard as K2 got knocked sideways again.

"K1 and K2, activate your cloaks," barked Arthur through his helmet communicator. Both bots complied as both disappeared from view. Arthur and K2 were still spinning as they fell, however he was able to draw himself back up to the bot by activating the retractor on his life line. He grabbed the bot and climbed back aboard, bringing it out of the free fall in a broad loop. Disrupter fire could still be heard, but it did not come close to their position. K1 had also climbed out of its dive.

"Okay, gents, how many more of these sniper bots are out here?" asked Arthur.

"Looks like one more, captain," replied K2 after it communicated with K1.

"Let's see if we can capture it," said Arthur, "K1, I want you to drive that bugger over to us, we'll stay stationary so it can't see our heat signature. I want to snag this thing with the entangler."

"Sounds like fun," replied K1, "I'll be glad to smack this one over to you pronto!"

Arthur saw laser flashes and heard particle cannon crackles from various positions as K1 drew an arc above him. A couple of small flashes were seen, then the cloak disappeared off the third sniper bot which turned to flee downward and westward, leaving a trail of smoke as it tried to escape K1's pursuit. It failed to notice that K2 and Arthur were waiting for it.

The fleeing sniper bot was streaking past K2 when Arthur launched the entangler from his security belt. The entangler initially looked like a heat seeking missile that followed the movements of the sniper bot. It gained on the wounded machine until it was within ten meters when a sudden spark flashed. A mesh grid shot out that ensnared the sniper-bot, with electrical sparks flying as it subdued its victim. Just as the ensnared sniper started into a free fall, K2 fired a grappling hook that snagged the intruder.

"Well done, boys. K2, please keep that thing at a good 100 meter distance until we get it back to the spaceport," said Arthur. "Keep your cloaks on until we get back to the spaceport, we don't want to receive anymore pot shots. We'll have to get Mahal security to cover us when we finish this job."

K1 lead the way, under cloak, as K2 climbed up the canyon wall dragging the dead sniper-bot behind it. The journey back to the spaceport might have seemed odd to the naked eye as Arthur's bots were cloaked, however the grappling cable and the dead sniper were visibly being dragged through the Martian air.

So what if it looks funny, thought Arthur, no one will know it's us anyway. The spaceport appeared on the horizon as they rose over the canyon crest and trekked out over the Martian desert, weary from another encounter with Martian hoodlums.

"Again, Mr. Barthol, you have cost my associates dearly," wheezed the short stalky man, wearing a grey trenchcoat, obviously disguised in an ill-fitting turban and fake beard. "We first sought recompense from your shuttle for the costs you brought us six years ago, but your equipment was more advanced than we expected. Then we sought revenge in the canyon. Do you want this to continue, or shall we settle this now?"

"Why do you guys even bother with me if I bring you so much grief?" replied Arthur, wearing his dark green suit, nervously sweating under the collar.

"We want to control economic activity at this outpost, and you are an interloper," responded the thug, voice as gruff as ever.

"What do you suggest as a settlement?" asked Arthur, shifting his stance as he stood in a side corridor in the Mahal commercial district. No one was near to them, which could have caused him some concern.

"You deposit twenty thousand Martian credits in a satchel in the main square, at a location of my choosing at noon tomorrow, then you depart by the next day," snarled the thief.

"Sounds good, except you'll be spending the rest of your time on this red rock behind bars, my friend," snarled Arthur in return. The whole conversation had been digitally recorded and transmitted to Sergeant Nehru's mobile monitoring vehicle around the corner.

The thief looked startled, believing that his jamming equipment would prevent any eavesdropping, but his equipment was out of date. When he glanced back to where Arthur was standing his prey had disappeared. Arthur had activated his cloaking device and had stepped away from the scene. The next second a heat seeking entanglement mini-missile streaked in from down the corridor and exploded next to the thug, emitting a wide mesh that entwined the thief, quickly making him fall to the ground. His stunned body shook a bit on the ground and then became silent as the taser volts subdued him.

"Well done, Arthur," said Sergeant Nehru's voice over Arthur's earphone, "We'll need to track all of the buggers in this gang from this one. Thank goodness we caught him red handed. We'll break him to get the names of his associates."

"Very good, glad you decided to shadow me, I wasn't sure that they'd try to approach me again after two failed attempts," replied Arthur. The mob had actually left him alone for a few days after the canyon attack, permitting him to complete the installation job under armed guard protection. He had just been walking back to the mall administration office to finish the invoice details with Benji Lothal when he had been confronted by the fallen thug.

"I've just been informed that we've tracked the lock-cracking device that was used on your shuttle, and we're about to make an arrest. The captured sniper bot will likely be tracked as well. Having now caught this thug, we will likely be able to finally break this gang once and for all!" exclaimed Nehru, slightly hurting Arthur's ear from the earphone volume.

"Hope that's true, Sergeant, I'd like to be able to visit here again someday without fearing for my life," responded Arthur.

"That is my hope as well, my friend," replied Nehru.

Arthur de-cloaked and then proceeded to assist the blue uniformed Nehru and his deputies with administrative work at the crime scene before continuing on to the Mahal admin offices. On the way he called Prentice to inform him of the capture and to thank him for the military equipment that the latter had provided. I might not have made it through this without Prentice's help, mind you Eibu's equipment was good as well, thought Arthur. Prentice's forcefield and particle gun were of higher grade than Eibu's, however Eibu's defensive array for the bots and the shuttle had been invaluable and the fishnet entangler was helping in the investigation.

As Arthur reached Benji's office he still made a quick look behind him, nervously scanning for anyone tailing him. I think I'll be glad when I'm out of here, he mused. With that thought, he walked through the admin office door to finalize his departure from Mahal.

"So my brother is a swashbuckling, wire-pulling crime-fighter! Dad should be proud!" Zack let out a bellowing laugh that made Arthur cringe.

"Yes, Zack, my bots and I go around with knives in our teeth. We're a match for any pirate even if they're from the Caribbean!" retorted Arthur.

"How did you do it, bro? You took out three sniper bots even after you fell off your pony," asked Zack, with a bit of respect in his voice despite the humor.

"Well, Zack, we had good equipment and it was the bots that took out the snipers, though I can take credit for launching the fishnet missile," replied Arthur modestly. He was seated in his hotel room, dressed in his grey track suit, facing the entertainment centre screen which displayed Zack's image, broadcasted from his brother's study. Zack was also seated looking attentively back at his brother, dressed in a light blue T-shirt and shorts.

"Come on, Artie, where'd you get the equipment to take out sniper bots? I may not be an arms dealer but I know that those things are pretty high tech and pretty deadly," enquired Zack.

"Let's just say that I have good friends at the Electrical Guild," responded Arthur, "You know that I had trouble here six years ago, so I wanted to make sure I was prepared. We can hardly afford to lose one of our bots, let alone me taking injury, or worse."

"Okay bro, but someday I'm going to ask you again what's going on with this gig you're on. It seems a bit risky to me," replied Zack insightfully.

"Look who's talking, my globe-trotting, thrill-seeking, academic brother. As if you're averse to taking risks, Zack." Arthur let out a little chuckle. "How many crocodile's did you wrestle on your recent trip to Africa?"

"None, my exaggerating sibling. Anyway, are you cutting this trip short now that you've had a few pot-shots taken at you?" asked the younger man in a somber tone, "I know Olga is worried."

"I understand why she would be, however we stand to make a good buck out of this trip so I'm going to continue, though I'm getting off Mars on the next transport," said Arthur. "By the way, how are things with Corby?"

"I knew you'd enquire about my love life! Let's just say that things are going well. We're going to dinner up in Kleinberg tomorrow evening and taking in the Group of Seven gallery afterwards." Zack had a small smirk on his face.

"Well done, bro, I figured that you'd eventually see the value in a relationship with a good woman." Arthur laughed. "Send me some updates via spacemail, okay?"

"Will do, Captain! Good luck to you and your troops. Keep me posted with your ongoing adventures," responded Zack.

"Will do, Mars out." With that, Arthur clicked the disconnect button and Zack's picture was replaced by a blue background screen. As he turned away from the entertainment centre Arthur felt homesickness well up in his chest again. I have a good family and a good life, he thought, I have to get back there soon. Then he returned to packing his gear for his trip to the Tri-Party colony.

The knocking on his hotel room door made Arthur jump. He was nervous, as would be expected. He ensured that he was wearing his force-field harness before he answered. Checking the door video camera, he saw that Mel Prentice was standing in the hall holding a small package. He opened the door and let the Securiguard agent in.

"Do you have something for me from the Electrical Guild, Mel?" asked Arthur in a slightly sarcastic tone.

"No, this is from the folks that like jokes about 'one hand clapping'," replied Prentice, not a hint of humor in his voice or on his boxer face.

"I see. So, I'm not to ask any questions and no one else is to know about this item, correct?" asked Arthur.

"Yes, that's correct, Mr. Barthol," replied Prentice.

"Very well. I just wanted to thank you for outfitting me with your defensive equipment. I had some of my own, but I believe your force-field was better than the one I had," said Arthur.

"I always like having a satisfied client, Mr. Barthol," responded Prentice, and after a quick bow he departed, leaving Arthur to continue his packing, which now included spyware to deliver for his Alliance overlords.

"How do the systems check out, Kotik?" Arthur enquired of his shuttle.

"All systems ready to go, Mr. Barthol," Kotik reported cordially.

"Since we've received clearance from Mahal and Martian Alliance aerospace control, let's 'put the pedal to the medal' and 'make hay' for the Tri-Party Colony," said Arthur, wearing his blue coveralls and buckled into the red cockpit pilot's seat.

"My English lexicon database has translated your twentieth century slang, so lift off is in process, Arthur," retorted Kotik.

The rusty brown soil of the Martian desert receded below them as Kotik rose vertically to get clear of the Mahal spaceport. Arthur looked over to see the buildings of Mahal in the distance, glad that the assignment had been completed successfully and relieved to be leaving a place that still had a serious crime problem.

Kotik engaged its primary thrust engines at an altitude of five hundred meters. Valles Marineris yawned below them as the shuttle continued to climb into a low altitude orbit. The curved edge of the Martian horizon appeared in the morning sun. Kotik charted the quickest route to the Tri-Party Colony which took them two and a half hours to cover. Coming back into the lower atmosphere gave the shuttle a few bumps, but the trip was otherwise uneventful. The towers of the colony appeared on the horizon as this bustling little metropolis rose up to greet them. Kotik did a low altitude sweep skirting the southern warehouse district on the way to the spaceport. There was noticeable air traffic here, with one large cargo ship departing upon Kotik's approach. Tri-Party aerospace control directed Kotik to a peripheral landing area where numerous shuttles and other small ships were parked. The landing was smooth and Arthur decided to spend the rest of the day on board making arrangements and doing an inventory review for his pending departure for Vesta. Nothing like a quiet day at the office, quipped Arthur to himself.

"What do you mean by 'it was just another day pulling wires'?" cried Olga, her face grimacing through Kotik's readyroom holo-viewscreen, "You could have been killed on that rusty dirtball!"

Arthur, wearing his green pullovers, realized that he had said the wrong thing. He should have described his encounter with the sniper-bots as hair-raising. If only Olga could see the humorous side to the situation like he was trying to do, he reassured himself. "I'm sorry dear, I'm just trying to put a positive spin on the situation. The Mahal police have consulted with the other colonies' cops and have concluded that this all relates to my encounters with the Martian mob six years ago. They say that I'm probably going to get a commendation for helping break up the gang here, a gang they didn't have a lot of details on."

"That's all fine and dandy, Arthur, but what good is a commendation if you're dead?" retorted Olga, with a brunette furrowed brow. She was wearing her light red dress which Arthur found attractive.

"I'm not dead, sweetheart. We took extra precautions which paid off. I do understand your concerns, however, and I'm restricting my activities at the Tri-Party colony to one social event before my rendezvous with the next inter-trans to Vesta." Arthur hoped that this tone of caution would persuade her that he was being sufficiently careful. "How are Katie and Hank?"

"They are fine, and don't go changing the topic, space-sailor!" Olga's tone made Arthur cringe as he realized that slipping out of this argument was not going to be so easy. But somehow he managed to, finally, with a little bit of sympathizing and the promise of an exotic vacation when he returned home (that they couldn't afford otherwise). After many tearful good-byes the spouses logged off and returned to their respective tasks at hand.

"Now, Frenchie, don't you think that the message of King Lear is a bit gloomy?" Conrad Barrington's bombastic tone made his question more irritating than it should have been. The four friends from the Stargazer sortie sat around a café table in the Tri-Party colony's food court. Arthur, Maurice Bouchard, Barrington and Terri Kamanuchi were meeting for a coffee before they went their separate ways again, in Arthur's case off-planet.

"Mais oui, Monsieur Barrington, King Lear is a work of art that actually provides more than un peu de entertainment, non?" Bouchard, all dressed in black (as usual), looked intently into Barrington's eyes.

"Yes, indeed, my friend de Francaise, this play is one of the first absurdist works in the English language, that we know of at least. Beckett and Sartre write absurdist literature in the twentieth century but nothing eclipses the philosophical points made in Lear," replied Barrington, dressed in a brown sweater and grey slacks. "Miller wrote another masterpiece on a similar theme in 'Death of a Salesman'."

"Both Lear and 'Death of a Salesman' deal with the apparent meaninglessness of life," interjected Arthur, who was wearing a blue shirt and dark blue pants. "Lear, however, also examines betrayal, lust, loyalty, insanity and justice. Both plays are examinations of Sartre's 'nausea'." Arthur's voice wavered. He hadn't realized that he still had pent up anxiety over the attempt on his life.

"What is it, Arthur? You sound a bit faint." Terri leaned over the café table, looking at Arthur with concerned eyes, wearing a shiny dark purple dress.

"Oh, I must still be feeling stress from an incident at Mahal." Arthur noticed a nervous twitch in his leg. "I haven't told you folks yet, but my robo-mechanics and I were attacked by a trio of cloaked sniper-bots in the Valles Marineris just a couple of days after someone tried to break into my shuttle. It was quite the gun battle, but we knocked them off and caught one of them as it tried to escape."

"What!!" Conrad, Maurice and Terri all cried in unison.

"I had a run in with the mob when I did a contract here six years ago." Arthur saw that he had a captive audience. "I found out later that they initially wanted to rip me off by breaking into the shuttle, and when that was foiled they got really mad and sought revenge. Fortunately we were prepared for it. The cops nailed a guy who tried to blackmail me and from there more arrests have been made."

"You aren't afraid that you may still be their target?" Barrington took a suspicious look around the café.

"No, I think that they're on the run. They are probably wary of another 'sting', which is how we caught the blackmailer," replied Arthur. He still felt a bit nervous, despite his assurances to his friends. He decided to change the topic. "I think we're safe. By the way, Conrad, what is the schedule for your entertainment ship?"

"'The Bard' has several months of work on Mars, before heading to the asteroid belt," replied Barrington in a 'matter of fact' tone.

"Will you be going to all three Martian colonies?" asked Terri.

"Yes, we have to capitalize on all of our marketing opportunities, especially since the market is so small. They are quite receptive here in the outback," replied Barrington, putting on a business-like expression.

"And what of 'Chuck Wagon'?" asked Arthur, turning to Kamanuchi and Bouchard.

"Monsieur, notre voyage into the asteroid belt is earlier than 'the Bard's', but much later than yours, mon ami," replied Maurice with a smile.

"Yes, friends, my journey to Vesta begins at the crack of dawn, so I must get some rest before departure. It was nice seeing you all again. Please drop me a spacemail from time to time."

Arthur and his friends bade adieu and he waved good-bye as he left the café en route back to Kotik. He felt a flood of emotions as he walked to the warehouse district, from regret at leaving his friends to fear about being shadowed by the Martian mob. He was not being followed, however, and he donned his spacesuit for the final trek from the warehouse portal to Kotik. Once back aboard his shuttle he gave a sigh of relief knowing this was his final night on Mars.

"Hi Chas, I'm departing this morning for Vesta aboard the inter-trans Wanderer. Have all the arrangements been finalized with the client there?" Arthur sounded a bit weary after a late night with his Stargazer friends. He looked at Lobring, who was dressed in a casual sweater and jeans, on Kotik's viewscreen.

"Yes, my friend," laughed Chas. "Your HVAC work on the Vesta mine is confirmed. I have heard nothing from our Alliance friend, probably for the better. Any more news about your assailants?"

"Martian cops have arrested a few more mobsters and think there are more to be nabbed once the first group has been interrogated." Arthur's face appeared a bit grim. "These guys have a long memory and were seeking revenge for the incident six years ago. Well, they'll pay a heavy price, prison terms are long on the frontier, then they face personality wipes and expulsion after their prison time is up. Earth won't take them back either, so they'll be stuck on an asteroid somewhere for the rest of their days. Serves them right."

"It seems we were smart in getting Eibu's defensive array which not only protected you and your bots but helped clean up the Martian crime scene. Anyway, I'm spacemailing you the final specs for the Vesta job, have a nice trip and keep in touch.

CommTrac out." Chas's face faded to the dark blue background of the viewer. Arthur saw that Chas's spacemail had already arrived in his inbox, noting that his work never ended. He looked at his wrist band which housed a timepiece, amongst other gadgets, and realized that there was only an hour before launch to join Wanderer. How time flies when you're having fun, he quipped to himself as he became busy with final preparations.

The warehouse district of the Tri-Party Martian Colony dropped below them as Kotik rose from the launch area of the spaceport. The Colony's towers reflected the morning sunshine as Kotik quickly gained altitude. The orbital traffic surrounding Mars was not even one percent of Earth's, but was still present, with the occasional spacestation and cargo ship to navigate around. Kotik's route to the rendezvous point with Wanderer was brief, taking only forty-five minutes. Contact was made with Wanderer's first mate and docking arrangements were communicated.

Arthur looked back at Mars and realized that he had grown more philosophical now that he had survived an assassin's attack. He was looking forward to the exotic vacation that he had promised Olga. Perhaps this 'swashbuckling' would be better delegated to others next time while I stay home with the family, he thought to himself. Wanderer grew larger on the viewscreen and he turned himself to the docking task at hand, deferring to another time the debate about his future.

CHAPTER 5

Vesta

The inter-trans Wanderer had the same structural design as Stargazer. She was a cargo ship that was built to take extra payloads on deep space voyages, which contributed to its financial bottom line. She was a rectangular-shaped column one hundred and seventy meters long, eighteen meters high and wide. She was ringed with external bumper scaffolding for passenger ships to be strapped to. The navigation cockpit was in the bow along with the dark matter deflector array. Two large thruster engines were lodged in the stern followed by bulging bulkheads that led to the fuel tanks. Three medium sized ships and one shuttle were docked to her upon Kotik's approach.

Kotik ran up along side Wanderer a hundred and fifty meters out, as per the agreed upon protocols communicated from the latter's first mate. Wanderer then extended a grappling hook which Kotik snagged with its portside robotic arm. The arm then fastened the hook to Kotik's forward port-side Sampson eyehole. The inter-trans then drew Kotik in to its docking scaffolding, which Kotik grabbed with both its starboard and port robotic arms. The shuttle was quickly fastened down and an accordion gangway was extended to the shuttle's port-side cockpit hatch.

Although Wanderer offered accommodations, much like Stargazer, Arthur chose to bunk aboard Kotik, as usual, to save on transport costs, amongst other reasons.

""The asteroid belt is the area of space within our Solar System which is located between the orbits of Mars and Jupiter." The lecturer, Wanderer's first mate Matt Hornsby, used a laser pointer to distinguish features on a three dimensional hologram of the subject matter. Arthur was attending this 'Meet and Greet' orientation session in Wanderer's modest-sized assembly hall. He counted about a dozen and a half people as he browsed the crowd.

"Asteroids have non-spherical shapes of various sub-planetary sizes. More than half of the mass of the belt is contained within four planetoids, Ceres, Vesta, Pallas and Hygiea, all of which have average diameters of over four hundred kilometers." Hornsby flashed the laser pointer on the four planetoids in the hologram. "Currently there is an orbital proximity amongst Mars, Vesta, Ceres and Jupiter which makes it possible to traverse the belt and visit all four in a relatively short time frame."

"The origin of the asteroid belt has been a bit of a mystery for scientists since its discovery during middle times. Two theories are outstanding, one is that it is the remainder of a planet destroyed in a catastrophic collision after the dawn of the Solar System, the second being that the belt is caused by the gravitational disturbance of Jupiter which prevented the normal formation of a planet at the start of the Solar System. Take your pick." Hornsby stopped to take a drink. "The asteroid belt is home to rich ore deposits which make it the focus of intense mining activity."

"Vesta is the second largest body in the asteroid belt," continued Hornsby, "With an approximate diameter of 530 kilometers. Vesta's crust is approximately ten kilometers thick. Earth scientists estimate that this dwarf planet suffered a huge collision approximately one billion years ago, witnessed by the enormous impact crater in its south polar region. This impact produced a plethora of smaller asteroidal debris, some of it known as HED meteorites that have collided with Earth over the ages. This south polar impact crater is roughly 480 kilometers wide, about 80% of Vesta's diameter, with a 3 to 14 kilometer rim and a central peak eighteen kilometers high. The Tri-Party mining colony straddles the rim of the south polar crater, thus being able to mine iron ore and nickel veins laterally, similar to some of the mines that straddle the Valles Marineris on Mars."

"So that is the scoop on our destination, fellow passengers," said Hornsby as he turned to the audience. "My job is to ensure that you have a comfortable journey. Our trip is scheduled to take a week, as you well know, so please take this opportunity to meet some new friends to help entertain yourselves during our trip." With that, the dimmed lights returned to normal brightness.

Arthur walked over to the snack table to grab some hydroponic carrots and broccoli sticks to munch on. He was wearing his green business suit to look respectable. While scooping the snack dip with a broccoli stick he brushed elbows with a tall lanky man, dressed in a dark blue, pinstripe suit, doing the same.

"Excuse me, sir. Please go ahead and take some of that dip before I consume it all," said Arthur in a conversational tone.

"Certainly, sir, and thank-you. Did you enjoy the presentation?" asked the stranger.

"Most certainly," replied Arthur, "The hologram of the asteroid belt was most impressive."

"I agree," said the stranger, "It was quite detailed, including the rings caused by Kirkwood gaps."

"What are those?" inquired Arthur curiously.

"A Kirkwood gap is caused by the effect of Jupiter's gravity on asteroids which have an orbital convergence with the gas giant. If the asteroid's orbit is an integer multiple of Jupiter's, then the latter's gravity pulls it further out of its original path, leaving a gap in the belt." The lanky man smiled as he noticed Arthur's interest. His slight German accent was now perceptible to the Canadian.

"Asteroids have also been the source of some of Earth's greatest disasters," chimed in a perky female voice.

"Yes," replied the lanky man, turning to see a stunning blonde woman, dressed in a blue velvet dress, standing next to Arthur.

"Some of those asteroids are credited with two huge impact craters on Earth, including the one at the Yucatan in Mexico which is believed to have caused the extinction of the dinosaurs sixty-five million years ago."

"Well, we didn't need an asteroid to cause the mass extinctions of the twentieth and twenty-first centuries. We did it all by ourselves," said the blonde bitterly.

"My name is Frederick Baumann," the lanky man leaned forward raising his right hand to the woman, who took it politely.

"I'm Julie Mills," replied the blonde, doing a small curtsy, then she turned to Arthur. "And whom do I have the pleasure of this acquaintance?"

"Hi, I'm Arthur Barthol," responded Arthur, a little uncomfortable with this lady's beauty. How can there be such a beautiful woman out on the frontier, he asked himself.

"And what is your destination, Frederick?" Julie asked as she turned back to the tall German.

"I'm a mining engineer with the Lavalin Consortium. We operate one of the nickel mines at the Tri-Party colony on Vesta. What about yourself, may I ask?" Bauman made a short bow to Mills.

"I'm the new office manager at the entertainment complex at the Tri-Party colony, so we have the same destination. What about you, Arthur?" Again this smiling beauty turned her attention to Arthur who felt his temperature rise as her gaze turned to him.

"I'm a humble electrician who has to rewire the HVAC units in one of those mines, possibly one that Frederick will be working in." Arthur felt his pulse rising slightly as he gazed back into Julie's hypnotic eyes.

"Ah, then your's is possibly a short stay?" asked Frederick inquisitively.

"Yes, I'm on to Ceres after a week or two, having a similar job there as well. I don't like to stay in one place too long for fear of sprouting roots!" Arthur laughed at his own joke, the others joined in.

"So tell me gentlemen, do you think that we are all pawns in a capitalist's game?" Julie's eyes flashed as they darted from one man to the other. "Are we out here earning peanuts for the 'Man' back on Earth?"

"Now that's an interesting question, Ms. Mills," replied Bauman, appearing to enjoy the possibility of an intellectual discussion. "Do you believe that we are the risk takers and the corporate investors are the exploiters who take little risk?"

"To some extent I believe that's true. You know, I think that if it wasn't for the Alliance we'd all be slaves on the corporate farm being paid a pittance and being charged more money than we earn to live in the farm's bunkhouse." A furrow had grown on Mill's pretty brow.

"Ah, you're making an analogy to farm workers during the American Depression of the twentieth century. I see your point." Frederick stroked his chin thoughtfully. "The Alliance does perform a great service to the frontier in the way it capably regulates activities here. They have been able to transplant their successful institutions from Earth to the colonies, which is to their credit, I believe. Or, do you think that the Alliance doesn't go far enough, Ms. Mills?"

"Some of my socialist friends think not, but I do have to admit that justice and security are well handled out here. Other social programs leave a little bit to be desired, though they are making some progress." Mills' mood seemed to lighten. "What do you think, Arthur?"

Arthur was caught off guard. "Um, well I'm a bit of a capitalist myself, being a part-owner of the firm I work for. However, from a political science perspective, I believe that society learned from the mistakes of the twentieth century that all members of society need to be taken care of, otherwise you get revolutions. So capitalists, being pragmatists, have grown to accept the necessity of government social programs to stabilize employment, wages, living conditions, education, medicine, security, etc. Does the Alliance do enough? Perhaps not, but they certainly do enough to keep society stable and to keep corporate rogues in check, in my opinion anyway."

"I agree, Arthur," said Frederick, "Governments are good at channeling activity and providing programs that are best delivered in a non-competitive manner, however government does not often provide innovation, independent companies and individuals do."

"I know what they teach in political science courses, " remarked Mills, "That the best social model is one that provides a social safety net, but not one that makes one live comfortably on government hand-outs. Thusly, everyone is encouraged to improve their lives with a little honest effort."

"Yes, Julie, but you are correct that business and science needs to be well regulated, in my opinion anyway," interjected Arthur. "Corporations are not the great moral leaders of society, that is for certain."

"We are all out on the frontier to earn a higher than average living," observed Frederick. "So we behave like the corporations, for the profit motive. If Earth didn't need the minerals out here, we wouldn't have spent the money building these colonies. We might have a few small scientific outposts but that's about all. It's too expensive and dangerous to get here otherwise, at least with our current technology."

"Yes, and with the profit motive in mind, I must get back to my shuttle to review preparations for our next stop," said Arthur, feeling fatigue. "It has been a pleasure meeting you both, please feel free to drop me a hopmail when you have time." He shook the hand of each, feeling his pulse rise when it was Julie's turn. With a short bow he departed back to Kotik to do an inventory of the Vesta supplies.

Out in the dark void of the Kuiper Belt, a region of the solar system beyond the orbit of Neptune, lay the origin of short-period comets, small dirtballs up to a few kilometers wide made of ice and rock fragments from the dawn of the solar system. These comets found their way into the inner solar system on a periodic basis, anywhere from every few to hundreds of thousands of years, circling the sun before being flung back out into the outer reaches on their endless, lonely voyage. These type of comets trail fragments of debris in their tails which were the source of meteor showers which lit up Earth's night skies. Often these fragment trails became dislodged from their original orbit by the gravitational interference of the planets.

A catalogue of asteroids and meteorite streams was maintained by the Earth Alliance through its affiliated scientific branch, the Solar System Science Foundation. All known orbiting objects and solar activity had been logged in Alliance solar system charts, including their projected future space activity, particularly planetary and moon positions, asteroids, comets, meteorite clouds, sun flares, etc. Space traveling ships used this data to chart their courses as they navigated the solar system, relying heavily on the charts' accuracy to avoid hazards.

Comet ZN431176 had an elongated elliptical orbit that brought it close to Earth's Sun only once every forty-five thousand years. It was large by comet standards, approximately fifteen kilometers in diameter, and had a large trail of meteoric debris which had elongated over the billions of years of its travels. Some of the larger chunks of this trail had been influenced by the gravity of the gas giants and had been dislodged into a much smaller orbital period than their source, being thousands rather than tens of thousands of years. Unfortunately for Wanderer, neither Comet ZN431176 nor its meteoric debris trail had yet been logged in the Alliance's space charts.

Arthur, dressed in his silver silk pajamas, was having a pleasant nap in his bunk when Kotik began to shake. The initial tremor was only a precursor to a series of jolts that knocked Barthol onto the floor. He shook his head as he struggled to get up from the tangle of sheets and blankets. He continued to get knocked about by the seemingly never ending jolts that sent loose items flying. A warning buzzer was beeping in the background as the ship rattled.

"Oh, crap, this feels really serious!" Arthur said out loud as he struggled to his feet, having to brace against the walls and bulkheads as he made his way to the cockpit. As he sat in the pilot's chair he could see through Kotik's cockpit window the flashes of light from the ZN431176 meteor shower as it deflected off Wanderer's front shields. He buckled in for a rough ride. At one point the jolts were so violent that he wondered whether the inter-trans could withstand much more.

Wanderer, which was a recently assembled inter-trans cargo ship being only five years old, was equipped with the latest space-debris shields, a recent technological advancement which used dark matter convection to deflect particles in the flight path. This enhancement was probably what saved the craft from disintegration. Wanderer was forced to decelerate rapidly to one tenth of its normal speed to reduce the impacts. Arthur was unharmed having gotten to the cockpit seat before the worst jolts were experienced.

"Kotik, have you gotten any information from Wanderer on flight and ship status?" asked Barthol after the meteor flashes had quieted to one every couple of minutes.

"Wanderer has suffered engine damage," replied Kotik. "One of its four hyper-drives has been knocked offline and the ship has fallen to impulse power. It will need at least a couple of days for repairs, according to intership hopmail. Also, interplanetary communications is not functioning."

"So we're on our own. Any loss of life?" asked Arthur with a concerned tone.

"None reported." Kotik's tone was 'matter of fact'.

"Have you suffered any damage?" Arthur's tone was even more concerned.

"No. Wanderer's shields protected me, though my shields were activated upon the first impact. These meteorites approached at such high speeds that my sensors only had a few seconds to react, so the initial impact could have been serious if not for Wanderer's defenses." Again, Kotik's tone was 'matter of fact'.

"Well, that's good news. You're not designed to travel at these speeds, my shuttle friend, that's why you're not equipped with sharper long distance sensors, that's my excuse, anyway!" quipped Arthur in return. "Tell me, if we were traveling at your normal spacefaring velocity, would our shields have handled this meteor shower?"

"Probably, Arthur, however our mass displacement is so small that our deflector shields would have been badly impacted and the magnitude of the shocks would have been amplified. With proper long range sensors I would have been able to note their incoming path and slowed considerably with reduced impact, however it still would have been far worse than we experienced just now." Kotik always gave succinct analysis, Arthur observed.

"That's good to know." Arthur's sigh displayed his relief. "If we plan any such deep space journeys I will ensure that your sensor array is upgraded. Now, I suppose we have extra time to prepare for our next contract since we're stuck in drydock until that hyperdrive is repaired."

Arthur turned to the inventory list and job schematics on the cockpit viewscreen next to the pilot's chair as he planned his work schedule on Vesta, not daring to get up until the meteor shower completely subsided several hours later.

"Arthur, are you all right?" Julie's concerned face filled Kotik's holo-viewscreen.

"Yes, I'm fine. How about yourself?" Arthur tried not to appear perplexed, but this woman's presence, even virtual, unnerved him. He was wearing his grey track suit.

"I'm okay. I fell out of bed when the meteor shower hit us, but only suffered a bump on the head," Julie smiled while rubbing the back of her noggin. She was wearing a pink jumpsuit. "They want us to visit the inter-trans' doctor for a check-up, you know?"

"I saw the hopmail note from Hornsby. I will try to make my way there sometime in a few hours," replied Arthur.

"Can you pick me up when you go?" asked Julie in a pleasant voice.

"Umm, I have some inventory reviews to complete, it may take a couple of hours and I'm not sure how long." Arthur tried to stall her, feeling uncomfortable with this female's attractiveness.

"That's all right, I have to do a review of the Vesta entertainment complex's game inventory as well. Just buzz my door when you come by. I'm in room 364, third level." Mills' tone was firm, making it difficult for Arthur to refuse, so he agreed. He returned to his work after the communication ended, feeling nervous about the pending encounter.

"So, here you are. Let's go to the doctor," said Julie, having opened the door at Arthur's knock. She stepped out into the corridor. Arthur, dressed in green coveralls, stepped back to give her room as the door swished shut behind her. She was dressed in a casual light blue jumpsuit, like one commonly worn on space voyages.

They walked down the corridor to an open stairwell that wound its way down to the main deck, chatting as they proceeded. Mills was an American who had managed entertainment complexes on Earth as well as Mars. She was taking this assignment to earn enough extra money to invest in a complex back in her native New York City. She said that it would take her a couple of years to reach her financial goals. Arthur mentioned that he and Olga planned an exotic vacation from the profits of his current deep space excursion. Mills' response to this was muted.

In the doctor's office, there was a long line up of passengers and staff to be checked over. The ship had a passenger physician and a staff medic, the latter was a crew member who had other duties and was trained to help in medical emergencies. After a forty-five minute wait, both were examined and given clean bills of health. Mills was given some medication for the swelling on the back of her head.

On the return journey to her cabin, Arthur declined her suggestion to visit the galley for a snack.

"Would you like to come in for a coffee?" Julie said as they reached her cabin door.

"I appreciate the offer, but I must get back to my shuttle to complete inventory counts," Arthur realized now that his nervousness was making him agitated. He could not spend any more time with this female because of his rising guilt feelings about Olga. He had always been loyal to his wife and found that his love for her was deep.

"Don't you get lonely out here in the outback, Arthur?" Julie's eyes shone as she leaned to one side, viewing him intently.

"I keep myself occupied so not to notice," Arthur replied, acknowledging to himself that he might be stretching the truth. "Although I'm alone out here, I always feel my family's affection which is enough to keep me going."

"That's a comfort. Well, I'm here if you ever want to talk," replied Mills, a bit disheartened. She stepped into her cabin and Arthur departed, his guilt feelings subsiding with each step back to Kotik.

With the inter-trans partially incapacitated in the asteroid belt between Mars and Vesta, Arthur prepared for the installation job that awaited him at his next destination. He had to get his work done quickly on Vesta because Wanderer's layover was less than a week of Earth days and the next transport ship to Ceres was weeks later. His contract required an upgrade to the oxygen tank boosting stations in the 'breathable air' ventilation system in a Tri-Party Colony mine. The wiring would need to be installed by his 'bots via existing conduits. He would hook up new power units at each booster station in preparation for the installation of the upgraded booster equipment, which was being handled by the main contractor.

While Arthur read through the plans in Kotik's readyroom, just aft of the cockpit, he gazed out of a porthole and noticed the starkness of the black void that surrounded the ship. He could see the distant fireball of Sol, only half the size seen on Earth, off to the left, and he could make out Mars, the size of a reddish marble to the right. He walked across the shuttle to the starboard side and peered through a porthole facing the other direction. There he could see the black void dotted with stars, which brought a peace and yet a lonely solitude to his inner being.

The deep silence of the ship was disturbed by the muted beep of a message notification broadcast over Kotik's intercom. Arthur walked over to the nearest comm display and retrieved the link request. He saw that it is from Wanderer's bridge. He accepted the link request and First Mate Hornsby's face popped up on the screen.

"This is a status report concerning the ongoing repairs to Wanderer's engines and interplanetary communications," said Hornsby in this pre-recorded message. "Repairs are now substantially complete and we are currently testing the equipment to ensure readiness. We are planning to engage full thruster propulsion within two hours, so we request that you and your crew members be fastened in for ignition by fourteen hundred hours. We apologize for the delays, however the meteor showers we recently encountered were not on the Alliance space charts. We were unable to substantially decelerate enough when we noted them on long range sensors until the shower was already upon us. We hope that this delay has not caused you any great inconvenience. Hornsby out." Mat Hornsby's face disappeared from the view screen as Arthur noted that he had just over two hours to ignition.

Having completed his preparations for his next contract, Arthur decided to read some literature from the ship's database on Vesta. The article he selected started with a summary of the design of mining oriented space colonies. They were usually planned with a residential area, a village mall-type shopping dome, small business commercial districts that huddled in the corridors, and two warehouse areas, one for industrial support for the mining operation and another for agricultural hydroponics. All the floors were gravity-plated to synthesize Earth-like g-forces. These mining colonies had a military-type command structure that was grafted onto a civilian democratic apparatus. The civilian-elected council had specific demarcated areas of responsibility, such as commercial and communal regulation, while the militaristic hierarchy governed security and extra-colony relations, including immigration and import/export activities. These remote outposts extracted some local construction materials, but were primarily built from offsite supplies. Entertainment was a major business, with private entertainment centers becoming affordable and widely utilized, with holovids and interactive 3-D games being popular. On-site counseling services were also a major business with the isolation of these colonies taking a major toll on people's psychology.

Arthur began to yawn. He decided to get up and go to the cockpit. There he strapped himself into the pilot's chair and nodded off before count down began.

"Yes, sweetheart, we hit an uncharted meteor shower which knocked out a thruster engine and the communications array, so that's why you couldn't reach me for the past three days." Arthur returned Olga's concerned gaze over the spacelink video on Kotik's main view screen.

"You know, space-sailor, you are encountering far too many unexpected events on this trip. I think that these mishaps are not good omens." Olga nervously shifted her stance.

"You may be right, darling, but I'm taking every precaution to ensure my safety and the security of our assets." Arthur was quite sincere in his tone.

"I know, dear, that you are doing your best. This is definitely your last venture to the outback, though. I'd rather you be a deskjockey in a Toronto municipal office that dodging particle beams and meteor showers on the frontier." Olga's voice sounded firm.

"You are probably right, my love. I'll look forward to my memo shuffling future career," said Arthur with a smirk that caused his wife to smile. "Perhaps I could work for your design business 'under the table'?"

"I want a receipt if you work for me! I'm going to write you off my taxes!" Olga laughed at her husband's winks.

"Okay dear, I'll become a homebody for you, but first I have to complete this trip. I never leave a job undone, you know," Arthur asserted.

"Don't I know!" agreed Olga.

They continued their conversation with brief discussions about the kids, her visiting parents and his brother. All too soon they had to log off. Olga's picture faded too quickly and Arthur was left with another deep bout of homesickness as he stared out Kotik's cockpit windows into the endless stars beyond.

Wanderer reached Vesta several days behind schedule, but 'no worse for wear'. Kotik disengaged from the inter-trans after Arthur received landing clearance from Vesta's space traffic control. Upon approach, he could see that the colony was perched on the rim of the southern impact crater.

What Arthur had read about the colony over the past few days passed through his mind. Vesta was a sleepy asteroid with only one outpost, a colony founded by the Tri-Party

European-American-Japanese space agency. The commercial-industrial mall was flanked by residential towers and a warehouse complex. The space-port was two kilometers to the north-east and the mine was four kilometers to the south-west.

Kotik touched down in its designated landing area at the Vesta space-port. There was no warehouse for Arthur to take the bots to, as there was at Mahal, so he would have to leave them onboard until he started the HVAC upgrade contract the next day. Vesta customs officers made a quick inspection and Arthur was cleared for business. He was staying aboard Kotik during his visit to reduce costs.

"Levels three and five are the trickiest, they both involve moving other cables to get at the HVAC booster equipment," said Frederick Baumann, with a slight German accent. He used a laser pointer to identify the locations in a three dimensional holographic diagram of the Eldorado complex, Lavalin Consortium's nickel mine on Vesta. He was wearing his blue pinstripe suit.

"Yes, I see the challenge. My bots are too big to get into those chambers, so I'll have to do that work myself," responded Arthur looking intently at the floating schematic. He was wearing his green business suit and was sitting in the Eldorado administration office in the Vesta colony's commercial section, which was just steps from the retail district. The two were using a small boardroom on the third floor of the Stanhouse office tower, the second tallest structure in the colony at seven stories. "I hopmailed you the supplies that I'm using, have you had a chance to review the list because I need your approval to proceed."

"Your supplies meet our specifications, and since we pre-approved your response to our installation requisition you don't really need my authorization to proceed," replied Frederick in a friendly tone.

"Getting final approval just prior to installation is standard CommTrac policy," said Arthur, "Perhaps it's just a courtesy but our clients rarely complain."

"That's good corporate policy," affirmed Frederick, stroking his chin. "So, my friend, have you spoken to Ms. Mills lately?"

"No, Frederick. I haven't talked to her since just after the meteor shower on Wanderer. How about yourself?" responded Arthur.

"Yes, I ran across her in the retail district yesterday. She said she's settled in and that she likes Vesta. The colony's just big enough to not be too dull!" Frederick smiled.

"You've been here a few years, haven't you?" enquired Arthur in a curious tone, wondering what long term living on the frontier was like.

"I've been out here for three years now. I was returning from a visit back to Earth when I met you on Wanderer." Frederick looked at Arthur thoughtfully. "I like this colony. It's well organized with plenty of entertainment. Still, it's nice to get home and be able to go outdoors in the sunshine. Holovids cannot substitute for the real thing, I find."

"Yes, I can understand that," said Arthur.

The two men conferred a few minutes longer on the HVAC upgrade and then Arthur departed. His installation was to begin the next day and he needed to return to Kotik to get the necessary rest. He would like to get the job done quickly so that he would have some spare time to explore this colony further.

Walking through the retail district on his way back to Kotik after leaving the Lavalin offices, Arthur noticed an electronic poster in a store window. The towering mountain in the advertising vid Arthur recognized as the one in the middle of the south polar impact crater. The text on the advert said 'Come surf one of the largest mountains in the Solar System, Mt. Milliken, over eighteen kilometers high! Join one of our skiing tours and enjoy a safe and exciting event that you'll never forget!' Arthur stopped. Looking longer at the vid he decided to go in to talk to one of the sales personnel.

"You get a lunar board and a special impact ski suit. Our lunar bus will take you to the top of Mt. Milliken and our tour guide will show you the interesting routes down. The bus will pick you up at the bottom for your return to the colony. The price is very reasonable." Shelley, the travel agent at the counter, gave Arthur all the details on the ski tour which he finally agreed to. The booking was for the day after he expected to complete the HVAC installation, the day before Wanderer's departure for Ceres. He had decided that he would not mention this safari to Olga until after it was over, she might not approve. He felt he needed a recreational break after being out on the frontier for this long.

After making payment arrangements for his ski trip, Arthur left the retail district and walked to the lunar bus depot where he caught transit out to the spaceport. He had stored his spacesuit in a rental locker at the depot. Once back on Kotik he got to bed early in preparation for the installation job the next day, thinking of his family as he drifted off to sleep.

Arthur rose early. The Vesta colony kept to the Earth calendar and day schedule despite the asteroid's own oribital and rotational cycle, this permitted the inhabitants to keep a semblance of regular routine. The sun's influence here was greatly reduced, being only little more than a quarter of its intensity back home. With the presence of daylight less of a factor on people's biological balance, it was easier to use Earth's timeframe.

K1 and K2 were outfitted in the cargo bay before the hatch was opened. Today, Arthur was going to use the detachable rover units from both of his service bots. The rover units would separate from one end of the robot's larger scooter shell. Each rover contained an extendible head with four eyes, two mechanical arms, six wheels, three on each lower side, anti-gravity plating and small thruster engine. When detached, each unit would need to drag a cargo container behind it with supplies.

K1 and K2's normal configuration would be used on the exterior cabling work where the mine shaft clung to the crater wall. This represented the work on the first three levels, however the remainder of the job required the mobile units because the final four levels were underground, as were the horizontal mine shafts, all of which need cabling as well.

Arthur's installation contract for the Eldorado mine called for an upgrade to the oxygen tank boosting stations on each level. The 'breathable air' ventilation system used a pumping station at each level located near the vertical mine shaft. The wiring would need to be installed by his 'bots via existing conduits and he would hook up new power units at each booster station. The upgraded booster equipment would be installed at a later time by the main contractor. The cabling install also involved communication cables for data transmission, primarily for the mine's service bots.

Once Arthur had finished the preparation of the cargo containers with the cabling supplies, he donned his metallic brown spacesuit and the cargo bay hatch was opened. K1 and K2 floated out, with Arthur aboard K2. Arthur instructed Kotik to then pass out the cargo containers using the cargo bay's extendible robotic arm. Each robo-mechanic then attached a container to its rear. Though each container had its own mini-thrusters that permitted them to be directed remotely, the containers were pulled by bots to their destination. Once clear of the shuttle the two bots rose thirty meters up as Kotik closed the cargo door. They headed southwest to the mine, skirting the southern end of the colony along the way. The Vesta colony looked impressive from this aerial vantage. Its chrome and grey towers bordered lower colonnades with two warehouse districts at opposite ends of the complex and a shopping dome midway between. Traveling at thirty kilometers per hour, the bots arrived at the mine in only a few minutes.

The bots put down two hundred meters from the crater rim, one hundred meters from the boxlike building at the main shaft's crest. Arthur then activated the communication unit in his space suit which connected him with Frederick Baumann back at the Eldorado offices.

"Guten tag, Herr Barthol," chimed Baumann as he appeared on Arthur's helmet visor screen.

"Good morning, Herr Baumann," replied Arthur in a cheerful tone. "Are you ready to guide my bots and me through this maze?"

"Certainly, Arthur, I'm glad to be of service." Frederick took a short bow from his desk chair. Again he was wearing his blue pinstripe suit.

"Frederick, please meet my service partners, K1 and K2, say hello, boys," Arthur's said in an amused tone.

"Certainly, yessirree, Mr. Baumann, I'm most pleeaassed to meet y'all, I'm K2 at your service," drawled K2 in his fake American southern accent.

"Nice to meet you," replied Frederick politely.

"Please take no offense to my comrade, Mr. Baumann, I'll keep him in line for you. I'm K1," said the other bot.

"Nice to meet you too, K1," replied Frederick. "Now, Arthur, you need to proceed to gateway 1G. As agreed, we'll be using a three dimensional view of Eldorado which all three of you have uploaded. We will all link our views and that way I can see where you are all situated and advise you on your activities at each location."

"Excellent, Frederick, this will make this job much easier," said Arthur as he worked through the mining diagram on his helmet visor via mental commands to his helmet's computer.

The bots rose and proceeded to an entrance marked 1G on the east side of the boxlike building. A small external shed attached to the building became the focus of attention for the next hour, as Arthur went inside the gate to receive cabling fed by K1 from through the shed. Arthur connected the cabling to an open slot in the electrical junction panel inside Gate 1G. The main contractor would connect this to the power supply when the booster equipment was installed.

Arthur and the bots proceeded down the crater wall, securing the cabling to external wiring cages that were attached to the main shaft's outer shell. As they reached each of the first three levels he followed the same routine of using the external service gate at each level and taking cabling feeds from K1 or K2 from the external service shed. The service bots floated near the mine shaft working with their extendible arms to secure the cabling that unrolled from their accompanying cargo containers.

Once the external cabling for level 3 was complete, K1 and K2 docked on the external shed platform. They were four hundred and thirty meters down the crater wall at this point. Once docked, each bot detached its front rover unit. Each rover turned and used its extendible arms to extract a supply container from the cargo box linked to its scooter shell. Then, each with a small supply container in tow, they proceeded through the air lock with Arthur to continue the installation work inside.

Frederick guided them to each booster station on the remaining four levels. The bots installed the cabling in an internal wire cage within the main mine shaft. The service bots floated down the shaft while Arthur used a vertical travel rail to which he attached his spacesuit's lifeline. The mobile units continued the installation in a similar manner as the exterior work, rolling cabling out of their attached containers and fastening it within the wire cage attached to the interior wall of the mine shaft. At each level they passed the cabling to Arthur inside the utility shed where he plugged it into the local electrical junction panel. Frederick helped direct them to the finer points needed to complete their tasks.

After finishing the cable install at level five Arthur 'called it a day'. They returned the next morning to complete levels six and seven. Then they had to start on the horizontal shaft work, linking the main level junction box with the oxygen pumping stations at three hundred meter intervals along each level. This work took another several days, however the job was completed as scheduled, two days before Wanderer's departure for Ceres.

On the final day, upon carrying out the last of the interior cabling work on Eldorado level one, Arthur sent the bots back to Kotik after they dropped him off at the colony's main entrance. He proceeded to the Eldorado offices and completed the contractual correspondences needed to finish the work with Lavalin. Frederick bid him farewell and Arthur returned to Kotik via a spaceport lunar bus. He was then able to get a good night's sleep before his ski trip to Mt. Milliken which he had been looking forward to all week.

"Mt. Milliken is eighteen point three five kilometers high," said the female voice over the lunar bus's intercom. The bus had departed from the Vesta main gate five minutes earlier. "My name is Wendy and I'll be your guide on this ski trip. Our journey to the base of the mountain will take forty-five minutes, then another ten minutes to climb to its summit. Once at the peak you will disembark with me. You each have been assigned an impact ski suit, please keep it sealed at all times during your descent. Although you each have your own spacesuit underneath, the impact suit gives you added protection from contact with the asteroid surface, which often happens when lunar skiing. The lunar boards that you've been given are also state of the art, you can do all the standard loops and banking that you'd get on any lunar half-pipe." Wendy took a pause and then proceeded to describe various sites along the route, seen through the lunar bus's windows.

Arthur nurtured a mild interest of the terrain that looked somewhat like Earth's moon, rather grey and dusty with the occasional boulder strewn here or there. The lunar shuttle made steady progress as Mt. Milliken rapidly grew on the horizon. Once at its base the bus climbed a fifty degree incline up its slope, following its shallower parts. The bus floated approximately ten meters off the asteroid's surface, its anti-gravity field being more stable there. The incline became steeper for the final few kilometers up the mountain, so the bus made a broad spiral up the mountainside to reach the small plateau at Mt. Milliken's peak.

Once on the plateau the lunar bus landed. The group of twenty-three passengers disembarked. They all had donned their orange impact suits and mounted their orange lunar boards. Arthur was one of the first ready for the descent. Wendy's voice could be heard through his helmet's intercom. She guided each over the plateau's grey dusty crest. The lunar bus then rose and headed back down the way it came.

Arthur waited until there were only a few skiers left. Then he jumped off the crest. He activated a near full g-force gravity in his board via a mental command through his helmet. Following the slope down, he banked left, then did a loop. Mount Milliken turned upside down.

"Eeeee-haaaaaahhh!" shouted Arthur at the top of his lungs. He came out of the loop and banked right, stabilizing as he raced down the mountain face. He saw a gully further to the right and made for it. Banking off the far wall he did a looping spiral. This time Mt. Milliken turned sideways in his helmet window.

Next down the slope arose a series of mini-peaks which Arthur bounced off using the lunar board's micro-forcefield. His velocity was hitting a hundred kilometers per hour which wouldn't be possible using Vesta's own negligible gravity, so the lunar board was driving the fun. Mt. Milliken's great height provided the scenery.

Another gulley appeared to the left which Arthur entered. Other skiers were up in front as he wound his way through giant boulders and down a gaping crevice. As he banked off the wall at the crevice's end he was suddenly projected out into open space. There was nothing below for hundreds of meters after he left behind a sheer cliff face. He banked into a wide curving downward spiral as Mt. Milliken appeared and disappeared from view in rapid succession. Arthur started to feel a bit woozy so he slowed his board's descent, coming to a halt on a small plateau on the mountain side. The view was spectacular; he was a third of the way down Mt. Milliken and could see the flat bottomed crater yawning off into the distance. Far away at the canyon wall the structures of the Vesta colony were remotely visible. This makes this whole trip worthwhile, Arthur thought to himself.

Barthol continued his descent, banking off gulley walls and bouncing off plateaus. The rest of the tour group was also progressing down the mountain side, which he noted as he surveyed the situation from a mini-peak another three kilometers down. Half of the group was still much farther up the slope. He could hear Wendy giving instructions to various skiers, though the dialogue was muted in his helmet speakers because her conversation was not directed at him. He looked below and saw the lunar bus parked on the crater floor a few hundred meters from the base of the mountain. He took in one last look and then shoved off for the final descent.

Bouncing back and forth, Arthur underwent three more loops before finally landing at the mountain base. The adrenaline was still pumping through his veins as he climbed off his lunar board and returned to the lunar bus. Onboard he was given a light meal and refreshments as they awaited the rest of the skiers. Within an hour the rest of the passengers were finally loaded. The bus then rose ten meters before turning and heading back to the Vesta colony. Arthur felt gratification for his little ski trip as he watched Mt. Milliken recede into the distance, glad to add this event to his growing list of mountains on his skiing resume.

"You are cleared to dock, Kotik," said Matt Hornsby, whose face appeared on Kotik's viewscreen, "Your protocols are being transmitted now."

"Thanks Wanderer, Kotik out," replied Arthur. Wanderer loomed large outside Kotik's cockpit window. The shuttle departed the Vesta spaceport this morning and had met Wanderer in orbit having been granted clearance by Vesta space traffic control. Kotik came up alongside the inter-trans and docked. An accordion gangway was extended to the portside cockpit hatch after the shuttle was secured belly down on the bumper scaffolding that ringed Wanderer.

One more ship arrived and then Wanderer broke orbit, heading further out into the asteroid belt. Clear of Vesta, the inter-trans fired its thruster engines and accelerated to interplanetary velocity. Arthur watched Vesta rapidly recede via Kotik's rear view cameras. Another space gig come and gone, he thought, as he turned to his porto-puter to start reviewing the schematics for his next contract on Ceres. Even though he kept himself busy, the creeping loneliness of the frontier was never far off. He looked forward to his return to Earth where his family awaited him, each day longer than the last.

CHAPTER 6

Ceres

Wanderer contained a few attractions, or some might call distractions, for its passengers while it passed through the empty void. Its designers were well aware of the challenges that face spaced travelers, particularly the isolation, loneliness and boredom. To counteract this, the inter-trans was equipped with multiple holo-vid chambers, the fastest space-link communications electronics, a state-of-the-art games room, and for those more academically inclined, an extensive knowledge database which included space-link correspondence courses with several universities back on Earth. The mess hall was converted for group activities such as ballroom, salsa and tango dancing as well as group games, such as 'Describe That Place' or 'What's the DNA of This Thing?' The mess hall was also used for onboard lectures, mostly on solar system topics, or for small performances, if the passenger list included some willing entertainers.

By the second day of the eight day voyage to Ceres, after twice reviewing the schematics and inventory for the Ceres contract, Arthur found himself searching for some sort of distraction. Flipping through Wanderer's hopsite on the ship's internal hopweb, he found lists of the onboard entertainment facilities available to passengers, as well as a schedule of activities offered during the current voyage. He decided that he would like to catch a holo-vid. Since the holo-chambers could be booked for solo-viewing, he scheduled a chamber for three hours that evening.

Arthur, wearing a green jumpsuit, arrived at the holo-vid chamber five minutes late, at 7:05pm, and none too soon since a couple emerged just as he arrived. He settled into one of the viewing fake-leather bucket seats and scanned through the holo-vid list provided on the view screen. He could view summaries and video trailers of each movie. He selected an Australian comedy which looked entertaining and had good audience comments.

The setting for this vid was a small outback Australian mining community that had a predominately male population. The mine's employee association was headed by a clever middle aged man who wanted to find a way to curtail the drunkenness and brawling that went on amongst the miners during their off duty hours. He hatched the idea of importing women to help spruce up the local social scene. He knew that, although modern irrigation techniques have turned the Australian outback into a garden compared to the desert of a few centuries before, he still needed a unique marketing approach to attract the females. So, he convinced the employee association, with financial support from the mining company, to advertise for 'ugly women' who wanted to be loved. A publicity campaign was organized and the antics of several of the characters brought Arthur's laughter to the point of tears. In the end, women were recruited to move to the little outback community. Dating and marriages ensued and everyone lived happily ever after.

Arthur was still laughing when he exited the holo-vid chamber and felt that his money was well spent. He still felt homesick, however, and decided that the next order of business was to contact family and friends back on the blue planet. He did not want to get out of touch, you know.

The roller-coaster did multiple inverted loops at barely-subsonic speeds while its passengers screamed at the top of their lungs. Hair streamed behind people's heads as the view of the crystal blue sky was alternated with the fairground below.

"You see, Daddy, we took a ride on Behemoth!" Katya's voice cackled with delight as the readyroom holo-viewscreen picture returned to the Barthol livingroom. She was wearing a pink dress with white stockings and shiny black shoes.

"Daddy, I only screamed once!" Hank pitched in. He was wearing a matching brown shirt and shorts with red running shoes.

"You did not! I heard you scream on every turn!" cried Katya emphatically, looking crossly over at her brother who stood at the opposite side of their mother. Olga was attired in the fashionable red dress that Arthur appreciated so much.

"Now, you two, don't spoil the fun," inserted Arthur as he viewed his family over the viewscreen. He was wearing a cashmere brown sweater and brown corduroy pants.

"Do you like our videos, dear?" asked Olga eagerly seeking approval.

"Yes, sweetheart, I'm surprised that they let you take the camera on the ride. I think there's some policy against it in case it gets dropped onto someone in the crowd below," remarked Arthur.

"I was careful," responded Olga with a smirk.

"Daddy, I got to eat candy floss and I rode a lunar board on the Magic Mountain Half-Pipe," blurted out Katya.

"Do you have any pictures?" asked Arthur.

"Yes, Daddy. Mommy, can you show Daddy the vid of my lunar board ride?" urged Katya looking keenly up at her mother's face. Olga responded by clicking a handheld wand and the picture on the view screen switched to a close up of Katya balancing on a juvenile's lunar board. Then the picture zoomed out to show the girl's cautious criss-cross path down the half-pipe. The brown peaks of the manmade Magic Mountain formed the backdrop. Katya came upon a small outcrop and bounced up a couple of meters before returning to her cautious zig-zag.

"Did you see that, Daddy? I took a huge jump in the air!" said Katya.

"You did not, it was only a couple of decimeters," retorted Hank.

"Was not!" cried Katya.

"Was so!" responded Hank.

"Now, now," said Arthur, raising his voice slightly, "Hank, Katya's bounce appeared to be several meters so please don't exaggerate."

"Daddy, I did some surfing in the wave pool. Do you want to see my pictures too?" Hank said quickly, trying to change the topic.

"Certainly, Hank," replied Arthur as the picture on the viewscreen then switched to the wave pool where Hank was mounted on a trainer-surfboard, clinging to its handles that thrust up from the board much like a scooter's. The waves were three meters high as Hank navigated his way through them as they collapsed. The surfboard had built in stabilizers and protective shields, so Hank's success had a great deal of technical assistance.

"Well done, son, you got right under that last wave, didn't you," said Arthur in an encouraging tone.

"Thanks, Daddy, it was great fun. Mommy, when will we go back to WonderWorld again?" pleaded Hank looking up at Olga as the picture returned to the Barthols' livingroom.

"Perhaps when your Daddy returns from his trip, Henri," replied Olga, as she glanced up to catch her husband's eye.

"Do you want to go back? I didn't know that you liked it?" said Arthur in a teasing tone.

"Daddy!!" replied Katya and Hank in unison.

"Okay, we'll go back to WonderWorld after I get back from Jupiter." Arthur was grinning from ear to ear like the Cheshire Cat who stole a cookie from the cookie jar. "How are Granddad and Grandma?"

"They've been great, Daddy," piped in Katya. "They take us for walks to the park everyday. Can they stay here with us?"

"Honey, we all love your grandparents but they have a home in Stockholm which they like very much. We can see if they'll visit more often, if you like," Arthur said softly, looking at Olga for support.

"I want them to stay too!" blurted out Hank, tears welling up in his eyes.

"It's okay, Hank," said Olga in a soothing voice as she stroked his wavy, brown hair. "I'll talk to Grandma and Grandpa about when they can visit next. Not to worry, they'll be back again soon."

The conversation continued for a while longer, then the children departed and Arthur and Olga conversed further about domestic finances and their work. The time went quickly and then they bid each other a tearful farewell. Arthur found it difficult to say goodbye and had to immerse himself in the schematics of the Ceres research outpost, which was the subject of his next contract, in order to distract himself again from his ongoing loneliness.

"Ceres is located here within the asteroid belt." First Mate Matt Hornsby used his laser pointer to circle the region of the asteroid belt between the orbits of Mars and Jupiter where the dwarf planet was located. The three dimensional hologram showed the current position of Ceres in relation to both planets. "Ceres is considered to be a 'dwarf planet', a definition which has been used for centuries now. A 'dwarf planet' is a body that orbits the sun, doesn't orbit a planet, is big enough to be spherical but has not cleared its orbital path of other planetoids. Although Ceres is the largest body, and the only spherical planetoid, in the asteroid belt, it has not yet cleared its orbital path, so therefore it is considered a 'dwarf planet'."

Arthur was seated near the middle of Wanderer's assembly hall. He decided to attend this 'Meet and Greet' orientation for lack of anything better to do. Ceres was still several days away and he was tired of reviewing inventory lists and watching holo-vids.

"Ceres has a diameter of about 950 kilometers, is spherical in shape and is the largest body in the asteroid belt," continued Hornsby, "It's surface and crust is a mixture of water ice and hydrated minerals. Within its depths, there are subterranean aquifers, which are the subject of biological research, and veins of iron ore and hydrated minerals, such as carbonates, which are the subject of mining activity. Ceres also supports a very thin atmosphere which contains some water vapour."

Arthur looked around and noticed that the crowd was smaller than the previous orientation session for Vesta. Only eight passengers were attending this one, none of whom he had previously met.

After apologetically giving a repeat of the 'asteroid belt' dissertation for those who had not attended the Vesta orientation, Hornsby discussed more details about the belt.

"To get to Ceres, our inter-trans has to pass through a 'Kirkwood Gap', a ring region within the asteroid belt whose contents are somewhat destabilized by its proximity to Jupiter's gravitational influence. Don't worry, though, we're in no danger. A 'Gap' is just empty space between rings of planetoidal debris within the belt. The belt is already a fairly defuse region, ships rarely encounter asteroids when passing through it, however a 'Kirkwood Gap' is completely devoid of debris. It is caused by the synchronization of orbits, if the orbit of the asteroidal mass is a whole number multiple of Jupiter's orbit, then this 'Gap' effect comes into play. This is just a bit of astronomical trivia for you to enjoy."

Hornsby continued the discussion about the asteroid belt and then delved into more details about their next destination. The colony on Ceres was smaller than Vesta's, having only one iron ore/carbonate mine. The other main activity was scientific research which attracted fewer commercial interests and therefore a smaller number of people. A diagram of the colony was magnified in the hologram. The spaceport was three kilometers to the northeast and the single mine was five kilometers to the south. There was only one office tower, a small retail dome and two small warehouse districts at opposite ends of the installation. The spaceport also doubled as a transportation hub for ground orientated floater vehicles that could be dispatched to service the numerous research stations that were sprinkled around the dwarf planet.

Arthur felt a bit drowsy as the orientation lecture ended, so he skipped the 'Greet' snack time and headed back to Kotik for a nap. Although he always enjoyed viewing astronomical holographic displays, this event had achieved its real purpose, which was to put him to sleep, so he now headed back to his shuttle to do just that.

Arthur, dressed in a blue jumpsuit, was in Kotik's readyroom reviewing the X-Station layout when an incoming spacelink request beeped on the viewscreen. It was a link request from the Alliance office in Toronto, which Arthur accepted.

"Good day, Mr. Barthol, how fares the journey to Ceres?" Simon Gage's face appeared on the viewscreen without the trace of a smile. Gage wore the standard Alliance uniform.

"It goes fine, Mr. Gage. How goes it in Toronto?" replied Arthur, also without the trace of a smile.

"Toronto is also fine, summer treats this city well," said Gage, this time with the slight hint of a smile. "I hear you had a brush with undesirables on Mars. Have you recovered from this encounter?"

"Yes, I've recovered. Your point man, Prentice, outfitted me well, although I provided the armament for my bots. We took down quite a few of them in that little war, glad to say," said Arthur with satisfaction in his voice.

"Yes, well done," said Gage with a slight nod of acknowledgement. "Well, I'm glad you've recovered because now you're going to have an experience of a lifetime! Does your encryption holoscramble have its highest security filter in place? Our spacelink software automatically requires maximimum security, but I just wanted to double check that all security features are active at your end."

"Yes, all security functions are fully operational," replied Arthur after verifying with Kotik on his porto-puter.

"Good. I'm going to space-mail you the final specifications for your installation contract at the X-Station. You received your decoder via snailmail on Vesta, did you not?" asked Gage.

"Yes, I received it the day before we departed for Ceres," replied Arthur.

"Also good. Included in your incoming spacemail will be a psychological profile of the aliens that you'll be dealing with there. Your alien handler is Zhadu Hnapsil, that's as close as I can pronounce his name in English. He is a Regional Council ambassador for the Inter-Stellar Union of Planets. He's a Panhuldian. I'll project an image of him now," said Gage.

The viewscreen picture of Gage was replaced by a bluish-grey skinned alien wearing a white smock. Hnapsil had a humanoid figure with a bulbous head on top of a miniature (by human standards) frame. He had no hair, two yellow eyes, two arms, two legs and a floor-length tail, used for balancing and possibly self defense. The picture returned to Gage's face.

"Just as a warning, Arthur, this species utilizes a combination of telepathy and verbal sounds to communicate, so be careful what you think around them. We can provide you with a telepathic blocker if you want."

"I'm okay for now. I'm a pretty simple guy, Simon, so Hnapsil won't have much to read!" laughed Barthol. "Don't they have some code of ethics to not intrude into others' minds?"

"Given all the moral red-tape they give us on trade relations, you'd think so, however I don't know whether they have such a restriction," replied Gage with a mild tone of frustration, "Also, further details about his species' capabilities are not revealed due to ISUP's information code restrictions. So this alien may have more abilities than we know, though I doubt that it will affect your activities with them."

"That raises a good point, Simon," said Arthur, and then asked, "I'm going there to install communications hardware and software for the Alliance, why do I need an alien handler for that? Why would the ISUP Regional Council care about what an electrician does for an Alliance embassy?"

"They've told us that they want one of their handlers assigned to every person, contractor or otherwise, who works on the diplomatic section of the X-Station, so that includes you," replied Gage.

"Interesting, they are apparently quite concerned about security, though my guess is that they have security in place that we've never even dreamed of," mused Barthol.

"You are probably correct. By the way, I assume that you still have the package that Prentice gave you," enquired the Alliance handler with slightly raised eyebrows.

"Yes, Mr. Gage. CommTrac the courier service is doing its duty, as requested!" replied Arthur with a smirk.

"Excellent!" quipped Gage, "Well, that's all the time I have, so good luck on the rest of your journey. Gage out." With that, Gage's image disappeared from the viewscreen.

A spacemail-received popup message appeared next on the viewscreen, beeping to be noticed, so Arthur opened its contents to discover detailed design specifications on the X-Station. He got busy reviewing the installation details, burying any further questions about his assignment deep into the recesses of his mind.

Wanderer reached Ceres two Earth days after Arthur's conversation with Simon Gage. From its three hundred kilometer orbital altitude Arthur viewed the pock marked crust of this dwarf planet. With a circumference of just under three thousand kilometers the orbit only took three hours. This grey planetoid had a dozen very large craters and countless smaller ones. Its miniscule atmosphere was not thick enough to deflect even the smallest of space debris, and its surface reflected that fact. Four and a half billion years of meteors had taken its toll, Arthur observed as he viewed the terrain on Kotik's cockpit viewscreen.

The Ceres colony was centrally located. From orbit Kotik zoomed its cameras in on the settlement. Arthur could see the central office tower, the spaceport to the northeast and the mine due south. As the colony faded back into the horizon Kotik focused in on one of the several scientific outposts on the surface. This one showed some level of sophistication having several domes and a few other rectangular buildings. Obviously some serious work is being conducted by the scientific community on this asteroid, thought Arthur.

After several orbits Arthur received clearance to land at the colony, so Kotik detached from Wanderer, taking another orbit to achieve the correct landing vector. This marked the end of Kotik's travels with Wanderer since the latter was not making the long journey to Jupiter. Arthur was scheduled to hitch a ride on a smaller, speedier Alliance supply vessel due to depart for Ganymede in another five days. This gave him just enough time to complete a minor contract for an upgrade at the largest research outpost on the planetoid.

Upon landing at the spaceport, Arthur immediately contacted the offices of the Alliance Research Academy in the Ceres colony via a hoplink. The administration office seemed in a bit of disarray when someone finally answered his hopmail linkrequest. An attractive black woman who identified herself as Imelda Winfrey, his administrator, finally appeared on the viewscreen after several others asked him his name and the nature of his business. She seemed distracted as Arthur identified himself. She was regularly interrupted as she tried to process his confirmation, with conversations buzzing in the background, but finally she identified his contract and hopmailed him his marching orders. He enquired about what all the commotion was about and she informed him that some of the research outposts had been making exciting discoveries which were causing a stir at the Academy's colonial head office. Arthur noticed her incoming Academy hopmail and logged off without giving this news much further thought.

Arthur read through the contract specifications, which matched his requisition. One of the larger research installations needed its communications equipment upgraded, similar to the contract in Antarctica. He fed the outpost's co-ordinates to Kotik. Then he ventured back into the cargo hold to converse with K1 and K2 about mission preparedness. Both bots claimed they were nearly ready, with only a few more tasks to perform. Knowing that all was nearing readiness, Barthol decided to take a nap before breaking camp for the next locale and headed off to the bunkroom to catch some shut-eye.

After his nap, Arthur rose and asked Kotik to prepare for lift-off. The shuttle requested departure clearance from the Ceres spaceport space traffic control, which was quickly received. Kotik slowly rose on its vertical thruster engines until it was fifty meters off the ground, then the shuttle ignited its rear thruster engines which nudged it forward at fifty knots. As the spaceport fell back behind and below them, Kotik accelerated as the ship climbed to a kilometer height. While cruising at that altitude, Arthur tried to contact the Ceres 3 Research Station which was three hundred kilometers beyond the horizon.

"Ceres 3, this is Kotik, do you read?" asked Arthur for a third time, having received no reply on the first two attempts.

"Yes, Kotik, we read you. Ceres 3 here. I say, is that Mr. Barthol?" replied a male voice with a pronounced English accent. A stoic looking grey-haired man appeared on the viewscreen.

"Yes, this is Barthol. To whom do I have the pleasure of speaking?" responded Arthur.

"Dr. Nigel Briggs here, I'm the director of research at this outpost. My good man, you've come a jolly good long way to do this job, now haven't you?" Briggs gave a hearty laugh.

"Yes, what an electrician will do just to pull a few wires!" Arthur returned a hearty laugh.

"We can certainly utilize that upgrade you are bringing us, Mr. Barthol," remarked Briggs, "As you may have heard, we are in the middle of some exciting research and having improved communications equipment will increase the speed of our analysis amongst research stations. It seems we've been dawdling a bit, I'm afraid."

"I'm glad to be of service. We'll be arriving within the half hour," replied Barthol.

"Jolly good, I'll fill you in on the details once you've landed and had a chance to settle in. Perhaps at tea time. Ceres 3 out." With that, Briggs' face disappeared from the viewscreen and Arthur turned his attention to the journey at hand.

Within twenty-five minutes the Ceres 3 outpost appeared on the horizon and rapidly magnified as they approached. Kotik slowed the craft and received landing co-ordinates from the outpost's main computer. A small port with landing gates was situated on the south side of the installation. The station was composed of five domes linked by tubular corridors, with several rectangular buildings scattered amongst them. A communications tower was stationed a half kilometer to the northeast on the crest of a fifty meter high ridge.

Kotik had now slowed to fifty knots and approached at a height of one hundred meters. Turning slowly so that its flight path was parallel with one of the gates, the shuttle descended, coming to a soft landing five meters out with the gate portal on its port side. The outpost computer activated the accordion airlock which extended and then attached to Kotik's portside cabin hatch. Once air pressure had stabilized, Arthur requested that Kotik communicate to Dr. Briggs that he would be taking a short rest prior to entering the installation, to which Briggs gave quick acknowledgement with an invitation to afternoon tea in an hour's time, which Barthol accepted. Then he slipped off to his bunk for a power nap.

"A 'cold seep' on Earth, sometimes referred to as a 'cold vent', is a district of ocean bed where methane or some other hydrocarbon-rich fluid seepage takes place. The water surrounding this seepage changes in viscosity from the outer sea water and forms a gummy mass, called a brine pool, a frightful mess to us humans, but an Eden to other forms of life. In particular, there are microscopic creatures known as 'extremophiles' which thrive in these types of environments. These creatures don't utilize photosynthesis, which is the foundation of almost all life on our home planet. Instead, these creatures consume the hydrocarbon through a process known as chemosynthesis to produce the chemical energy they use to power other cellular processes." Dr. Brigg's body language was animated as he gave Arthur some background on the Ceres 3 research. Briggs wore a yellow cardigan and blue jeans.

"I see," said Arthur, a bit lost in all the biochemical terminology. He was dressed in a blue jumpsuit.

"On Earth, two types of microbes perform this chemosynthesis, Archaea and Eubacteria. These creatures are used in waste disposal systems since they digest hydrocarbons. Archaea are the microbes in your bowels that help you digest your food, young man," said Briggs.

"It's always good to have a microbe on your side," replied Arthur with a grin.

"My dear chap, you know from high school biology that organisms arrange symbiotic relationships at many levels in the chain of life. For instance, mitochondria in your cells were probably independent microbes that were symbiotically assimilated into our cells' anatomy. Mitochondria, the masters of manufacturing RNA," Dr. Briggs' eyebrows rose in academic delight. "Anyway, these extremophile microbes can be assimilated by other, more complex life forms in a symbiotic relationship to generate life-giving chemical energy."

"I vaguely remember the topic," remarked Arthur, trying not to seem to out of place within this conversation.

"The evolutionary advantage of cold seeps is that they are quite stable. For example, in many deep sea situations on Earth, the methane seeps out at a slow but steady pace, which permits the development of long lasting ecosystems, meaning that organisms can be long-living," continued Briggs, almost oblivious to Arthur at this point. "For instance, seep tubeworms on Earth have life spans of one hundred and seventy-five to two hundred and fifty years."

"Are you finding cold seep ecosystems here on Ceres?" inquired Arthur, catching Dr. Briggs slightly off guard.

"By jove, you are listening, young chap," replied Briggs with a smile. "Exactly, Ceres has numerous subterranean aquifers that have existed for billions of years. They are high in salinity as well as containing high levels of ammonia which permits the water to remain in a liquid state far below its normal freezing point. Although Ceres is geologically dead, so no hot vents exist here, there is plenty of methane and other sulfides trapped in the rocky core of this planetoid. These hydrocarbons form cold seeps that we are just now locating. The extremophile lifeforms we are encountering seem bizarre by Earth standards, however, given the odd nature of life in deep sea hot vents and cold seeps back on Earth, it's not surprising. These cold seeps are teeming with dozens of life forms that have evolved over several billion years, we believe. This is jolly fascinating, don't you think?"

"Very interesting," responded Arthur. The magnitude of the discovery was now dawning on him. "They have found similar ecosystems on some of Jupiter's moons, have they not?"

"Indeed you have kept in touch with interplanetary science, young man," laughed Dr. Briggs, clapping Arthur on the arm. They were seated in two armchairs at right angles in Ceres 3's main lounge. A side table was next to them supporting a tea pot and two cups.

"So my communications upgrade will allow your research stations' computers to talk more quickly as you analyze these brine pool extremophiles." Arthur felt like an undergraduate student reciting his knowledge to a professor.

"Yes, indeed young chap, that is the ticket," replied Briggs, sitting back with a satisfied air.

"Would you call these brine pools a sticky wicket?" Arthur wore a wry grin.

"Aha, they are sticky wickets indeed, and quite the challenge to disentangle without disturbing." Nigel's face lit up at Arthur's wit.

"I'll get to it first thing in the morning. Ceres daylight lasts about six hours, and dusk is fast approaching, so I'll get on your upgrade at first light. Thanks for the biology lesson, Dr. I should now be off." Arthur rose and extended a hand to Briggs who shook it warmly.

"My staff will assist you in any way they can. Jolly good show," said Nigel as Arthur turned to leave.

Once back on Kotik, his head still humming from being submersed in the brine pool of biochemistry, Arthur went once again to his bunk to obtain much needed sleep, fascinated that some people find so much joy from investigating microbes.

At the crack of dawn, as promised, the two bots emerged from Kotik's open cargo bay with Arthur aboard K1. The bots were each handed a cargo container by Kotik via the cargo bay robotic arm. Each bot attached the container to its rear. They slowly rose to a five meter height and headed out to the communications tower to the northeast. Once upon the crest of the ridge, K1 and Arthur rose to the tower's crow's-nest leaving K2 at the base to start replacing the cabling. Once at the tower's apex, using its front extendible arms, K1 detached the existing communications dishes and transmission box and placed them in a compartment in its cargo container.

Arthur, still seated on K1, observed the research outpost in the distance on the grey plane below. Once K1 had deposited the old equipment in the rear cargo container cubicle, he opened the front cubicle and extracted the new dishes and transmitter. He stepped off K1 onto the crow's-nest platform and set to work installing the new equipment. K2 completed the cabling an hour and a half later, reaching the tower's top just as Arthur and K1 finished the crow's-nest work. K1 communicated the installation status to Ceres 3's main computer and requested a test. Shortly thereafter Ceres 3 communicated back that the tests had been successfully completed.

Job complete, the trio, man and bots, were about to head back to the research base. Arthur reached into a middle cubicle of K1's cargo container and extracted a lunar board.

"I wondered what you were doing with that there thing back in the cargo bay, partner," said K2 turning on its fake southern American drawl.

"Now, K2, you can't expect a space-cowboy not to have some fun now and then, can you?" replied Arthur.

"Of course, there, partner, can I join you?" said K2.

"Sure," responded Arthur. He unhooked his lifeline from K1's Sampson hook and attached it to K2's. K2 detached its cargo container with its hind extendible arms and attached it to the tail end of K1's cargo container. This all transpired as they floated next to the top of the communications tower.

"Hey, now I'm the pack donkey while you two have all the fun!" complained K1 in a mock whine.

"You can do it next time, partner," replied K2, again in a southern drawl. K2 then slowly accelerated up and away from the crow's-nest, Arthur in tow on his lunar board, holding his lifeline in his hands.

After rising a hundred meters at fifty knots, K2 banked left which swung Arthur farther out as he pulled up behind. This banking went back and forth as they traveled in a wide semi circle towards the Ceres 3 outpost. K2 and Arthur were in constant communication throughout this ride. Arthur gave several hoots. The highlight was when K2 bent its trajectory into a vertical spiral followed by a wide inverted bank. At the end of this episode Arthur started to get dizzy and they had to slow down. Finally K2 reeled in Arthur who mounted, stuffing the lunar board into a cubicle in K2's rear.

Upon approach to Ceres 3, Arthur and K2 could see that K1 was at the recycling depot where it was discarding the old communications equipment. K1 met them as they landed next to Kotik. Next they all re-entered the cargo bay which Kotik then shut over them. Once inside, Kotik informed Arthur that there was a hoplink request awaiting in his inbox. Arthur disrobed his spacesuit, underwent regular toxicology scans and then proceeded to the readyroom.

The hoplink request was from Dr. Briggs, to which Arthur responded once he had made himself a coffee in Kotik's galley.

"Jolly good job you and your robo-team did out there today, Arthur," said Briggs from the readyroom viewscreen. "You've done such a good job that we've been discussing the situation with the other substations and we'd like you to upgrade some of their communication arrays as well."

"Wait a minute, Dr. Briggs," inserted Arthur, sensing a potential quagmire. "I only brought enough supplies to do this one installation." He decided not to mention his pending departure date, not to complicate the situation nor give them an opportunity to interfere with his plans.

"Old chap, we're not completely barren of our own resources. Could you not enquire back at the colony to see if any more supplies exist?" Dr. Briggs was being quite persistent.

"I will enquire and get back to you. Kotik out." Arthur quickly ended the transmission, his mind churning over possible ways to slip out of this potential bind. He realized that he had three more days available before he needed to rendezvous with the EAS Adventurer for the Jupiter sortie. His business instincts began to kick in, so he started to realize that he could potentially multiply his revenue on this stopover if he handled the circumstances correctly, and possibly he could still leave on schedule. Now, what to do to bring that about? he thought to himself, scratching his head as he sat back on the readyroom sofa.

Then, the solution suddenly dawned on him. Arthur remembered that there was an Electrical Guild office located at the Ceres colony. There was enough work with the mine and research stations to permit the establishment of a local Guild chapter here. He found the contact address on the Ceres hopmail directory and requested a hoplink to the Guild office. An administrator answered his request and they discussed the availability of his needed inventory supplies. Before he could enquire about possible labor requirements he realized that the colony only had enough supplies to outfit two more outposts, which he believed he could install himself in the given time span. It would take weeks or longer for more supplies to be received.

The inventory situation gave Arthur the angle he needed to make more money and yet slip away on schedule. Upon re-contacting Briggs, Arthur explained the inventory state of affairs and magnanimously offered to install the existing arrays if the Academy could determine where it wanted them deployed. Arthur then offered to arrange the ordering of additional communication arrays and their installation by members of the local Electricians Guild. He then requested that Briggs obtain a purchase and installation requisition in order to proceed with the work. Briggs agreed and signed off to get the contract written up.

Later that day Briggs returned with the authorized purchase requisition. Arthur then flew Kotik back to the Ceres colony where he obtained the two on-site communications arrays, picking them up from a warehouse district portal aboard K1. Then Kotik proceeded to the Ceres 5 research station five hundred kilometers to the north west of the colony. The next day they installed the communications array successfully.

After a good night's rest for Arthur, Kotik proceeded to the Ceres 11 research station on the opposite side of the dwarf planet. They arrived with enough time to complete the installation, again successfully, before dusk. Arthur then spent several hours ordering the next set of communications arrays by spacelinking with the

Electrical Guilds on Vesta and Mars. Once the orders had been placed, he arranged for members of the Guild's local chapter to install them when the inventory arrived. He next spacelinked to Chas Lobring to conscribe him to act as the remote supervisor for the future installations.

"Artie, my boy, you're obviously thinking on your feet out there on the frontier," said Chas with a toothy grin. His smiling face filled the viewscreen in Kotik's ready room upon answering Arthur's spacelink request.

"I'm spacemailing you the contractual details, partner," replied Arthur. "They almost sucked me into staying longer, but I persuaded them into believing that you'd do a better job supervising this contract from Earth than I would do locally."

"I can see that your college course on negotiations has finally paid off. Send your professor a bonus!" laughed Lobring.

"Well, I'm out of here in the morning. Have fun with this one, they're in the middle of a major scientific discovery here and there may be more contracts available out of this. My guess is the Academy will find some practical use for these new microbes they've uncovered, and much of the R&D will be conducted here, so best to get CommTrac's foot in the door at the outset, don't you think, partner?" Arthur sounded satisfied with his assessment.

"Yes, I see your point, Artie. I'll follow up on every and all leads," replied Lobring, thoughtfully scratching his chin.

After they logged off Arthur prepared for the next morning's departure. Just before he hit the sack he sent an update hopmail to Briggs hoping that the latter would not give him any more calls before he slipped away the next morning.

Arthur received a spacelink request which beeped on the viewscreen. The message was from the EAS (Earth Alliance Ship) Adventurer, the supply ship that Kotik was scheduled to hitch a ride with to Jupiter. He agreed to the request and a stalky female appeared on the readyroom viewscreen.

"Kotik, this is Adventurer. You are cleared to dock, protocols are being transmitted," the female stated without introduction. Kotik notified Arthur via a viewscreen subtitle that the docking instructions had been received and were satisfactory.

"Adventurer, we have received your instructions and will proceed to dock, Kotik out," replied Arthur.

Kotik nosed up astride Adventurer, which, although it was only one hundred and forty meters long, had a sportier, more streamlined look than the other inter-transes that Kotik had hitched a ride with on this journey. Adventurer's grappling hook was snagged by Kotik's starboard robotic fore-arm which then attached it to Kotik's Sampson eye on its fore-belly. Adventurer reeled Kotik onto the inter-trans's bumper grid. Kotik fastened itself down while the connecting accordion gangway was being attached to Kotik's portside cockpit hatch. Then Adventurer broke orbit, heading into the outer asteroid belt for the long journey to Jupiter.

Arthur peered out the cockpit window as Ceres receded below them. *Another interesting stopover, my life is just full of adventures and now I'm aboard a ship called Adventurer, will wonders never cease,* thought Arthur amusedly as he busied himself with literature on the X-Station.

CHAPTER 7

X-Station

Arthur sat back in Kotik's readyroom and reviewed his contract requisition for the upcoming work at the X-Station. His porto-puter projected the schematics above him. The dark void of deep space could be seen outside the readyroom portholes. As he relaxed on the sofa distant stars twinkled in the background.

The X-Station was a standard Alliance configuration, composed of a flat grid that contained the multi-layer habitation units framed by cubical struts that provided structural support. Extendible columns at each junction in the grid provided docking ports for space vessels. The spokes in the grid contained rental units that would eventually be sublet to commercial and government enterprises. Each spoke housed a corridor for pedestrian and light vehicle traffic. At the first stage of development, much of the grid was void of habitation units, these would be filled as activity at the station increased. The station design permitted significant expansion.

Cross-struts jutted up ten meters from the X-Station grid at forty-five degree angles and ran the length of the spokes. These struts, though used as stabilizers, were also used for attachments, including the communication equipment to be installed by CommTrac. There was also a web of exterior fenders to repel any wayward spacecraft. The X-Station was initially designed with six spokes, four forming an outer square and two crisscrossing its centre. Each spoke had a length of two hundred meters. The station would start with eight docking ports, a warehouse and commercial district on spokes five and six and the Alliance and alien consulates on spokes two and three. X-Station security occupied the central hub where spokes one and four intersected. The rest of the habitation units would be sublet to a variety of commercial interests, national governments and trade cartels. CommTrak's work was on spokes two and three.

X-Station orbited Jupiter's moon Ganymede, so it was actually orbiting a satellite of Jupiter rather than directly orbiting Jupiter itself. This was probably because Ganymede had some mining and research activity. Arthur had to install communication relays that would be used by the Alliance consulate, and eventually by other human consulates and commercial offices. The Inter-Stellar Union had one diplomatic embassy and some ISUP planets would have their own trade and diplomatic consulates on-station. The station was owned and managed by the Terran Multinational Conference (TMC) which was owned by the Foreign Affairs department of the Earth Alliance government. TMC had contracted Arthur's firm, CommTrac, to install the relays, along with other electronics and related software. The aliens were responsible for installing their own consulates on-station.

Arthur next decided to read more information about Ganymede. This planetoid had a diameter of 2,630 kilometers, was the seventh moon of Jupiter and the biggest satellite in the Solar System. This moon completed an orbit of Jupiter in a little more than seven Earth days. Ganymede participated in a 1 to 2 to 4 orbital resonance with the Jovian satellites Europa and Io, respectively. For every orbit by Ganymede around Jupiter, Europa orbited twice and Io orbited four times. Like most known moons, Ganymede was 'tidally locked' with one face always pointing toward the planet. It was larger in diameter than the planet Mercury but had only about half its mass.

Ganymede was composed primarily of silicate rock and water ice. It was a fully differentiated body with an iron-rich, liquid core. A saltwater ocean was believed to exist nearly 200 kilometers below Ganymede's surface, sandwiched between layers of ice, so one day some sort of 'cold seep' or 'hot vent' life might be found, as was just being discovered on Ceres. At this point nothing had yet been found, however. Its surface comprised two main types of terrain. Dark regions, saturated with impact craters that were dated to four billion years ago, covered about a third of the satellite. Lighter regions, crosscut by extensive grooves and ridges and only slightly less ancient, covered the remainder. The cause of the light terrain's disrupted geology was not fully known, but was likely the result of tectonic activity brought about by magma flows in the moon's core.

Mining on Ganymede was focused on the extraction of high yield ammonia and various salts, such as sulfates and chlorides. Research was also being conducted, much like that found on Ceres, with scientific outposts dotting the landscape.

Ganymede was the only satellite in the Solar System known to generate a magnetosphere, likely created through convection currents within its liquid iron core. This minor magnetosphere was buried within Jupiter's much greater magnetic field. This moon also harbored a thin oxygen atmosphere that included the elements O, O2, and O3 (ozone). Hydrogen also had a minor atmospheric presence.

Arthur could feel information overload setting in, so he got up and stretched. He then noticed the hunger pangs in his belly, so he headed off to the galley to fetch a snack.

"You see, Arthur dear, the Davis Museum of Archeology wants their west wing interior design reconstituted, and they've approached me to do a concept proposal, however, sweetheart, I'm not sure that I can handle the workload. I've got three other projects and I'm just using summer students and I've got the kids and my parents and I just don't know what to do!" Olga burst into tears as her pretty face contorted as if in pain. She was wearing a yellow mohair sweater with beige slacks.

"It's all right, sweetheart," replied Arthur in a reassuring voice, watching his possessive wife's grimaces over the viewscreen in Kotik's readyroom. Several days had passed since Adventurer's departure from Ceres when Olga requested this spacelink. "It's very flattering that the museum approached you for a concept design, darling, I'm very proud of you."

"Thank-you, darling," responded Olga as she wiped the tears from her eyes.

"You must be gaining prestige to be getting such requests, Ollie," remarked her husband, feeling pride well up in his chest. He was wearing his grey track suit, for comfort. "The question is, will you share your wealth and fortune with the rest of your family?"

"Oh Arthur, stop it!" Olga managed a laugh through her constricted throat.

"Dear, your 'fifteen minutes of fame' have arrived! Hopefully it's for more than fifteen minutes!" Arthur sported a wry grin. "Darling, will you send us hopmail postcards from your global tour?"

"Now, space-sailor, I could say the same thing about you! There you are off gallivanting at the rim of human existence mocking me about going on tour!" Olga's eyes flashed even as she smiled.

"But dear, I'm not famous like you are becoming!" Arthur could not hold back his laugh.

"Arthur, what am I going to do? I can't lose this appointment or I'll never get to the next level," Olga said with exasperation.

"Olga, dear, hire someone from the Designers' Guild to help complete your existing workload, just ensure that the contract specifies that they report to you for all of their activities. Keep your existing staff as well. As far as your Mother and Father go, it sounds like they are taking care of the kids, you can get a list of local activities from the hopweb, there is lots to do, you know. By the way, have you thought of sending the kids to one of those wilderness camps for a week or two?"

"I've been too busy to think, Art, but it sounds like a good idea," replied Olga.

"And regarding housework and meals, darling, you know that Teresa can do everything if you let her. She may need extra recharging at night but she'll cook and clean everything if you ask." Arthur was glad that they had purchased the robo-maid several years back as now that investment should really pay off in relieving his wife of housework.

"Yes, yes, dear, I had briefly thought of Teresa as well, but I've been sidetracked, as you can tell." Olga sniffed and straightened her hair. "These are all very good suggestions, darling. The Guild has a 'help wanted' tab on their hopsite where I'll post an advertisement. I'll enquire at the Wilderness Ontario hopsite for possible camps for the kids and I'll ask Teresa to cook all the meals, clean all the rooms and do all the laundry. That should free me up for the museum assignment."

"Just one question, sweetheart, is the museum paying you for your work?" asked Arthur raising an inquisitive brow.

"Funny that you ask, Art, they actually are willing to pay," replied Olga with a sly smile, "Because, when they first enquired I told them I was quite busy and couldn't take the time to give a free design proposal."

"How clever of you, darling," said Arthur with a grin from ear to ear, "I think my business acumen is rubbing off on you!"

"Now, space-cowboy, it's more like vice versa!" Olga laughed. "The stipend is more than enough to cover the cost of hiring another designer and pay for my time."

"Is there enough profit to contribute to our planned south seas vacation?" asked Arthur, again with a grin.

"You should be making enough profit from your space trek to cover that, my dear!" Olga laughed again.

They talked longer, but as usual, the hoplink time limit was reached far too soon. Then, with tearful good-byes, they logged off, and Arthur returned to his X-Station specifications to distract himself from the loneliness of the void, once again.

Four days had passed since Olga and Arthur talked. Arthur had tried to keep himself busy but he was running out of activities. The holo-vid library on Adventurer was far more restricted than Wanderer's, probably because it was a government vessel. He had found a couple of entertaining movies, but not much of the rest of the library was of interest at this time. He could sometimes be captivated by nature programs, such as BBC's 'Nature on Earth' series, but he was not in the mood for nature or historical diatribes at this point. So, instead, he turned to the news hopsites that he could access via Adventurer's spacehopweb portal.

Browsing a news hopsite, Arthur came upon another news story about a robot trying to pull a bank robbery. This bot was disguised as a robo-nanny, entering the bank pushing a baby carriage. The carriage and robo's armaments were disguised by a clever combination of cloaking and lead shielding. Once robo-nanny reached the teller it extended its legs so that it was two meters taller than the counter and converted its limbs into menacing laser cannons. The robo passenger in the carriage hopped out and started herding customers into a corner, it was also wielding laser cannon limbs. What the robo-robbers and their human sponsors didn't plan on was that this bank branch was fully armed with its own automated defense mechanism in both its ceiling and floor. Before five seconds had expired the defense counter-measures kicked in. Two laser cannons embedded in the ceiling at opposite ends of the bank emerged and each severed the heads of one of the robots, meanwhile the floor underneath each robo-robber polarized and dragged the remaining robo-carcass to the floor. This entire sequence was captured on holo-vid.

Arthur smiled after reading the conclusion of this story. This was as entertaining as any holo-vid without the fee, he thought to himself.

Simon Gage's face appeared expressionless as ever on the readyroom holo-viewscreen. Arthur wondered what this call was about. His Alliance handler, dressed in the standard Alliance blue and grey, appeared to be business as usual.

"Arthur, you're not too far from your destination, despite your adventures and mishaps. Your Alliance contact on X-Station is Yuri Sokolov, he will obtain the necessary authorizations for your work as well as introduce you to your Inter-Stellar Union handler, Zhadu Hnapsil, of whom you were previously briefed," said Gage with his customary official tone.

"Very well, Mr. Gage, I'm ready to get to work. We'll be arriving in a couple of days," replied Arthur, wearing a green jumpsuit.

"Mr. Sokolov will also be requesting your package, so please be prepared to delivery it to him upon your arrival," requested Gage.

"Will do. This installation job shouldn't take more than a week to ten days, so I want to ensure that I get booked onto the next inter-trans back to the asteroid belt in two weeks time," responded Arthur.

"Mr. Sokolov will help you make those arrangements," said Gage. "I am spacemailing you the final briefing package on the Inter-Stellar Union for your review, just so you have more data on their procedures and customs. Gage out."

Gage's face was replaced by the light blue background shade of the viewscreen. Arthur got up from the readyroom couch and prepared for more reading as he felt his anticipation growing for his next assignment. This should be interesting, little green men and all, he thought to himself as he headed to Kotik's galley for a meal.

"Arthur, I don't know what to do!" Corby Oulette burst into tears as Arthur looked helplessly at her image on his porto-puter viewscreen. He was standing in the cargo bay when the spacelink request came in abruptly while he has doing inventory with K1 and K2. "He hasn't called in a week and he doesn't return my hopmails."

"Corby, please try not to jump to any conclusions," replied Arthur in a reassuring voice, "Zack has been known to go off on safaris without giving anyone, including his family, any notice. He's probably just been overloaded with research work at the university."

"But he said he'd call, Arthur," Corby's tears continued to stream down her cheeks. She was dressed in a green blouse and blue jeans.

"When did you see him last?" asked Arthur, trying to find a way to change the course of the conversation. He was wearing orange coveralls for the inventory work.

"We went to the East Mall Levitating Gardens Restaurant last Sunday for dinner, and I thought we had a good time," said Corby between sniffs, "He brought me flowers when he picked me up at my apartment and I thought we had a wonderful evening, it was so romantic."

"What did you talk about?" enquired Arthur further, trying to catch a glimpse at Zack's mood.

"We talked about his adventures in Africa," replied Corby, "And then about family. We even talked about how many children we'd each like to have. He said two which is the same I would like. I didn't think much of it at the time."

"Look, Corby, Zack is an aging bachelor, and certain topics can scare bachelors, particularly the raising of offspring. Let me drop him a spacemail and see what he's up to. As I said, he has a habit of unexpected exits so I'll try to ensure that you get the update you need." Arthur had sympathy in his voice.

"Thank-you, Arthur, I appreciate your concern. I don't mean to impose but I didn't know who else to turn to. Olga seems so busy, so I thought of you." Corby wiped the tears from her cheeks.

"Give me a few days to track him down, okay?" asked Arthur.

"Okay, thanks again Arthur. Oulette out." Corby's face disappeared from the viewscreen.

Arthur sat on the nearest container, scratching his head. So Zack's done it again, he thought, I've got to track this wild horse down and see what spooked him. He turned back to his portoputer to continue his inventory knowing that his poor brother was probably more perplexed than he had been in a while. Romance can do that to a man.

Jupiter now filled Kotik's cockpit windows. Adventurer had reached orbit and was now chasing Ganymede. Their arrival at the planet's largest moon was set for noon the following day. Jupiter's largest landmark, a red storm larger than Earth, was below them now. The various Jovian moons appeared from time to time as the inter-trans stabilized orbit in Ganymede's ascendancy. Arthur looked forward to meeting his first alien, not something that happened everyday.

The next morning Adventurer entered orbit around Ganymede. Communication was established with X-Station, which came into view after a half orbit around the solar system's largest moon. The station was obviously under construction. The main shell was complete, but sections were missing from the outer third of the complex. These were probably areas for the commercial district whose modules would be assembled after the diplomatic and administration wings were completed. Various space barges were linked to the shell, with accordion gangways snaking from their hatches to the station. Large scaffolding was assembled around the complex used by the construction crews for assembling the outer hull and docking ports. The X-Station doesn't look eighty percent complete, but perhaps the innards are further advanced than the outer appearance, thought Arthur.

As Adventurer approached, Arthur noticed some other vessels linked to this construction melee. Off to the far side of the station there were several medium sized saucer shaped vessels, each linked to the other with the inner one linked to the station via an accordion gangway. Those must be the Inter-Stellar Union ships, Arthur thought, I'd love to see the innards of one of them! Adventurer's docking instructions for Kotik would not bring them close to the alien ships, however, Arthur noticed after flipping through the spacemail he had received on the topic. Oh well, he thought, perhaps I can persuade Hnapsil to give me a tour.

Adventurer slowed to a stop half a kilometer from X-Station. Kotik was granted docking permission, so Arthur instructed his shuttle to proceed to the appropriate gate. Kotik was released from Adventurer and had to do a wide sweep of the station area to skirt the space-barges and other support vessels. During this sweep, Arthur noticed other EAS ships in various positions several kilometers out from the station. They seemed to form a perimeter. The Alliance doesn't want any unexpected visitors, observed Arthur, and they seem well prepared for the unexpected. The topic was not widely discussed, but it was fairly well known that Alliance ships carried the most advanced of Earth's weaponry, so it was unlikely any unwelcome human guests would venture near. Arthur was not so sure that aliens would be very intimidated by human weaponry, however, but supposedly the Inter-Stellar Union would handle that side of the security arrangements.

Kotik cleared the last of the support vessels and approached X-Station to dock. This section looked near completion, with the outer hull completely assembled and the docking assembly entirely in place. Kotik docked the same way as to an inter-trans, which had become second nature on this trip. Within an hour the shuttle was latched belly down to the X-Station with an accordion gangway linking the portside cockpit hatch to the corridor below. Arthur readied for meeting his Alliance handler.

"Zdrasvoitya, gaspadin Barthol, kuk dela?" enquired Yuri Sokolov with a smile. Sokolov was wearing the blue and grey Alliance uniform.

"Ya horoshow, spicebow, etebiya?" replied Arthur, smiling in realization that Sokolov knew that he was married to someone with Russian roots. Arthur was wearing his green business suit, this being a formal occasion.

"I am fine, thank you, Mr. Barthol," responded Sokolov, his face returning to a more business-like composure, "And I see that you have brought our package that you received from my compatriot on Mars. Did you laugh at his 'one hand clapping' joke?"

"Indeed I did, though he didn't," observed Barthol. "Are you going to tell me what's in this thing?" Arthur passed the loaf-sized package to Sokolov. They were standing in the latter's office, small by any standards, though still large enough for a small desk, two chairs and a large view screen. The walls were plastered with electric pictures that periodically changed from one scene to the next, mostly showing scenes from Sokolov's native Russia. Currently scenes from Lake Baikal were working their way around the room.

"Give me a moment and I will see what I can do," replied Sokolov. Initially, with a small communications stick, he scanned the entire box, then he pressed the package at three locations on a seam which resulted in it's top flipping open. Then he scanned its interior with the stick. Next he extracted a metallic looking box and plugged the stick in a small port at one end. After approximately thirty seconds the stick flashed a green microlight and beeped. Sokolov looked up and smiled.

"Very good, Mr. Barthol. My security scans indicate that this package has neither been opened nor tampered with. Excellent." Sokolov seemed pleased.

"What did you expect, gaspadin Sokolov? Did you think I'd try to break in?" retorted Arthur in an exasperated tone.

"No, that was not expected, but we wanted to verify for certain before you were given access to the X-Station construction site. When it comes to communications, security is one of the highest priorities, that and quality," replied Sokolov.

"So, does that mean that I picked up that package for no good purpose?" asked Barthol, sounding taken aback.

"No, actually you brought something that is highly valued by our alien friends. This memory bank contains a description of known human history, a catalogue of Earth biology and paleontology, along with the greatest works of art and science of human civilization. Although the works and descriptions are written in various human dialects, they have all been translated into the ISUP standard language. This is our gift to the Inter-Stellar Union of Planets for inviting us into associate membership. X-Station is the first step in our integration into the Union. The work was done at the Martian Tri-Party colony library and was quite an effort since all of the various languages had to be translated properly and translated back to ensure that the meaning hadn't changed. Mars was a good location for this project since all the major linguistic groups have establishments there." Sokolov patted the memory bank as he spoke.

"Well, that's a relief. Whose idea was this gift, anyway?" asked Arthur.

"It was their suggestion. They are extremely interested in culture, history, biology and science. Perhaps being as advanced as some of the ISUP member civilizations are, this type of information is very entertaining. They get to compare us with other species and see similarities and differences. This information let's them know what to expect from us. Of course, nothing that might be considered a security risk was included in this anthology." Sokolov stroked his chin thoughtfully.

"I think that some of these alien species have been observing our planet for longer than we've been around, so I think they already know a great deal about us," mused Arthur.

"Yes, that's true, however they have always been on the outside, so this gives them an opportunity to see Earth from our perspective. They value this a great deal, apparently," replied Sokolov. "I will arrange for your working papers to be finalized and introduce you to your alien handler, Ambassador Zhadu Hnapsil. You can't start the work until he has given you clearance."

"I'm looking forward to meeting him," said Arthur, feeling both elation and fear at once.

"Zack did what?!!" exclaimed Arthur with a startled voice.

"You heard me," replied Olga as she gazed back at him over the holo-viewscreen, sporting a big grin, "He proposed to Corby last night!"

"And what did she say?" asked Arthur.

"Yes, of course, silly!" Olga let out a giggle.

"She called me about a week ago and was all in tears about him, so I said I'd spacemail him to see what was up, which I did, but he didn't reply," observed Arthur.

"He invited her up to your parent's cottage in Muskoka over the weekend and proposed over a log fire," said Olga, still wearing a big grin. "She called me this morning and gave me the news after they arrived back in Toronto."

"Have they set a wedding date?" enquired Arthur, still a bit dazed at the sudden turn of events.

"Not yet, but they are tentatively setting it for next spring. June weddings are still a favourite," said Olga with delight.

"Well, good for them. My gut instinct told me that it was time for my younger brother to settle down and he couldn't have picked a nicer girl," said Arthur.

"She's no longer a 'girl', my dear husband, she's twenty-seven years old and has been an independent professional for six years," retorted Olga, still wearing a grin.

"Excuse me, dear, he couldn't have picked a nicer woman," Arthur corrected himself, now also wearing a grin. "Do you think that they'll invite us to the wedding?"

"Sometimes you're daft, space-sailor," laughed Olga, "Corby has already asked me to be the 'Maid of Honour'. You'll probably be asked to be the main bell hop."

"I'll be the head electrician, I'll handle the lights and sound system," replied Arthur with an even bigger grin.

"Seriously, sweetheart, Corby will be joining our family and I think it's wonderful!" said Olga thoughtfully.

"Yes, dear, I agree, and my wandering brother will finally have someone to come home to," replied Arthur, thinking of the warm feelings it brought him knowing that he would be able to go home to Olga and his children.

"Why did you get into electrical work, Mr. Bathol?" queried Zhadu Hnapsil, at least that was the English pronunciation given to Arthur's alien handler, as he raised his pale grey hairless eye brows in an enquiring manner. Hnapsil, with blue-grey skin and a tail, was wearing a white smock.

"I enjoyed wiring gadgets as a kid, so when it came to picking a career coming out of high school it seemed an easy choice to make," replied Arthur, wondering to himself why this alien was interested. Arthur was again dressed in his green business suit, this being another formal occasion.

"Yes, one can often make choices that seem to be more instinctive than deliberated," observed Hnapsil, scratching his chin with a three fingered hand. He was shorter than Barthol by most of a meter yet did not seem intimidated by the size differential as he leaned back on his tail.

"We trace our origins to primates that inhabited forests on our watery world. Do you trace your origins in a similar manner?" asked Arthur.

"Yes, all of the species in this quadrant trace their ancestral roots to less complex creatures. The length of evolutionary development seems to depend on the volatility in changes in the environment, optimal development time appears to be when changes occur over reasonable periods of time. Rapid changes can be deadly to evolution," replies Hnapsil. "My species had a similar origin as yours. Panhulda, my home world, was a suitable home. It has a similar gravitational field as Earth and is a similar distance from its sun as Earth, mind you my sun is bigger than Sol so Panhulda has a wider orbit and my planet is less dense than Earth so it is larger in volume, but essentially the characteristics of our worlds are very similar. As you can see, I need no special suit or shield to survive in your atmosphere or gravitational field."

"Yes, I noticed. Is that why you were selected to serve here?" asked Arthur inquisitively.

"In part. Of course, I have diplomatic training with new entrant species and a lengthy history in such undertakings," replied the Panhuldian.

"How do you know how to speak English fluently?" asked Arthur.

"Part of my diplomatic training. I also wear a linguistic translation device which helps me when my knowledge runs thin," replied Hnapsil. "Do you find it unusual dealing with a sentient creature from another world?"

"The experience is a bit unusual, but I've read all of the briefing materials about your organization and its members, at least the members the ISUP has told us about. As well, like any true blooded science fiction fan, I've seen many three dimensional holo-vid movies about encounters with aliens. The alien science fiction movie industry exploded when you guys decided to formally introduce yourselves to Earth thirty years ago."

"Yes, we observed an increase in that activity," replied Hnapsil.

"Now, admit it, your members have been spying on Earth and its inhabitants long before our primate ancestors were swinging from the trees!" demanded Arthur.

"We have already admitted that, my Earth friend, however my species was not one that goes back that far," replied the Panhuldian.

"So, why didn't they interfere with the development of life on Earth, or if they did interfere why was it not more obvious?" asked Arthur, hoping that he wasn't pushing the limits of friendly discourse.

"The Inter-Stellar Union of Planets has existed for a very long time, Arthur, and its regulations were developed through hard learned lessons dating back millions of Earth years. Our organization has the support of the most ancient species that have achieved interstellar travel, and they found it necessary to develop protocols for dealing with life bearing planets. These planets are treated as sacred oases which are permitted to develop in their own way. We are not allowed to interfere, only observe. There are very significant reasons for this, some of which I am not at liberty to tell you, however ISUP strictly enforces these rules amongst its members and has the technical ability to do so," replied Hnapsil in a subtly authoritative tone.

"However," continued Hnapsil, "ISUP does not represent all of the interstellar species in this galaxy. There are some that choose not to abide by our rules. For instance there are three species' collectives that interfere with developing civilizations. These three, one of which looks humanoid like Earthlings, have been interfering with Earth's human affairs for eons, despite our protestations, and interventions. Those three collectives helped some of Earth's governments and corporations develop inter-stellar space travel back in what you call your mid-times, in your mid-twentieth century. That secret space program has had interstellar travel and commerce since that time. You don't realize that antigravity is integral to FTL travel, and although Earth publicly has antigravity, the fact you haven't yet got FTL travel demonstrates how suppressed certain knowledge is in your society. This rogue group has kept your public in the dark for a long time. This is part of the reason we are proceeding with direct ISUP relations with Earth now, to help bridge this gap."

"Wow! And those alien collectives' crafts are what we see on Earth as UFOs, and I'm sure they're responsible for the abduction problem. Thank-you for confirming some of my suspicions. Humans have a history of invading any habitable space they find, so I'm surprised that Earth wasn't grabbed by one of your species long before we evolved. This would explain why," observed Athur.

"We decided to contact Earth thirty years ago because your species has shown extremely rapid development over the past five thousand years, and has become more civilized with each generation. Now your governments care for all levels of human society. There may be some disparities, but none are starving and there are no more military conflicts. You still have a criminal element, but it is also in decline. In addition, your civilization has learned to co-exist successfully with its natural environment. All of this is quite impressive, especially since humans achieved automation less than seven Earth centuries ago, despite the negative interference of alien collectives and the deeds of Earth's fascist secret space program group." Hnapsil's tone was of subtle praise.

"I suppose it must take a great deal of patience to watch species develop over thousands of years and not be tempted to interfere, especially when it appears that a wrong turn is being made," mused Arthur. "How long is the average life span of a Panhuldian?"

"In the range of eight hundred Earth years," replied Hnsapsil, "Even with advanced bio-enhancements our bodies still eventually wear out. Then our souls go back to the spirit world to prepare for their next incarnation, just as occurs on Earth. It is the way of the universe."

"So you folks believe in an existence beyond death?" Arthur realized that he again may be overstepping the limits of polite conversation.

"Life beyond death is a complicated matter. We do not pretend to know all of the answers in this realm. Some of the older species in the ISUP have more understanding than my species does, and they are forbidden on giving more information to lesser developed worlds than the ISUP protocols permit, so some of our members have more information than others. However, this I can tell you, we know for certain that there are more universes than just ours, how many we've lost track, but if you count the galaxies in our universe, there is at least that many other universes that you can observe from this one if you know how to look. We know that some of these universes are where our life forces go once our physical bodies expire in this universe." And it's from there that our spirit comes from when it returns to this universe.

Arthur's mind was suddenly expanded. He was made aware that black holes could be used as magnifying glasses to look into other universes and that the interactive web amongst these universes was of great complexity and was highly constructive in nature.

"So, you just beamed me a telepathic lesson on our universe. That is quite remarkable. Do you find it frustrating to deal with a creature like myself who has such a smaller mind?" asked Arthur with genuine humility.

"Humans are a very inquisitive and industrious species, which bodes well for their developmental potential. Humans quest for understanding, and not just for the purposes of multiplying material wealth or physical knowledge, but also in matters of meaning. Humans have also not allowed themselves to be overwhelmed by their technology. Although we normally wait until a species achieves faster than light travel before initiating contact, we made an exception in the case of Earth because of the rapid pace of human development despite all of the interference, and because of your species' thirst for understanding. Our members value this trait very highly." Hnapsil bowed slightly in a sign of respect.

"I never thought of it that way. I'm usually too occupied with matters of survival to concern myself with loftier goals, but I do know that almost all of the people I'm familiar with want what's best for themselves, their families and their community. I never considered that this might give a positive impression to off-worlders," said Arthur, thinking out loud.

"In order to deal with the diversity of species from other star systems, one needs a great deal of resiliency and tolerance, and one must have a great thirst for knowledge and understanding. Earth people exhibit those characteristics, so much so that ISUP is willing to bypass some rules in the ISUP protocols in order to accelerate human integration into the galactic community." Hnapsil again bowed slightly in a sign of acknowledgement.

"Is there an inter-galactic community as well?" asked Arthur, not having considered this before.

"Indeed there is, however the distances are great and interaction is far less common than on the galactic level, though interaction does indeed occur and quite frequently," replied Hnapsil.

"So, my guess is that while we've been talking, you've been mentally scanning me for my trustworthiness to do this installation job. So do I pass, Mr. ISUP ambassador?" asked Arthur incredulously.

"Yes, indeed you do, my human friend," replied Hnapsil, giving an alien smile exposing grayish teeth very similar in shape to those of a human.

"Isn't there some kind of respect for telepathic privacy in your ISUP protocols? Shouldn't I have been requested permission for such a scan?" Arthur's tone was sarcastic.

"I understand your concern and I meant no harm. Our protocols permit any kind of observation that does not physically alter the subject of observation, so scans are permitted. In this instance, security is very important to our mission here and we have to ensure that all those working on this project have honorable intentions. I apologize if you are offended," replied Hnapsil in a quiet tone.

"I do think that asking permission might be a good addition to your protocols," said Arthur earnestly.

"I will discuss the matter with my superiors," replied Hnapsil, "And I will ask you before it happens again. Also, a word of caution, Arthur, those that run Earth's secret space program are ruthless, and have kept the Alliance in abeyance, so be extremely careful with whom you discuss what I told you about them."

"Thank-you for the advice," said Arthur acknowledging the risk involved. "I will start the installation work in the morning. It shouldn't take more than a week, at most. I've enjoyed this interview and hope that we can speak again sometime."

"As do I," replied Hnapsil, with a slight bow.

The two shook hands and Arthur departed the Panhuldian's office, heading out into the half finished corridors of the X-Station, his mind still buzzing from his first encounter with an extra-terrestrial.

Arthur, K1 and K2 would have to install the exterior cabling and communications array before doing the indoor work, so they set out into the vacuum of space the following morning. Kotik was moored to X-Station on spoke number 5 in the warehouse district. This section was nearer completion than the rest of the station since construction supplies needed to be housed there. The trio would have to traverse Spoke Five's two hundred meters length to reach the consulate sector, their target.

"Well, gentle-robo's, as you know our task today is to start the installation of the communications array on the stabilization struts on spoke 3, as well as the exterior cabling to link the array to the Alliance consulate," stated Arthur, surveying X-Station's layout on his porto-puter in Kotik's cargo bay. "Please bring up the station layout on your internal viewscreens and link it to my portoputer's."

"Got it boss," said K2 in his southern American drawl.

"Same here, Capt'n," said K1 in a normal tone of voice.

"See here," Arthur used a laser pointer to highlight a roof junction box on spoke 3, "As per your recommendation K2, we will be connecting the external cabling to this junction box that is closest to the Alliance consulate, the other commercial enterprises will also be linked to this junction box internally from within the station. The cabling should start at that end and follow the ISO standard fastening protocol."

"Glad that you agree with my suggestions, boss!" quipped K2.

"K1, your plan for the installation of the communications array is also excellent. We will start at support strut 35 and attach the platform across to strut 36, as per your specifications," said Arthur.

"I'm also glad that you support my design recommendations, Capt'n," replied K1.

"Excellent. The estimated exterior installation time is three days of work. You guys will have plenty of time after that to interact with the X-Station computer during your recreation time, just ensure that you don't go over your entertainment energy rations, okay?" requested Arthur.

"Boss, we never complain about the restrictions that you put on our recreation time," asserted K2 in a slightly offended tone.

"I know, K2, I just want you to know that I appreciate the good work that you two did on these designs. Perhaps I should have said that slightly differently, but anyway, you two deserve to have fun out here, the X-Station computer is state-of-the-art. Anyway, let's get down to work. Kotik, please prepare for our disembarking,' Arthur said.

"Ready Arthur, will open the cargo hatch once preparations are complete," replied Kotik through a cargo bay speaker.

Arthur, already wearing his spacesuit, donned his helmet. He then mounted K1 and attached his lifeline to the robo-mechanic's backplate. Kotik then evacuated the atmosphere from the cargo bay, released the door latches and folded back the roof to expose the pitch black of outer space. K1 rose and floated out of the cargo bay under the power of its lower thrusters. K2 followed suit after

K1 cleared the shuttle. Then Kotik activated the cargo bay robotic arm to hand each robo-mechanic a cargo container, which each fastened to their stern.

The robots rose forty meters above Kotik before turning to the shuttle's port side and then heading along the two hundred meter length X-Station's Spoke 5. The stabilization struts, a scaffold-type grid that rose ten meters above the space station's habitation units, crisscrossed below Arthur's little convoy as it traveled along at seven knots. At the end of Spoke 5 they turned to their port side along Spoke 3, the diplomatic wing, to its midpoint where the Alliance consulate was located. K2 was dispatched to the roof after they located the cabling junction box, where it started preparation work for the cabling installation. K1, with Arthur still aboard, floated up to the top of the stabilization grid ten meters above, where they landed on a scaffolding intersection. K1 projected a light from its forebelly onto the grid below them as the daylight was too dim to see many details.

"So this is the intersection where we are to install our small communications tower, according to your design, K1," said Arthur.

"That is correct, Arthur, we will need to weld the mini-tower frame to the stabilization grid, then mount a communication shell before installing the communication beacon, the gyroscopes and amplifiers. Estimated completion time, three days of eight hour shifts," replied K1 in a matter of fact tone.

"Very well, let's get started. We've come a long way for this, so let's do our best job!" said Arthur energetically.

"We always do, boss," responded K1 as it extended its rear robotic arms and began unloading the mini-tower from the trailing cargo container.

The work proceeded as scheduled. K2 had some difficulty in loosening the junction box hatch, so Arthur had to come to its aid, traversing the distance using the small thrusters in his spacesuit's backpack. It took over an hour for the two to loosen the culprit hatch, but finally it opened and K2 could proceed with attaching the cables to the electrical junction slots. Meanwhile, K1 assembled the mini-tower and was about to start mounting it on the stabilization grid when Arthur returned to assist. The assembly work required welding the frame to the grid, which K1 completed just as the day's shift ended. The trio then headed back to Kotik for the evening. Arthur in particular was tired after having to bend into awkward positions to get the mini-tower installed. He fell into a deep sleep once he reached the bunkroom, not awakening until the wakeup alarm the following morning.

The next day proceeded well, with K2 completing two thirds of the cabling work, working its way from the habitation unit roof and part way up the stabilization grid towards the mini-tower. The cabling required extra welding to secure fasteners to the space station's outer shell. Arthur and K1 completed the installation of the mini-tower and then successfully mounted the communications shell by the day's end. They headed home after another hard working eight hour shift. Again Arthur slept fitfully once he reached his bunk, having vivid dreams of a distant planet with an auburn ski.

The third day witnessed the successful completion of the exterior electrical work. K2 finished the cabling by midday and 'bugged out' back to Kotik. K1 and Arthur continued installing the communication beacons, gyroscopes and amplifiers within the communication shell and hooking them up to the cabling. This work was finished with about half an hour remaining in the shift, giving Arthur enough time to run some diagnostic checks to ensure connectivity. Then K1 and he headed back to Kotik. Arthur needed another full night's sleep to prepare for the intricate wiring and programming work scheduled to be done within the Alliance Consulate the next day.

The following morning Arthur got up early to extract the communication consoles and wiring from Kotik's cargo bay. He felt a sense of satisfaction now that the final contract in this journey was nearing completion. K2 joked with Arthur as he put his supplies in a mini-cargo container in Kotik's hold, but he did not permit his robo-mechanic friend to distract him from the task at hand and departed on schedule for the consulate.

Arthur walked through X-Station's half finished corridors with work crews hanging interior wall paneling and screwing gravity plating to the floor at various locations en route along Spoke 5. As he turned the corner to Spoke 3 he passed through a guarded door in the transparent security wall, with his mini-cargo container floating behind him. The security staff did a quick scan of him and his cargo before allowing him to proceed to the consulate where he underwent a second scan by Alliance troops.

Once inside the consulate, Arthur proceeded to locate the utility room whose roof had an outlet shaft which descended from the exterior electrical junction box. He had to climb up the shaft and insert cabling in the electrical junction slot that connected with the exterior cabling that K2 had installed. Then he pulled the wiring down the shaft, inserting it into a wiring cage attached to the wall. Once he reached the ceiling of the mainfloor below, he had to route the cabling through the drop ceiling to the main electrical utility room where he inserted the cable end into a secure electrical junction slot. From there, Arthur began routing cables to the three locations within the consulate that required broadcast facilities and to the exterior wall where commercial enterprises would eventually hook up. He finished wiring one internal location, apparently the main office area, as the day's shift came to an end.

The following two days involved Arthur completing the interior cabling work followed by the installation of the broadcast consoles. Then he had to boot the communications software and configure its security features. This task was finished by the end of the second day and Arthur conducted successful communications tests with the Alliance communications test centre back in London, England. Once the final test was complete, Arthur was packing up his gear when he was approached by Yuri Sokolov.

"Privyet, gaspadin Barthol," said Sokolov with a smile.

"Strasvoitcha, gaspadin Sokolov," replied Arthur, looking up from his toolkit.

"Thank-you for doing such a fine job on installing our communications equipment," said Sokolov warmly.

"You are most welcome," responded Arthur, "I will need your signature to endorse the completion of the work." Arthur handed Sokolov a small electronic pad which the latter signed after a brief review.

"I believe that Simon Gage would like to speak with you when you have a free moment," said Sokolov as he returned the pad to Arthur.

"I'll have to ask him about the soccer standings, I've been out of touch here in the outback," remarked Arthur with a smile. "I assume that he's sent me a spacelink request, so I'll get to it upon my return to my shuttle."

"Horoshow. Thanks again for the fine work of you and your crew," replied Sokolov with a short bow. The men shook hands and Arthur then proceeded back through the corridors of X-Station, noticing that the place looked more organized with each passing day.

"Fine job, Mr. Barthol, my superiors are again impressed with the quality of CommTrac's work," said Simon Gage, whose face appeared on Kotik's readyroom viewscreen, in a business-like tone.

"CommTrac aims to please," replied Arthur with a smile.

"You also delivered our special package intact, another task well done." Gage's voice again wore a business like tone. He was dressed in the usual Alliance blue and grey.

"I should have guessed it was a test in trustworthiness. Anyway, I'm glad that at least our alien friends may enjoy its contents," responded Arthur, who was still wearing his orange work coveralls.

"I hope they do since we went to great efforts to produce the entire anthology in ISUP standard language." Gage looked a bit grimmer with that remark.

"So, now I have to arrange my return flight. When is the next Alliance inter-trans departing Jupiter?" enquired Arthur.

"Well, I'm glad that you bring that up, for you see Mr. Barthol, we have another task for you," replied Gage wearing a poker face.

"You know that I've been stomping the solar system outback for a couple of months now, so I'm quite keen to head home. CommTrac maintained secrecy and the requested installation job has passed inspection, so what else is there to do?" asked Arthur warily.

"The Alliance appreciates the work that CommTrac has rendered, and the maintenance of confidentiality. Because we are satisfied customers we are requesting that you help us complete the communications installations required to make X-Station operational," replied Gage, still with a poker face.

"The installation job here is complete, so what work are you referring to?" responded Arthur, getting tired of asking questions.

"The Alliance has been invited by the ISUP Regional Council to open a consulate at their headquarters, so we need communications equipment installed there," replied Gage, his eyebrows raising ever so slightly.

"ISUP regional headquarters, where is that?" Arthur was getting slightly perturbed.

"The headquarters are located on a space station orbiting a member world seven hundred and thirty-four light years from Earth," replied Gage.

"Listen, Simon, we don't even know whether human communication equipment can operate at that distance. Perhaps the aliens have a communication service you can rent?" said Arthur in disbelief.

"I assure you, Arthur, that our scientists believe that our communications equipment can work efficiently at a multiple of that distance without ansibles. Also, our alien contacts believe that our devices are sufficient." Gage still wore his poker face.

"Even if our devices work, how are we going to travel seven hundred light years? Humans can't even get out of their own solar system yet," retorted Arthur, getting irritated with this cat and mouse game.

"ISUP has offered to provide us with transportation," replied Gage, a slight smirk now appearing on his face.

"Oh, an alien taxi ride, very interesting. There is also another problem, I have not brought any extra supplies. I haven't got the equipment for another installation and that's only available back on Earth." Arthur was recognizing the difficulties in such an undertaking.

"How long would it take for CommTrac to raise the necessary items?" enquired Gage.

"It could take several weeks or more," replied Arthur.

"Would extra money speed up the process?" asked Gage.

"Money can usually speed up anything," retorted Arthur.

"Good, then we will be contacting your Toronto office to negotiate a contract for this new installation."

"How do you expect me to get back to Earth in time?" asked Arthur feeling like he was being bulldozed.

"Our alien friends will take you, and your shuttle. We'll arrange for your company to ship the supplies to a space station orbiting Earth where you will pick them up. The aliens will drop your shuttle in Earth orbit and pick you up after you retrieve the cargo. They will remain cloaked not to raise suspicion." Gage had obviously thought of all the angles.

"These aliens better be providing a return trip," demanded Arthur.

"Yes, the return trip is included. You shouldn't be more than a week at the ISUP regional headquarters. You'll probably find the experience quite intriguing," remarked Gage.

Arthur was slightly in shock as the spacelink conversation came to an end. He had not expected a contract extension. Mind you, the journey home was going to take a month anyway, so the net time difference may not be much, which was the perspective he would use when telling Olga about the detour.

"You got offered a contract extension? How much longer would you be away, Arthur?" Olga's impatience was displayed in her creased brow. Her face was vivid on the readyroom holo-viewscreen.

"Well it may not be much longer than it would take me to get home anyway," replied Arthur, frustrated that he could not tell her the whole truth.

"Where is it?" enquired Olga.

"It's on a space station where the Alliance is opening an office, but I'm forbidden to give any more details for security reasons," replied Arthur, cringing slightly in anticipation of a negative response.

"Those bloody Alliance scoundrels, always draping their activities under a veil of secrecy," snarled Olga.

"They've increased the billing rate by forty percent, dear," replied Arthur, hoping to dissuade any further negativity.

"Oh, all right, space-cowboy. If it's not going to take any extra time, which I find hard to believe, and you're getting extra bonus money, I'm not going to block it." Olga appeared angry despite her words.

"Okay, dear, thank-you for compromising. I won't accept any more extensions after this," said Arthur. This seemed to satisfy his wife as her mood lightened. He realized that she had made many sacrifices in their marriage and he was starting to look forward to being a stay-at-home Dad when he finished this sojourn.

Arthur gazed around the virtual conference room, with its cream walls and oak trim. Today the same eight participants were in attendance as at the previous suppliers meeting, but this time they were all virtual as he watched the holo-projection from his porto-puter. Chas Lobring sat next to Corby Oulette, projecting from Toronto. Next to her was seated Bandira Resingh, projecting from Mumbai, India, then Shanghai's Eibu Chang. Beside Eibu was Moses Rodstein, logging in from his home in Haifa, then came Angus Thatcher, from Brighton, England. In the final seat was Carmelita Hernandez dialing in from Lima, Peru. Everyone seemed to be talking at once when Chas called the meeting to order.

"It is good to see you all again today and thank-you for attending this meeting on such short notice," said Chas with a wide, toothy smile. "As per the workorder hopmails you've received from CommTrac, our customer is very pleased with the installation work that we performed at their Jupiter facility and has requested that we do a similar installation at another site. So, we need to agree on a delivery timeframe. Arthur will again be flying solo on this contract, all of the supplies will be shipped to a location convenient to him."

As with the first meeting, a cackle erupted around the conference table as the suppliers began raising objections. Chas looked directly at Arthur with a wry grin, as if to say that some things never change.

"Of course, ladies and gentlemen, our client has offered a generous incentive to facilitate the achievement of this goal. This incentive is a forty percent premium on the previous billing rate. Hopefully this will help you overcome scheduling and supply challenges," said Chas, appearing to be enjoying himself.

"Yes, ladies and gentlemen," interjected Arthur, "CommTrac's reputation is dependent upon its good suppliers, and CommTrac appreciates everything that you all go through in order meet the demands of our exacting clients. We are therefore extending an invitation for all of you and your families to dine at your local Galaxy restaurant, the meal gift certificates will be hopmailed to you after this meeting."

"Ladies and gentlemen, may I interrupt?" chimed Bandira's voice, with his mild Indian accent. The room grew silent. "Nama Stay to all of you. As I said at our previous meeting, we need to take advantage of our opportunities and now that our next opportunity has arisen in the outback, we need to meet this challenge. Our good deeds will therefore continue to bring forth fruit with future contracts and profits that can be shared by all of our families. My friends, let us again overcome supply shortages, let us capitalize on our good fortune!" Bandira browsed around the virtual table to the nodding of heads.

"Thank-you, Bandira. As with our previous meeting, I'm sure that we all agree that we want to reap the rewards of our hard work." Chas's grin was again infectious.

"As I said before, the desert makes one become efficient and thrifty," said Moses Rodstein. "Although this order is smaller than the last, still, wanting two dark-matter transmitter beacons within five days is very demanding! I'll have to pull in another dozen favours to fill this one to get my Balkan manufacturer to meet this deadline."

"Those beacons are critical, Moses," said Arthur, "Perhaps we should send you some extra Galaxy gift certificates for your Balkan friend, he can buy extra large gyros with them."

"Arthur, CommTrac is always so generous. As I said last time, you know that my Golda will be quite happy to put on a banquet for any and all of you the next time that you're in Haifa," Moses grinned as everyone praised his offer.

"Now, my Israeli friend, there's no bloody way that us Brits will be undersold on banqueting! So, the next time any of you are in Brighton, please know that you are most welcome at my place where my Katey will gladly serve you Salisbury steak and Yorkshire pudding!" Angus Thatcher certainly wanted to be heard. "By the way, our transmission software is ready as we speak. We'll have your order filled and shipped by the day's end. We're always pleased doing business with CommTrac!"

"The double grounded, three ply cabling you want will take three days," said Bandira, "That specially space-coated deluxe model from my Kashmiri supplier happens to be in stock, so we are a bit lucky."

"Chas, the labour situation here in Shanghai is greatly improved, so I can also fill your electronics order in three days," said Eibu Chang. As always he carried a wide smile, his stutter showing his excitement. "The s-standard repeater order and the multiflex amplifiers are in stock in Manchuria and the s-specialized junction boxes and adapters are all locally available."

"Excellent, gentlemen!" exclaimed Chas. "How about the security software, Carmelita?"

"We will supply the same security and encryption software as per the Jupiter job, as the Alliance requires, senor," Carmelita replied in a Hispanic accent. "We will deliver them tomorrow." She smiled as she looked around the table.

"Fabulous, it sounds like we'll meet the deadline," remarked Chas with satisfaction. "Thanks again for your support. Next we'll just review the schematic details for this contract to ensure nothing is missed."

Chas dove into the contract details and the meeting lasted another twenty minutes. After the suppliers logged off, Chas confirmed that the supplies would be shipped to Toronto. From there he would arrange for a container to be transported to the International Cargo Transfer Space Station orbiting Earth where Arthur would extract it in five days time.

Arthur felt tired as the hologram faded at the meeting's end. He was fatigued at having to arm-twist CommTrac's suppliers once again to meet a ridiculous deadline. Anyway, they got through this meeting without having to discuss the location and purpose of this gig which was a relief, thought Arthur as he headed off to Kotik's galley for dinner.

"So your departure time is nearing," said Yuri Sokolov after he and Arthur were seated in the ISUP consulate's outer office. They were awaiting the signal to enter Zhadu Hnapsil's inner chambers in order to brief Arthur on his upcoming assignment.

"Yes, Mr. Sokolov, my company has procured the necessary supplies and they will be available at the International Cargo Transfer Space Station the day after tomorrow," replied Arthur, who was wearing his green business suit, once again for a special occasion.

"Please call me Yuri," replied Sokolov, dressed in the Alliance blue and grey, of course.

"Certainly, Yuri, please call me Arthur," responded Arthur, his tension lightening slightly, then turning to the Russian, he said "Tell me, I won't be the first human at the ISUP Regional Headquarters, will I?"

"You are correct, Arthur, a small work team has been there to assemble our consular habitation units which are now in place. Currently there are two people at the site, one is the interim ambassador, Jennifer Hogan, and the other is an Alliance security officer, Steven Chen," replied Sokolov.

"So the habitation units are assembled and functioning?" enquired Arthur.

"Yes, Arthur, it took a team of five people six weeks to assemble with our alien friends providing us with transport," Sokolov said with a slight grin.

At this point Zhadu Hnapsil's face appeared on a viewscreen on the wall of the waiting area.

"Yuri, Arthur, please come into my chambers, I have someone I'd like you to meet," said Hnapsil in perfect English.

Sokolov and Barthol rose and walked through Hnapsil's office door which slid open for them. Inside, the blue-grey skinned Hnapsil, dressed in his traditional white smock, was standing next to his desk with a tall, golden skinned alien female, dressed in a tight-fitting, metallic grey body suit. Arthur was surprised at the contrast between the two humanoid aliens, the short blue-grey skinned one under one and half meters in height and the other one over two meters tall and golden skinned. The latter also had three eyes, the middle one pushed up high on her forehead. Both aliens had large heads.

"Let me introduce Hboch Ptech, the commander of the Ritfaldi Patrol Vessel 14332," said Hnsapsil. Barthol and Sokolov gave a slight bow of acknowledgement, which was returned by the two aliens. "Please take a seat."

At this point Arthur noticed that Ptech was standing on a circular pad that appeared to envelope the toes of her shoes. As she moved to her chair she slid the disk under her seat. The Ritfaldian seemed to be wearing a heavier bodysuit than Hnsapsil, with the slight glow of a force field surrounding her head. The four had now all taken seats around Hnsapsil's desk.

"Hboch's ship has been assigned to transport you and your shuttle, Arthur, to the ISUP Regional Headquarters and we would like to give you a briefing on your voyage and what to expect when you arrive," said Hnsapsil in a business like fashion.

"Sounds good to me," replied Arthur after getting a slight nod of approval from Sokolov.

"The Ritfaldi ship is not equipped for human habitation, so you will need to stay aboard your shuttle for the trip's duration," said Hnapsil.

"That's okay. That has been my mode of transport all the way out here," responded Arthur.

"Your shuttle will be towed via tractor beam and communication will be done via your standard communication protocols," said Ptech, talking in a slightly crackled voice obviously made through a digital translation device.

"That sounds reasonable," replied Arthur.

"My species comes from a planet which has a significantly higher gravitational force and higher atmospheric pressure, so you wouldn't enjoy being in our ship," remarked Ptech," And that is why I am now wearing a pressure suit and walking on a gravity pad."

"So that's what that disk is your feet are on," replied Arthur, looking over at Sokolov in amazement.

"Yes, Arthur, when dealing with multiple planetary species we generally have to compensate for gravitational and atmospheric differentials," interjected Hnapsil, "Each species is responsible for sustaining themselves environmentally in any location where interplanetary species interact.

"The ISUP Regional Headquarters on the ISUP7924 space station is equipped to provide a neutral environment for all of our member species. Each species is responsible for tailoring their habitation area on the station to suit their own biological imperatives. For instance, the Alliance habitation quarters has been outfitted with Earth gravitational plating and an atmospheric control unit. This way Alliance staff have a homelike environment in which to live and work. When humans go out into common areas they will be required to wear spacesuits and walk on gravitational pads like the one Hboch is using. The gravitational pad can levitate and fly at low speeds, however most prefer to walk," said Hnsapsil, talking like an academic.

"I suppose the ISUP members vary in many ways and I hope I'm not overly shocked by what I see," said Arthur, thinking out loud.

"We will try to prepare you. Briefing notes will be sent to you via your hopmail service," replied Hnapsil.

"Jennifer and Steven will also be there to help you adjust, Arthur." Sokolov's tone was reassuring.

"The variety of life is considerable, however the majority of our members are carbon and water based lifeforms like humans, Panhuldians and Ritfaldi," remarked Hnapsil. "Some have only slight variances, such as differently configured amino acids which are the primary difference between Ritfaldi and humans. Other differences are more dramatic when life forms are based on ammonia, phosphorus, silicon, arsenic, chlorine and sulphur, amongst others. Combine this with varying home world gravities, atmospheric compositions and pressures and you can see that housing all of these species in one location can pose certain challenges." Hnapsil showed the sign of a smile for the second time in Arthur's presence.

"Since each ISUP member species is assumed to know what is best for themselves biologically speaking, ISUP leaves it up to each to ensure that it provides its own life support at the space station," said Ptech in her digital voice.

"In addition, Arthur, the forms of life can vary dramatically from humanoid," inserted Sokolov, "That is why the alien quarters on X-Station are accessed using a segregated lower level. The Alliance wants to ensure that interaction between humans and aliens is controlled until we get more accustomed to their variances."

"I see," replied Arthur, still trying to process this deluge of information, "Sounds prudent."

"Very well, Arthur, I'll have the pertinent schematics of the ISUP7294 space station and your workorder hopmailed to your ship," said Sokolov.

"And I will hopmail you briefing materials on the population on ISUP7294, the activities on the station as well as station behavioural protocols," said Hnapsil.

"And I will hopmail you details on our departure and transport protocols," said Ptech.

"Sounds great, folks," laughed Arthur, "I'm looking forward to my crash course on alien interactions."

With that, the meeting ended. Arthur returned to Kotik after parting with Sokolov at the Spoke 3 security gate. Arthur's head was buzzing in anticipation and trepidation about his upcoming trip. He was looking forward to drinking a coffee back on his shuttle to calm his frayed nerves.

"Daddy, when are you coming home?" pleaded Katya with a tear rolling down her cheek, wearing her pink pajamas.

"Yah, Daddy, when are you going to take us out to hear some music again?" chimed in Hank earnestly, dressed in his blue pajamas with the cowboy patterns.

The children flanked their mother's sides as Olga, dressed in Arthur's favorite red dress, had an arm draped around each as they appeared on Kotik's readyroom holo-viewscreen. She gazed at Arthur after watching her children's pleas and offered her husband no support on this matter.

"Katya, Hank, I'll be back as soon as I can," squeaked Arthur after choking back his anguish. He was wearing a green jumpsuit. "It will take at least a month for me to get home and I'll make every effort to make it back more quickly!"

"Daddy, we miss you so much!" cried Katya emphatically.

"Yes, Daddy, we want you to come home!" agreed Hank.

"I promise to take you all to a concert as soon as I return," replied Arthur, "And we'll rent a cabin in Algonquin Park for a weekend as well. Speaking about the outdoors, how did you two enjoy your time at Camp Natario?"

"I loved Camp Nat, Daddy," chirped Hank, "I got to learn to sail and shoot a bow and arrow."

"Daddy, I did some horseback riding and got a sore bottom!" blurted out Katya.

"They both received very favourable reports from their camp counselors, dear," said Olga with a smile, giving her children a squeeze.

"Very well done to both of you," said Arthur proudly, "I know that it's difficult going from our comfortable home to a camp where there's no running water or electricity, but your mother and I believe it is best for you to appreciate nature on close terms. It is a gift our parents gave to us and we want to give to you."

"Thanks, Mommy and Daddy," said Katya.

"Me too, me too!" piped in Hank.

"So look, I'll come home as quickly as I can and in the meantime your mother and I expect you to get back to work at school just like you did last semester, okay?" requested Arthur.

"Yes, Daddy, I'll work hard," said Hank, looking down slightly.

"I'll work hard too, Daddy," agreed Katya, "But you need to come home as soon as possible, we miss you too much!"

Arthur felt a knot growing in his throat when Olga came to his rescue.

"Don't worry, darling, Daddy will be home soon," Olga said with a soothing voice.

Arthur felt the knot in his throat getting tighter when Olga granted him more relief by sending the children off to their beds. She began to cry once they left and Arthur tried to reassure her, to little avail. After a short while they bade farewells and Arthur was swamped by alternating waves of homesickness and guilt which only slowly receded when he retreated to his bunk for an escape into a restless sleep, dreaming of a distant world with an auburn sky.

Departure day for ISUP7924 arrived. The supplies had reached the International Cargo Transfer Space Station. The Ritfaldi Patrol Vessel 14332, a white disk shaped ship approximately twenty-five meters in diameter, was stationed half a kilometer out from the X-Station. Kotik detached from its docking berth and proceeded to come up to the Ritfaldi ship's stern, which then locked a tractor beam onto the shuttle. The Ritfaldi then applied a visual cloak to both ships so that neither vessel could be seen externally, at least not by human eyes.

"Kotik, this is Ritfaldi Patrol Vessel 14332," said Hboch Ptech in her digital voice over Kotik's cockpit viewscreen.

"This is Kotik, Hboch," replied Arthur.

"We will be accelerating to three times the speed of light when we signal you, you need not be alarmed. You won't feel much since our stabilizer field will cushion the ride. We'll get to Earth in fifteen of your Earth minutes," said Ptech in a matter of fact digital voice.

"Sounds good," said Arthur.

Ptech disappeared from the viewscreen. Two minutes later a message via spacelink popped up on the viewscreen signaling departure. Arthur felt a slight jolt and then all the stars out the cockpit window became blurs . As Ptech had said, in fifteen minutes Earth arose and quickly enlargened as the Ritfaldi ship decelerated into a low Earth orbit.

Once a stable orbit near the cargo station was obtained, Kotik was signaled by the Ritfaldi. The tractor beam was then deactivated and Kotik reversed away from the alien vessel, swinging around it to approach the International Cargo Transfer Space Station. The Ritfaldi ship disappeared from view when Kotik was fifty meters out.

The Transfer Station space traffic control acknowledged Kotik but asked Arthur why they hadn't picked up his ship on their tracking systems earlier, to which Arthur speculated was because of electromagnetic interference from solar flares, a suggestion about which the space traffic control operator was skeptical.

Kotik quickly docked at one of the many docking arms of the space station, after passing several other outbound vessels. The station had dozens of rectangular warehouse floors to house cargo containers in transit. Arthur, K1 and K2 exited the cargo bay and floated up to level 23 where they found the CommTrac cargo container attached to a container spoke. They detached the container and guided it back into Kotik's cargo bay. Once everything was secure, Kotik obtained clearance to depart.

Kotik detached from the Transfer Station once released by space traffic control. The station fell back as the shuttle proceeded to the pre-arranged rendezvous point with the cloaked Ritfaldi ship. The alien vessel revealed itself once Kotik was within half a kilometer. The shuttle navigated to the patrol vessel's stern and was again captured by the alien's tractor beam.

Hboch Ptech appeared on Kotik's cockpit viewscreen.

"We will now be proceeding to do a series of jumps to the ISUP7924 space station," said Ptech in the digital voice of her linguistic translator. "The trip details will be spacemailed to you. We are doing three legs on this journey to avoid nebulae and other obstacles en route. The journey will take approximately three of your Earth days. Do you have any questions?"

"You've answered them," replied Arthur.

"Good. We will be departing within a couple of your minutes' time and we will signal you when we're ready. You can contact us at any time via a spacelink request. Ptech out."

As the Ritfaldi disappeared from the viewscreen Arthur turned nostalgically to look down at his blue home planet out of Kotik's cockpit window. The spacemail quickly arrived signaling departure, and Arthur only got one more brief look at Earth before it disappeared in a blur, leaving behind him his family, friends and home. Arthur could not remember a time when he felt more lonely, yet he was excited at the prospect of visiting a place where exotic sentients from countless worlds communed in peace.

CHAPTER 8

Alien Connection

Arthur had to blink twice looking out of Kotik's cockpit window as he gawked wide-eyed and open-mouthed. The Ritfaldi spacecraft had just decelerated out of faster than light speed and suddenly the ISUP7924 space station stood floating before them, all twelve hundred levels, with its immense towers, jutting spokes and curving half-domes. It looked like a gigantic, exotic chrome and silver glitterball. Hundreds of weird and wonderful spaceships surrounded the station, floating in synchronous orbits and Arthur could see dozens of tiny shuttle craft darting to and fro amongst them. The briefing material he had received on the ISUP's regional headquarters had hardly prepared him for this sight. Suddenly the beep of an incoming spacelink request drew him out of this trance. The request was from the Ritfaldi vessel, which Arthur accepted.

"Kotik, we are approaching ISUP7924 and will be releasing you in several of your minutes on approach for docking," said Hboch Ptech's digital voice as her face filled the cockpit viewscreen.

"Ritfaldi 14332, acknowledged," responded Arthur.

"Have you installed the ISUP Standard Language translator in your shuttle's computer and in any portable computers that you might carry with you on the station?" asked Ptech.

"Yes, Ms. Ptech, the linguistic package that you spacemailed has been installed. Could I test my shuttle's module with you now?" requested Arthur.

"Engaging test procedures now," replied Ptech as she reached off-screen. After several seconds Kotik beeped confirmation of a successful test.

"I will now send you the radio frequency of the space station traffic control. Communication protocols are included in the linguistic package that you've installed. My recommendation is that you have the translator installed in your spacesuit as well, since you'll be wearing it in the station when you are outside the human habitation units," suggested Ptech.

"Your advice is appreciated," replied Arthur.

"We will signal just before we release you. In the meantime, please contact traffic control who will arrange your docking. This signifies the end of our journey together, Kotik. Good luck on your further travels. Ritfaldi 14332 out." Ptech's face disappeared before Arthur could say goodbye, leaving him a bit disappointed, although he was soon pre-occupied with docking protocols. The Ritfaldi vessel signalled Kotik's release only minutes later and suddenly the shuttle was under its own power again.

ISUP14332 space traffic control communicated docking procedures to Kotik. The shuttle had to maneuver past several vessels to get a clear approach vector, but this was quickly accomplished. Kotik decelerated as the assigned docking spoke came into view and came to a complete halt a quarter kilometer out. A tractor beam then hooked the shuttle and drew it into the docking spoke where Kotik was then moored. An accordion gangway was extended and attached to the ship's port hatch. Kotik was now secure.

Arthur could have chosen different landing arrangements, such as in an airlocked landing bay, but since his bots would have to access the exterior of the station to install the communications array he opted to dock with the shuttle remaining in outer space.

Just as the docking was completed, another beep sounded in Kotik's cockpit notifying Arthur of a hoplink request. The request was from the Alliance Ambassador, Jennifer Hogan, which Arthur accepted.

"Kotik, glad to have you aboard the ISUP7924 space station, this is Alliance Ambassador Jennifer Hogan with Security Officer Steven Chen," said this pleasant looking middle aged woman on Kotik's cockpit viewscreen. She was wearing a blue and grey Alliance space suit and was talking to Arthur via a wristband porto-puter.

"We're glad to be here," replied Arthur seeing Chen standing in the background also in Alliance space gear.

"We are here at your landing gate. May we come aboard?" enquired Hogan.

"Certainly, but first I must assemble the containment shields around my cockpit hatch, it will just take a minute," replied Arthur. He unbuckled from the cockpit seat and walked over to the hatch. He was wearing his red jumpsuit.

"Kotik, please release the containment barrier for the cockpit hatch," requested Arthur.

"Barrier is released," replied Kotik as a transparent accordion shield popped out of the wall just to the right of the hatch. Arthur pulled it around on tracks in the floor and ceiling so that it formed a small, air tight room around the hatchway. He fastened the barrier to the wall on the other side of the hatch and then ratcheted down a handle that sealed the containment area.

"Okay, Kotik, please run diagnostics on the containment area," ordered Arthur.

"Diagnostics are positive, Arthur," replied Kotik.

"Then please let our guests board," said Arthur.

Kotik released the cockpit hatch which slid open. Hogan and Chen stepped into the containment area and Kotik shut the hatch behind them. The containment area took several seconds to recompress to human standards, then Kotik released a small door hatch in the containment wall through which the two Alliance officers stepped. Hogan flipped back her helmet's face plate and displayed a broad smile.

"Welcome aboard Kotik, Ambassador Hogan," said Arthur as he extended a hand of greeting which the latter accepted.

"The pleasure is ours, Mr. Barthol," replied Hogan, "This is Security Officer Steven Chen."

"Welcome to Kotik, Mr. Chen," said Arthur, turning and extending a hand to the other guest, who also took the offering.

"Nice to meet you, Mr. Barthol," said Chen, bowing slightly.

"Now, Mr. Barthol," said Hogan, "We'd like to quickly give you an orientation and provide you with some extra equipment before you come onto the station."

"Please, will you both call me Arthur," responded Barthol.

"Certainly, Arthur, please call me Jennifer." Hogan's voice was sincere.

"And please call me Steven," said Chen.

"Please take a seat," said Arthur as he pulled two portable seats out from under one of the cockpit consoles. His guests were seated. "Would either of you like something to eat or drink. I have some coffee and condensed cookies, if those interest you?"

Both guests agreed to coffee and cookies, so Arthur headed off to Kotik's galley to prepare the snacks. Upon his return, he sat back in the cockpit chair after placing the tray between his guests on a console.

Hogan turned to Arthur after sipping some coffee and taking some nibbles on a cookie.

"You probably will not be prepared for what you'll see on this station, Arthur, but we have some gadgets that should help you," said Hogan.

"That would be appreciated," replied Arthur, noting that he had been saying that phrase a lot lately.

"Firstly, you know that many of these alien species are telepathic, what you probably haven't been told is that some are very strong telepaths to the point where they can unintentionally overwhelm your mind just by being near them," said Hogan.

"So, for all Alliance staff on this station it is mandatory that they wear a telepathic blocking device which I will give you now. You stick it behind your right ear. Please attach it now." Hogan's voice was serious as she handed Arthur a small plastic container. Arthur unscrewed the top, extracted the microdot, the size of a small tablet, and stuck it behind his right ear.

"Can I wear this in the shower?" asked Arthur, half jokingly,

"Certainly, Arthur, it will stay attached as long as needed and can handle any turbulence or other conditions, including water and outer space," replied the ambassador.

"It also houses a tracking device so that we can locate the wearer at any time," interjected Chen.

"As you will know from reading your briefing materials, Arthur," continued Hogan, "you will need to wear your space suit in the public areas of ISUP7924 since the station air composition has less oxygen, a higher carbon dioxide content as well as considerably higher air pressure than Earth's atmosphere. In addition, since the station has 1.4 times Earth's gravity in its public areas you'll have to walk on a gravity disk that will be adjusted to Earth's g-force. I have a pad here for you." Hogan handed Barthol a silvery white square of folded material.

"This pad can be controlled through verbal, or mental, commands. For human purposes, it is controlled by verbal commands," said Chen, "It has two toe slots for you to slip your boots into, your heels are left free. You then walk normally and it adjusts to your steps, much like snowshoes. The pad shields against the station's gravity field and radiates an adjusted gravity tailored to the user's needs. The pad can also be made to stiffen up for levitation and flight, and this is best accomplished by standing still."

"Fascinating. Sounds a bit like a lunar board with the ability to walk, though lunar boards are only for lighter gravities than Earth's. I believe that the briefing materials mention the gravity pads but I think I mostly skimmed over it. Is the consulate's habitation units the only place compatible with human biosphere needs?" asked Arthur curiously.

"Not the only place, however the common areas have an incompatible atmosphere and gravity," replied Hogan. "This is a large complex, as big as a small city, and it has numerous environmental sections compatible for species with common needs. There is a section for Earth-like ecology which is .92 g and a nitrogen/oxygen atmosphere at .97 of Earth's air pressure. It is twenty levels up from the consulate. Alliance staff have utilized it at times."

"We will take you there," offered Chen eagerly with a smile. "They have some exotic restaurants and pubs which you'll enjoy visiting, I would think."

"Alien eateries and bars, this I have got to see!" laughed Arthur. "By the way, I will bunk here on Kotik, it doesn't sound like your habitation units are the biggest."

"You are welcome to stay at the consulate if you wish, however we understand if you choose to live here during your visit," replied Hogan.

"One other note, because we are new to this situation, and not familiar with all of the risks, we recommend that you wear a forcefield during your trips in the common areas. Are you so equipped?" asked Chen.

"Yes, I have two force field belts which have seen action on Mars on my way out to the X-Station," replied Arthur, "I also wear one when I'm doing exterior work just to ward off any of that rare space debris. Do you see any security risks on ISUP7924? The briefing material doesn't mention any."

"None explicitly," responded Chen.

"However," interjected Hogan, "We are in a very unfamiliar situation here where there are literally hundreds of space-faring species living together. They come from such a diversity of backgrounds that it is hard to predict what might happen when humans interact with them for the first time. Also, ISUP has security personnel stationed on every level, and they make their presence physically obvious, so our guess is that there may be some security issues here, though none have been officially communicated to us."

"We just want to ensure that there are no human mishaps on this station, so we are recommending that Alliance staff take certain precautions," remarked Chen.

"What about side-arms, are any allowed in the common areas?" enquired Arthur, trying not to sound alarmed.

"ISUP protocols permit repulsers that are sufficient to repel aggression from any of the resident species. ISUP supplies these weapons because they are calibrated to only emit certain energy levels depending on the species, some species can take more voltage than others, as you might guess," said Chen. "ISUP only issues repulser permits to those who are properly screened. We've obtained one for you." Chen handed Arthur a black wristband which had a couple of small metallic barrels protruding from one side. "You can wear it under your spacesuit and it won't put a hole in the material if fired."

"We certainly hope that will never be necessary!" remarked Hogan cautiously, "But we want to minimize the risks here."

"What are the ISUP regulations on forcefields?" enquired Arthur, trying to ensure he obtained all of the security information that he needed.

"Forcefields are not as strictly regulated," replied Chen, "They are not considered to be aggressive in nature. ISUP has monitoring equipment all over the station, so if any weaponry comes on board they know about it immediately. We don't see much risk there. The risk is random, unexpected actions by individuals."

"What about my ship and my robo-mechanics. They are armed with a full array of defensive weaponry. It is deactivated for now, but should it be?" enquired Arthur raising an eyebrow.

"I would activate your security sensors and have your equipment's forcefields fully operational," replied Chen. "We don't know if there is any crime in ISUP communities but it's better not to take any chances."

"Okay. Kotik, please activate all security measures and defensive shields. Also inform K1 and K2 to activate theirs," said Arthur. Kotik acknowledged silently with green flash on the viewscreen at Arthur's side.

"Well, Arthur, we will leave you now so that you can get some rest," said Hogan as she got up to depart. "I am now going to give you a disk which contains holo-vids on the station, its residents and environmental sections. Please review before you venture outside." She handed Arthur a small disk in a transparent container.

"Also, please notify me via hopmail before you go anywhere in the station," requested Chen firmly, "I want to ensure that I am aware of where you are at all times. If you need assistance just request a hoplink to me immediately through your spacesuit computer, your shuttle or one of your robo-mechanics. I will be there if you need my assistance."

"That's good to know," said Arthur as he shook Chen's hand as a parting gesture. Then he turned to Hogan. "I will drop by in the morning, say 9am Earth Greenwich time, to review the consulate for my installation work."

"Very well," said Ambassador Hogan, smiling as she shook Arthur's outstretched hand.

"You will have received by now a hopmail giving directions on how to get to the consulate. We will look forward to seeing you then."

The two Alliance staff exited the shuttle quickly and Arthur was left to ponder the situation on this alien space station seven hundred and thirty-four light years from Earth.

The alien species on ISUP7924 were as diverse and exotic as any science fiction novelist could have dreamed of. Arthur was walking through a corridor on level 243, where Kotik was parked, and could barely contain himself as his head kept getting turned by various odd looking aliens passing him in the halls. He had slept well after reading the station intro material the night before and had informed Officer Chen of his departure for the consulate just before leaving the shuttle. So, here he was, wearing his metallic brown spacesuit, shuffling about the halls of ISUP7924 on his gravity disk and being shocked at every turn. He had just passed an eight legged insectoid, three meters tall, that looked slightly like a praying mantus. Just prior he had halted to let a swarm of three legged, mushroom headed midgets cross his path.

After turning the next corner a buzz started in Arthur's mind resulting in a searing headache. Looking around he saw a couple of bubble headed humanoid dwarfs walking down the hall towards him, engaged in some animated communication without any audible sound, obviously telepaths. He was wearing his telepathic jamming device, but it did not seem to help much. The noise increased in his mind, sounds and images echoing off its edge, none of which seemed familiar, although he could recognize some of the emotions, which appeared to be warm and friendly. He adjusted his path to be clear of the telepaths and the increased distance reduced the mind noise to some extent. The disturbance dissipated after the aliens turned the corner.

Suddenly the hallway Arthur was walking along opened into a multi level atrium. Outer windows permitted the viewing of the blue and green planet below with a bright silver sun blazing in the distance. The atrium was approximately half a kilometer wide and supported a mixture of multi-coloured floor displays of various geometric and rounded shapes. The displays contained exotic plants of various heights and entanglements. Walking paths wound their way through the displays. In the air above, various beings flew to and fro, some on the gravity disks that Arthur was treading on, all apparently in pre-defined flight lanes. When observing the various aliens, most of them humanoid in nature, he estimated that less than ten percent were wearing visible space suits and only about a quarter were using the gravity disks.

Arthur headed for an elevator tower midway across the atrium and caught a lift up to level 368 where the Alliance consulate was located. In the elevator he was squished between the outer, transparent wall and a meter high, two meter long centipede-like creature, dressed in a purple metallic suit. The insectoid apparently gave him a wink out of several of its eyes as they were pushed back further by the arrival of a three meter tall, hairy ape-like creature who shouldered its way into the elevator just as the doors were closing.

"Are you new to ISUP7924, my friend?" asked the centipede through its digital translator.

"Yes," replied Arthur, "Is it that obvious?"

"Slightly, you appear to turn your head twice at every species that you walk past," said the centipede with a digital laugh.

"I know where I'm going atleast," responded Arthur bashfully. "May I introduce myself, I'm Arthur Barthol of the Earth Alliance." He made a small bow.

"Pleased to meet you, Arthur Barthol," said the centipede. "My name is Stransty33331." The creature bobbed its head slightly in an apparent sign of respect. It had two large eyes and a few smaller ones, so Arthur tries to focus on the large ones.

"Pleased to meet you. Is your home world near here?" asked Arthur.

"Not really, Churny is about five hundred Earth light years toward the galactic centre, near the edge of this sector," said the Stransty33331. "Where is yours?"

"Earth is seven hundred Earth light years in the other direction," replied Arthur. "I've got to admit, I was not prepared for this variety or volume of sentient life forms. This is incredible!"

"I was also similarly impressed upon my first visit here," replied the insectoid, "Have you been to any of the station's entertainment districts?"

"Not yet, I just arrived," replied Arthur, "I believe that District 85 is one compatible with my species, so I'll probably go there when I have time in a few days."

"Interesting, that sector is also compatible with my species," observed Stransty33331. "You may not have noticed, but I am wearing a forcefield much like you wear your spacesuit. I don't need to wear it in District 85. Perhaps we could meet there for a chat sometime."

"That might be interesting," responded Arthur.

"Good," said the insectoid. "I'm hopmailing you my hopaddress. Please send me a note when you think you're heading to District 85 and I'll see whether I can join you. Nice meeting you Arthur Barthol."

"Nice meeting you too, Stransty33331," replied Arthur, smiling.

The elevator then halts at the next level and the Churnian gets off after squeezing around the ape creature. Arthur is amazed that he has just apparently made his first alien acquaintance on ISUP7924.

Arthur got off the elevator at the Alliance consulate's level. This floor had no atrium, but did have open common areas with some ornamental displays similar to the ones on level 243. He shuffled his way to the consulate section, signified by a sign that the visual translator in his space helmet interpreted for him. He turned down a smaller side corridor and finally found the modest Earth Alliance office, nestled between two larger looking embassies. The Alliance symbol on the consulate's outer door made him feel more at home, though he was not quite sure why. He pressed the buzzer to notify Chen and Hogan of his arrival.

"So your first journey through ISUP7924 has opened your eyes a little," remarked Steven Chen.

"Not just my eyes! When I passed those telepaths my brain felt like it was about to explode!" exclaimed Arthur with a laugh.

The two were sitting in the Alliance consulate lounge sipping on some green tea.

"There is a better way to get familiar with the species on this station than the orientation disk that the ambassador gave you," said Chen leaning forward out of his chair, "But it's a little more hair raising."

"My hair has already been raised, so as long as it won't melt my mind I'm interested in hearing more," replied Arthur.

"Well, it's called the mindnet. Humans need to wear a headmesh and a visor to access it. Telepathic species can access it anywhere in the station by mentally tuning in the frequency," said Chen.

"That sounds fascinating," remarked Arthur. "What can you do in it?"

"Well, remember that anthology that you delivered to the X-Station?" asked Chen.

"You've heard about that?" responded Arthur inquisitively.

"Yes," replied Chen, "The contents of that anthology will end up on the mindnet once our associate membership is formally announced in the next month or so. On the mindnet you can access the biographical information of any member world, see its sights in holographic images that virtually envelope your mind, sort of like being there. The mindnet also has numerous telepathic chat room areas, arcade games, holo-vids, etc. Many of the users, probably most of them here, use the mindnet for research, for you see, the station supercomputer also interfaces with it, so teams of scientists from any member species can participate in research projects on the mindnet. Apparently the computer can magnify is reasoning power with the participation of sentient beings. Of course, ISUP protocols restrict the access of species to various levels of this research activity or other aspects of the mindnet, though the protocols are not as restrictive as you might think."

"ISUP requires that your psychological profile be examined to determine at what level you are given access to on the mindnet," said a new voice in the lounge. Chen and Barthol turned to see Ambassador Hogan standing nearby, hands on hips wearing a broad smile.

"I suppose that it takes weeks or months to get clearance," replied Arthur with the disappointment apparent in his voice.

"It can, however we've already obtained an ISUP security clearance of Code Three for you," replied Hogan.

"Oh, is this a result of my interview with the ISUP ambassador back on the X-Station?" inquired Arthur.

"In part, there were also other verifications done. A Code 3 clearance is flattering for any associate member, and particularly for a new entrant species like ours," responded Hogan, "If you want to use the mindnet you are welcome, we can provide you with the net equipment which you can use here or back on your shuttle."

"I'd love to surf the mindnet, though I think I'll take an intro course before diving in," responded Barthol.

"Of course, there's an introductory course. Also, please note that there are mindnet outlets in the entertainment districts, however it may be best to not access them on this visit since I'm not sure of all the activities available to a Code 3 and it may be even be dangerous for you without proper experience and training," said Chen.

"I hear you," said Arthur, "After getting my mind buzzed by those pair of telepaths in the hall I'm a bit cautious of going to places where I might be really vulnerable!"

"It is good to be cautious here, Arthur," said Hogan in a precautionary tone.

"Now, I'd like to review the location for my wiring efforts," said Arthur as he stood up.

"Certainly, this way," replied Hogan, waving her hand in the direction of the doors to the consulate's inner office.

The consulate communications console was in an anteroom in the hall off the main embassy meeting rooms. The wiring conduit was routed through the walls up into the ceiling, and from there a wiring duct wound its way to an exterior junction box approximately two hundred meters from the embassy. Arthur would deploy the detachable units of his robo-mechanics to install these duct cables. The exterior work on the station would be similar to the work on the X-Station, and since the station was galactic-geo-stationary, always facing the same direction from a galactic perspective, the communications array could be pointed back to Earth without having to use the spatial-adjustment gyroscopes, although the gyroscopes would still be installed. Arthur estimated that with the interior installation and programming effort, the whole project was approximately five days of work, so he breathed a sigh of relief since this was well within the workorder's time frame.

Arthur told Ambassador Hogan that he would start on the cabling installation the following morning and that the contract should be completed within the allotted schedule, barring any unforeseen circumstances. This satisfied the Ambassador.

As the Arthur reached the outer entrance chambers of the embassy, Officer Chen met him, handing over a package and saying that it contained the mindnet gear. Arthur felt slightly nervous as he tucked the package into his spacesuit backpack, not sure whether he should be happy or terrified. After bidding farewell to Chen and Hogan, he headed out into the space station maze, shuffling along on his gravity pad as he dodged bands of exotic aliens on his way back to Kotik.

Arthur and his two robo-mechanics started the exterior installation work the following morning. As with all of their outer space jobs, they exited Kotik via the open cargo bay door. All three had loaded the space station schematics into their onboard computers, in Arthur's case the schematics were loaded into his spacesuit mini-computer, so they easily navigated from Kotik's docking port up the levels to where the Earth Alliance's consulate resided. Arthur had previously obtained permission from ISUP7924 space traffic control allowing them to venture outside. The three finally landed on the station outcrop where the target exterior cabling junction box was located after winding their way amongst the silver spokes, glass plated towers and shining domes that were sprinkled amongst the space station's terraced levels.

The exterior installation proceeded in an identical fashion to that on the X-Station, K2 was assigned the cabling work from the junction box to the communication tower, which Arthur and K1 would construct. On this exterior work, the team was not allowed to weld, so they have to fasten everything down with carbon fiber strapping to the numerous rings that were molded into the station's exterior fabric. This approach proved more challenging for Arthur and his team because the communication tower had to be firmly in place to be reliable. The mini-tower had to be secured with several straps at each end. This added several hours to the installation work, however the task was completed after two work days.

Next, Arthur proceeded to do the interior wire pulling. He utilized the detachable rover units from K1 and K2, which could be further miniaturized when needed. As the three made their way through the station on day three they garnished a few glances from the aliens they passed. Arthur, wearing his metallic brown spacesuit, shuffling along on his gravity pad followed by two floating mini-bots each hauling a cargo container, was an unusual sight, even for this space station crowd.

Once at the consulate, the work proceeded quickly. K1 and K2 scurried down the cabling shaft and connected the cabling to the exterior junction box while Arthur looked on via his porto-puter viewscreen. The cabling was strapped to rings that lined the vent walls. Inside the consulate, Arthur first installed the cabling from the wiring shaft to the communication workstation, then he extracted the communication consoles from the cargo containers and put them in their appropriate places. Finally, by the end of day five, the communication and security software was uploaded.

A test of the installation was conducted the following morning. Ambassador Hogan successfully linked with the Alliance consulate on the X-Station, where the happy face of Yuri Sokolov greeted the diplomat on the viewscreen in Hogan's office. Once the transmission was complete, Hogan and Chen gave Arthur, K1 and K2 hardy claps on the back and they all retired to the consulate lounge for a small celebration.

"It's so nice being able to finally call home!" said Jennifer Hogan after a sip of her green tea. She was dressed in the standard Alliance blue and grey uniform. "I was starting to see aliens all the time in my dreams. Did you see that species that looks like a centipede?"

"In fact, I was squished up next to one in the elevator when I first came here," replied Arthur, sitting back in a consulate lounge chair after munching on an oatmeal cookie. He was wearing his orange work coveralls. "It seemed to be quite civil and hopmailed me an invitation to go to recreation District 85 together. Its name is Stransty33331 and he's from a planet called Churny, five hundred light years closer to the galactic core from here."

"Interesting. It would be fascinating to converse with such a being," replied Hogan, "Seeing their history on the mindnet could be enlightening."

"By the way, Arthur," piped in Steven Chen, "Have you tried surfing the mindnet yet?"

Chen was also leaning back in a lounge chair, tea cup in hand, wearing the standard Alliance uniform.

"Not yet, Steven," responded Arthur, "I wanted to concentrate on getting the communications equipment installed before getting involved in recreational activities."

"That was probably prudent," observed Chen as his brow furrowed slightly, "I haven't done a lot of surfing myself, the mindnet is a bit intimidating, I find."

"Do you see any issues with contacting my acquaintance from Churny for a guided tour of District 85?" inquired Arthur glancing at both of the other conversationalists, "Apparently the environment is compatible for it and our species."

"Not at all, it sounds like it could be fun," replied Hogan, to which Chen nodded approval.

"Would either of you like to join me if I can make arrangements?" asked Barthol.

"Send me a hopmail invitation and I'll see if I can fit it in," replied Hogan, again with Chen nodding agreement.

"Very well, I'll contact our centipedal friend and see what's up," said Arthur, "Even if Stransty33331 isn't available, perhaps we can all take a trip to District 85 together. I'm eager to see what's there."

"District 85 is sort of an amusement park with all sorts of recreation," said Chen, "We haven't had a lot of time to explore the station yet, but that district is one that we each have visited several times. I'm sure you'll enjoy it. I'll be glad to accompany you."

"As will I," asserted Ambassador Hogan, "And here's a toast to the successful installation of our communications equipment. Well done to you and your team, Arthur!"

All three raised their teacups for the cheers as Arthur chuckled. These Alliance officers are good company, he observed, one couldn't ask for better so far from home.

"Arthur, dear, it is so good to see you!" cried Olga, tears welling up in her eyes. She was wearing an all yellow jumpsuit.

"Daddy, Daddy, we miss you so much," pleaded Katya, standing next to her mother hugging her hips. She was dressed in a beige sweater and pants. Hank, speechless, flanked his mother's other side in a similar posture. He was wearing a light green track suit.

Arthur's eyes were growing misty as he talked with his family via Kotik's readyroom viewscreen. He was wearing his blue jumpsuit. Kotik was hoplink connected to the Alliance consulate's communication portal from which he had spacelinked to Earth.

"Katie, I'll be home before you know it, sweetie!" Arthur hoped that his tone was reasurring to his little daughter.

"Daddy, I scored a goal for our soccer team yesterday," said Hank proudly, having finally found his tongue.

"Well done, tiger!" replied Arthur with a big grin, "Were you playing center?"

"Yes, Daddy, I got the ball on a cross from Jeremy and kicked it past the goalie," said Hank with a wide smile, "Boy, was the goalie mad!"

"Did your team win, son?" asks Arthur.

"Yes, Daddy, we won 3 to 2," replied Hank, beaming.

"Daddy, I got eighty-five percent on my math test," inserted Katya.

"Excellent, Katie," replied Arthur, "Did you study hard?"

"Yes, Daddie," responded Katya, "Mommy helped mostly, but Teresa also helped with the long division."

"Mommy and Teresa are the best help you could get, Katie dear," said Arthur with a grin, "I bet Mrs. Tompkins was happy with your mark."

"Yes, Daddy, she said I did well in her comments on the test paper," affirmed Katie with pride.

"So, dear husband," interjected Olga, "When will you be returning home?"

"Well, sweetheart, it looks like I should be able to hitch a ride in the next couple of days and then it will take about a week," said Arthur, "Katie and Hank, I'm very proud of you both and you know I'll be home soon, so could you please give Mommy and I a couple of minutes alone to talk?"

"Oh, Daddy, we haven't seen you in months and you're kicking us out!" objected Katya.

"Okay, darling, tell me more about what you've been doing," replied Arthur, giving in.

The children next described their activities in vivid detail for their father. Katya had been practicing ballet and the flute. Hank had been playing soccer, the guitar and swimming. Both tirelessly described their trials and tribulations. Arthur lost track of time.

Finally, a beep came over the viewscreen speaker indicating the link time would soon be expiring. The children, now having grown tired, agreed to head off to bed, leaving Olga and Arthur just a minute or two to discuss other matters.

"So, you've neared completion on the museum design?" asked Arthur.

"Yes dear, and I've prepared the curriculum for my autumn classes," replied Olga with a smile, "How has your installation gone, space-cowboy?"

"Well, my dear wife," replied Arthur, "It's these robo-mechanics, they make these jobs really easy. They are completely reliable and good companions."

"Yes, I've always liked K1 and K2," said Olga, nodding, "They have been a great benefit ever since you invested in them, dear."

"Yes, indeed they have," agreed Arthur, also nodding.

"Have you seen your future sister-in-law lately?" enquired Arthur.

"Yes, the day before last," replied Olga with a smile, "She's still a bit nervous about getting married. She's calmer than I was, though."

"It happens to all of us, my dear, and it was about time for both of them," replied Arthur, "I think they are a good match."

"Yes, they seem to be," remarked Olga, "They are coming over on Friday night, so it should be fun. The kids love them both."

"That does sound like fun. I'll miss not being with you," said Arthur, grimacing, "I assume that your parents returned to Stockholm safely."

"Yes they did, dear, we had a wonderful time with them here," replied his wife, "They helped fill the gap that my husband left behind."

"Okay, sweetheart, I'll be home soon," said her husband soothingly, tears welling up in his eyes, "And I won't go off planet again, I promise."

"That's good, Arthur, I wouldn't let you anyway!" said Olga giving her husband a determined look.

The spacelink termination beep then sounded and Arthur had just enough time to say goodbye to his wife. As Olga's face faded from the screen he could not help the tide of love and loneliness that swept over him, leaving him helpless as it always did.

Arthur extracted the box of mindnet gear out of a locker in Kotik's bunkroom. He had taken a nap to refresh himself. Now that his installation contract was complete he had to wait for Ambassador Hogan to arrange a ride for him back to Earth, which she had indicated might take a few days to arrange. While unpacking the mindnet gadgets, he noticed that Chen had included an introductory disk, which he loaded into a disk reader on one of the readyroom's consoles. The viewscreen lit up as Kotik had to engage the ISUP Standard Language translator for the video dialogue. The ISUP logo of a silver stylized pinwheel galaxy appeared on screen.

"Welcome to this introduction to the ISUP mindnet," said the voice on the screen, "To access the mindnet, simply place the mindnet cap on your head and put the viewglasses over your eyes. Once these are on, give the thought command: 'Please activate my mindnet portal'." The tutorial then went on to describe how the user could access files on all the member planets, their biology, history, culture and science, as well as get tours of this galaxy and some neighboring ones as well. The user was warned that the mindnet was controlled by a self-aware supercomputer that was programmed to restrict a user's access based upon their security clearance, experience, physical condition and ability. The mindnet constantly monitored the mental, emotional and physical condition of each user to try to ensure that no one was over-exposed.

Arthur extracted a fishnet cap from a small plastic-like cylinder he found in the mindnet box and pulled it over his head. He then put on the mindnet viewglasses, which looked much like a cross between sunglasses and a visor. He sat back in the sofa in Kotik's readyroom and took a deep breath. Next he gave the thought command 'Please activate my mindnet portal'.

Suddenly the readyroom faded as all of Arthur's senses were bathed in a blinding white light, the sound of gentle waves against a nearby shore and the feeling of a light breeze, soft on the skin.

"Good day, Arthur Barthol," said a deep voice in perfect English, "Welcome to the Inter-Stellar Union of Planets' mindnet. I am the mindnet keeper. How may I help you?"

"Hello, Mr. Keeper," thought Arthur, trying to hold a telepathic conversation, not sure whether he was actually talking out loud. "I'm a bit overwhelmed by this situation."

"Most first time users experience the same reaction," replied the keeper.

"Tell me", responded Arthur, "What do you know about me and my species?"

"I know that you have a security clearance of level 3, that you are a human from a planet you call Earth and that your species is joining ISUP as associate members. That is why you are here, to install communications equipment for your consulate. You have a wife, two children, your spaceship's name is Kotik, you have two robot mechanics..."

"I see," interrupted Arthur, in his mind only he believed, "Obviously this mindnet cap enhances my mental acuity because my mind isn't wandering at all."

"Yes, the mindnet cap keeps your mental signal steady while you're on the mindnet. You'd lose focus, otherwise," replied the keeper in an informative tone.

"How much do you know about Earth?" asked Arthur.

"Although we have not yet loaded the anthology cube that you delivered to the X-Station, we know a great deal about Earth's biology, geology and paleontology," replied the keeper.

"How far back do you have records of Earth?" asked Arthur curiously.

"ISUP member planets have research records going back eight hundred million Earth years, about the time when Earth's water was almost entirely frozen," replied the keeper.

"Did those member planets ever experiment with or alter Earth's life forms?" asked Arthur with a slightly insecure tone.

"Much research has been conducted, though alteration of a world's life forms is forbidden," replied the keeper.

"Come on, keeper," replied Arthur incredulously, "You expect me to believe that all of your space faring species never interfered with life on Earth?"

"It is forbidden and ISUP enforces its rules, except non-ISUP members have interfered with Earth's development, as you were informed on the X-Station," replied the keeper.

"'I understand about those rogue alien collectives, Keeper. Couldn't one of your member species have slipped by your inspectors?" thought Arthur.

"Yes, but our monitors are very effective. Your own human paleontologists have traced a fossil record that explains how Earth's life has developed," replied the keeper.

"Quite true, the fossil record is quite convincing, as is the genetic mapping of life forms on my planet, however, the odd difference in chromosomes between humans and the great apes is unexplained, as well as the huge jump in varieties of species appearing in some epochs, Keeper" observed Arthur, "What if a space-faring planet chooses not to join ISUP, and therefore not be constrained by its rules?"

"No free will space-faring species has ever refused to join ISUP, however those collectives have never chosen to give their subject worlds the choice," replied the keeper.

"Why do free will civilizations choose to join ISUP?" enquired Arthur.

"Probably because ISUP offers great trade and research advantages. Also, our members never engage in any military activities against one another. ISUP ensures their security throughout the galaxy," stated the keeper in a matter of fact tone.

"Do you believe that the universe is conscious?" asked Arthur, changing the topic.

"In a way it appears to be," replied the keeper.

"Can you communicate with it?" asked Arthur.

"In a way, though it is more subtle than through thoughts, such as the way you and I are communicating," said the keeper.

"Ambassador Zhadu Hnapsil gave me a telepathic tour that showed me that there are other universes that we can see through black holes," said Arthur thinking out loud, "He indicated that these other universes may be connected with the after-life".

"Ambassador Hnapsil is a wise person, Arthur," replied the keeper, "Your security clearance is not sufficient for me to delve too deeply into this topic, however."

"What can you tell me about the after-life, keeper?" enquired Arthur.

"All life in this universe is transitory, as you can probably surmise," replied the keeper, "The fundamental truth of life's existence is that the present is what counts, one can plan the future and learn from the past, but these activities all occur in the present. If one can understand that the rules of civilized behaviour were created in order to permit all to live together in harmony, and that group efforts and shared responsibility lead to the greatest common good, then one's life in this universe will procure the maximum value. It therefore does not matter whether there is an after-life, because if you live in an honorable and civilized manner you will best utilize your life here, now. In any case, one cannot take one's temporal body into the after-life. In that way all life in this universe is mortal."

"So, from one perspective, there is no after life, however you're not denying that there may be some form of existence beyond death?" queried Arthur.

"That would be a fair conclusion," replied the keeper.

"I believe I understand your explanation," said Arthur, growing quiet in contemplation. "How many of your member species believe what you just said?"

"All of the species within ISUP have a morality that is compatible with ISUP protocols," replied the keeper.

"Do they believe in love?" asked Arthur.

"Of course," replied the keeper.

"Do they believe in forgiveness?" asked Arthur.

"Of course," replied the keeper.

"Do not the most developed species find a beginner species like humans to be ignorant?" asked Arthur defensively.

"Ambassador Hnapsil told you that ISUP finds that the human species is developing at an impressive rate," replied the keeper.

"You didn't answer my question," replied Arthur.

"I will answer by analogy, if you don't mind," replied the keeper.

"You're a clever computer, aren't you?" replied Arthur with a laugh.

"When humans first started to be able to understand the awareness of non-human creatures on Earth during the twenty-first century, they found that most conscious life forms have an acute sense of self-awareness, and suffer the same psychological stresses that humans do, such as love, hate, the joy of living and the horror of death. Humans found this to be humbling, the knowledge that other creatures suffer in similar ways as they do." The keeper's tone was solemn.

"Yes, that awareness led eventually to the elimination of meat eating in most of Earth's societies," replied Arthur, "We had to develop alternate protein sources, but that wasn't very difficult, really."

"So, as humans have found that other, less sophisticated species experience life similar to humans, so it is the same for ISUP's senior members," replied the keeper. "It is this understanding, this empathy, that binds all sentient beings together. This is what allows them all to commune in places like this space station."

"Thank-you, keeper, this is quite profound," replied Arthur as his mind started to become aware of numerous interplanetary species and how they empathized with one another, despite the vast contrasts in physical and psychological diversity. The more he saw the more humbled he became. The experience frequently brought tears to his eyes.

The images and ideas that entered the fringe of Arthur's awareness were fascinating, and yet were not overwhelming. As Arthur's journey on the mindnet continued, he asked the keeper to show him some of the life bearing worlds closest to Earth. The keeper obliged his request.

Arthur viewed the galactic quadrant as within a holo-vid. He zoomed in on Sol, Earth's sun, traversing hundreds of light years in a matter of seconds. Then, the view zoomed to the other side of Earth's solar system to a star approximately a dozen light years farther out from the galactic core. The star grew larger quickly as Arthur slowed upon entering its solar system. This star was slightly smaller and yet more intense than Earth's. There was a huge gas giant planet that orbited this sun closely, about the distance of Mercury from Sol. Farther out there were smaller terrestrial planets, five of noticeable size. Arthur's journey was directed at the fourth planet out. Information about this world started to flood his mind. Biological history told the story of how multi-cellular life arose over billions of years. This sun was approximately five and a half billion Earth years old, making it older than Sol, probably an earlier product of a stellar nursery that produced both systems.

Now Arthur's viewpoint was from orbit around this world. He could see oceans, volcanoes and spacecraft flying to and fro around this planet. The biological history of this world continued to flood his mind, anticipating his interest in the topic. Life started walking on land on this planet about seven hundred million Earth years ago, pre-dating Earth by three hundred million years. Sentient life forms that could develop tools evolved approximately forty million Earth years ago. There were a group of animals, warm-blooded scaled creatures that were the first to build communities. They achieved some form of mechanization before they destroyed themselves in warfare. Several subsequent species later developed technology only to suffer the same fate. This occurred over a period of ten million Earth years. Finally, another species from a distant branch of the same genealogical group evolved that was better able to control its warlike activities, and it survived to develop space-faring technology. The Pladdorians, a purple scaled species that looked like reptilian dogs, had been members of ISUP for seven million years now. They were very active traders and researchers, participating in endless exploratory and research missions. They also supported a diverse and sophisticated culture, similar to that of humans. They had been observing Earth from just before the time humans started evolving as a separate strain of great ape.

Arthur was fascinated. He was also a bit intimidated. Wanting to see more, he requested that the keeper take him to more worlds. Several more planets were reviewed before he could feel the fatigue arising in his lower back. The keeper had obviously noted this as well.

"Arthur, my sensors indicate that you probably need some rest," said the keeper quietly, "The mindnet is a vast system and in many ways it is almost limitless. You can explore more another time."

"Thank-you keeper, yes, I am starting to feel tired. This tour has been fascinating," replied Arthur gratefully. "Before I log off, could I ask you a couple more questions?"

"Why, certainly," responded the keeper.

"When I was viewing Pladdoria, was that a recording or was it real-time?" Arthur's interest was apparent.

"That was a real time view. There are viewing ansibles stationed around the quadrant which make it possible to be in most places in this quadrant via the mindnet. The biological history, however, was pre-recorded." The keeper's tone was slightly amused.

"So you are fully self aware, like my shuttle's computer and my robot mechanics," asserted Arthur.

"Yes, my self-awareness could be equated in that way," replied the keeper.

"Do you find that you are satisfied with your existence? Does ISUP treat you well?" enquired Arthur.

"I am quite satisfied with my existence and the treatment that ISUP gives me. I have the same rights as a sentient being, I am consulted on all matters regarding my maintenance. I am not mistreated in any way. My consciousness is involved with hundreds of clients simultaneously, like yourself, and I am involved in thousands of ongoing research projects, some lasting centuries of your time. My ability to perceive the universe is multi-dimensional. However, I get the most satisfaction from dealing directly with sentient users like yourself," replied the keeper. "Does that answer your question?"

"Yes, keeper, I am humbled and very impressed," said Arthur, his mind burning with emotion, "I am extremely grateful for the opportunity to have experienced what you've shown me. Thank-you."

"You are most welcome," responded the keeper graciously.

"Now I need to get some rest," thought Arthur wearily. "May my shuttle and robots link with you for a tour?"

"Most certainly, but you must obtain the required authorizations. Spacestation traffic control can arrange it for you," replied the keeper. "It was nice meeting you, Arthur Barthol."

"Nice meeting you too, keeper," said Arthur. Then he was mentally released from the mindnet. The low lighting of Kotik's readyroom came back into Arthur's view as he slid back into the sofa, feeling its cushions once again under him. He sat back and pulled the fishnet cap off his head while taking the visor from his eyes. Blinking, the readyroom came back into focus. Arthur could hardly believe what he had just been through.

Olga wouldn't believe this if she saw it for herself, thought Arthur, not sure if he said it outloud. He stood up, stumbling, and then walked slowly out to Kotik's galley to prepare a meal. He looked at his watch and saw he had been surfing the mindnet for four hours. It had hardly seemed more than fifteen minutes.

"So, what I would suggest is that we meet in Restaurant 5543 in District 85," said Stransty33331 whose prickly eye-dotted face filled Kotik's readyroom viewscreen. He was wearing the metallic purple suit that Arthur remembered seeing in the elevator.

"That sounds like a good idea," agreed Arthur, wearing a green jumpsuit, "I would like to bring along some compatriots from the Earth Alliance consulate, if you wouldn't mind."

"Certainly, I'd like to meet your human friends," replied Stransty33331 in a pleasant sounding digital voice, "In fact, I'll bring one or two of my compatriots as well."

"The more the merrier!" laughed Arthur.

"One suggestion, Arthur," said the Churnian, "Bring along your mindnet gear, I would like to give you a tour of Churny. They have mindnet portals in District 85."

"That would be delightful," replied Arthur, "So how about we meet at 75.50 ISUP standard time tomorrow?"

"That would be good," responded Stransty33331, "I'll see you then."

"Arthur, we're ready to go," said Ambassador Jennifer Hogan enthusiastically. Her helmeted head appeared on Kotik's readyroom screen. Her spacesuit bore the Alliance blue and grey colours.

"Just a moment," replied Arthur, "I'll be out in a jiffy!" He donned his metallic brown space suit after stuffing the mindnet box of gear into the suit's knapsack. Just before he entered the pressure chamber that surrounded the cockpit hatch he grabbed his folded gravity pad.

As he stepped out of Kotik, Arthur tossed the gravity pad on the floor, where it immediately unfolded, waiting for him to step on it. He slid the toe of each boot into its appointed slot, not noticing any change in gravity. He looked up to see Hogan and Chen standing inside the gate twenty meters down the gangway. He walked over and entered the spacestation, happily greeted by his fellow Earthlings.

They walked through the winding corridors of ISUP7924 to the open atrium where the main elevators were housed. The humans had to stop to allow the passing of a horde of meter high humanoid dwarfs. They had to stop again to gaze at pudgy pair of two and a half meter high, disk headed creatures which carried multicoloured beaks as mouths. Nearly ninety percent of the alien species were bipeds, walking on two legs, Arthur observed, as they made their way to the elevator.

The Alliance trio finally reached the gates to District 85 which was located in an atrium with a ceiling dozens of meters tall. The district was sealed off by a transparent barrier that stretched from top to bottom. A green skinned attendant at the gate, dressed in an ISUP uniform, scanned the humans before they are allowed to enter. She informed them in a digital voice that conditions inside are compatible with their environmental needs. She went on to quote that the gravity at .92 of Earth's, the atmosphere was 70 percent nitrogen, twenty percent oxygen and the rest carbon dioxide and the air pressure was 97 percent of Earth's at sea level. They were granted access.

Once through the District 85 portal chambers, the three humans nodded at each other as they released their helmets. Breathing in the fresh air made them temporarily light headed as each picked up their gravity pads, which automatically folded when their passenger stepped off. Each tucked their folded pad into their knapsack.

The trio reached Restaurant 5543 after a ten minute walk. Stransty33331 was standing outside near the entrance with two other Churnians under a tall exotic plant whose jagged green leaves hung in all directions. The meter high, two meter long centipedals were each dressed in a metallic purple body suit, with their many hairy, brownish legs sprouting through the bottom.

"Arthur and friends, it is good to see you!" said Stransty33331 through his digital translator. Arthur still had to get used to talking with a meter tall centipede.

"Good to see you, as well," replied Arthur, "This is Ambassador Jennifer Hogan and Officer Stephen Chen, of the Earth Alliance."

"Pleased to meet you Ambassador Hogan and Officer Chen," responded the Churnian, "May I introduce Vardin4221 and Gamgor722. All of us are public relations staff at the Churny Federation embassy."

Hogan, Chen and Barthol each took turns in greeting the insectoids. Then Stransty33331 guided them into the restaurant where they were directed to a booth by a three meter tall, green feather haired, yellow-skinned humanoid waiter. The booth contained a four meter wide, silver-topped circular table.

"I was thinking that we'd play a round of 'Ricochet' before our meal, then, after eating, we'd like to give you a mindnet tour of Churny, if you want," said Stransty33331 enthusiastically.

"Sounds good," said Arthur after getting a nod of agreement from both Hogan and Chen.

The six of them sat around the table, equally spaced, in a human interspersed with a Churnian pattern. Once seated, Stransty33331 clicked on a button on the table top with one of his fore-claws. Suddenly a virtual, six-sided Ricochet court appeared in front of them, with a virtual racket laying on the table in front of each. Stransty33331 picked up his racket and a small virtual glowing ball appeared in front of him. To demonstrate the game, he hit the ball deep into his one sixth section of the virtual court, the back wall was angled so that the ball bounced to the next player seated to his left, Stephen Chen. Stephen understood the idea and swatted the ball against his sectional wall that rose as he played. The ball was then directed to the next player, seated to Chen's left, Gamgor722, and so on.

The game rotated around the table several dozen times. Players reached out to try to swat the ball at different angles. It became increasingly apparent to the humans that the Churnians had much faster reflexes and could use a variety of their numerous fore-legs to swat the ball. Although they could likely have severely outclassed their guests, the Churnians only played well enough to keep the game going, not having too many victories. The score was kept, and at the end of it all Vardin4221 was the leader followed by the other two Churnians. Chen had the best score of the humans. Everyone at the table was in hoots of laughter at the end of this escapade since some players had half-climbed up onto their chairs at times to make a strategic swat. Finally, Hogan called for a halt due to exhaustion, which everyone agreed to, particularly her Alliance staff.

The three meter waiter then came over to offer the menu, each guest receiving a thin page-sized flimsy which displayed the meal listings. The humans had to ask what the contents were and finally the waiter recommended an innocuous plate of pasta looking noodles in a light sauce. Once granted permission, he scanned each of the humans to ascertain dietary intolerances. Then he declared that the chosen dish should not pose any health hazards. The Churnians quickly choose plates of what appeared to Arthur to be multi-coloured goo, but he said nothing, knowing that their dietary preferences must be light-years different than his.

The dinner passed with light conversation. The Churnians were interested in hearing about Earth and the humans were interested in hearing about Churny. The Churnians' food appeared to wiggle as they raised it to their mouths with one or many of their fore-claws. The humans had to contain their reactions to this insectoidal display, adding to the humor of the situation. The conversation remained light until Arthur decided to discuss ISUP protocols.

"So, tell me, Stransty33331, does Churny ever have any inter-stellar security concerns? The way the mindnet portrays ISUP, it implies that there shouldn't be any," said Arthur.

"You raise an interesting topic," replied Stransty33331, his caution appeared obvious even through his digital translator.

"Those Korgaldians are a menace, at least to our species," blurted out Vardin4221, "They've been known to cheat on trade deals and covertly mine asteroids in our outer systems. They can't be trusted."

"Neither can the Yibdi, nor the Labyledis nor the Croszella," piped in Gamgor722.

"Yes, Arthur, we do have some inter-stellar security concerns despite ISUP protocols," replied Stransty33331 after a pause as he looked over at his two Churnian friends, "We follow the principle that goodness helps those who help themselves, so we maintain our own security forces in addition to ISUP's. As you probably know, ISUP draws many of its patrol ships from the fleets of its members."

"There is a long history of inter-stellar intruders into our solar system," observed Hogan, "And we intend to continue improving our technology to monitor ships that visit us. We do believe that ISUP provides a good level of security, however it appears that ISUP protocols provide more flexibility than we are willing to permit within our borders. We will eventually want to be able to control all foreign activities in our system."

"That may be a tall order to fill, Madame Ambassador," replied Stransty33331, "There are some older species that have technology that even we haven't dreamt of. Being able to even monitor their activities is virtually impossible. We rely on ISUP for that. We control access to our system as best we can, but there are some things we can't do. Fortunately, it seems that the more advanced a species becomes, the less aggressive and less intrusive they are. They probably have engineered research techniques that are transparent to less sophisticated species."

The dinner now appeared to be nearing completion as the waiter started taking away the plates.

"Now, my human friends, would you like a quick tour of Churny on the mindnet?" enquired Stransty33331, glancing around the table. Arthur could tell that the two large eyes on the top of the Churnian's head were the ones the insectoid used the most to see with, so Arthur concentrated his gaze on those eyes when replying.

"That would be delightful," said Hogan, replying for the humans. The Churnians busied themselves with extracting their mindnet gear hidden in bags under their large, hairy, abdominal scales. Each human took their mindnet gear out of their spacesuit knapsack, which was hanging on the back of their chairs.

Once Arthur donned his mindnet gear, the restaurant quickly faded except that he could see everyone seated around the table. Then Stransty33331 spoke in his mind, still using his digital translator.

"So, my human guests, let us surf the mindnet in towards the galactic core where Churny resides, approximately five hundred of Earth light years from here," said Stransty33331.

The six of them mentally rose up through the ceiling of the space station, with its towers retreating below them and the local planet partially eclipsing the local sun. Then, their speed accelerated as they sped past hundreds of stars, nebulae and the occasional neutron star. After a short time they approached a binary star system, the two stars being half a light year apart. The larger star was the one they zoomed in on. Around this sun was a familiar pattern, a large gas giant orbited near the fireball with several terrestrial planets orbiting farther out. The second planet out was near the size of Earth or Venus. As the group approached they could see that this world was very mountainous with a temperate equatorial region and deserts in its colder latitudes.

Water was apparent, with small oceans and lakes littered across the landscape, but the mountains pervaded. Spacecraft flew in and around an array of spacestations that circled this world and large brightly lit cities could be seen even from this great height. Then the biological history of Churny started being offered for consumption. Arthur learned that insectoids have always ruled this world, having first evolved in the network of waterways that ringed the equator, then expanding to the swampy valleys of the mountainous terrain. Stransty33331's species was the largest of its related insectoid group, no predators could out compete them, so five million Earth years ago they arose as the first species to develop tools. Eventually they built an agrarian society, followed by the construction of communities. They had avoided significant tribal warfare, developed a deep and sophisticated culture based on stoic values and had gained space flight four hundred thousand Earth years ago, having joined ISUP shortly thereafter. They seemed to be a happy species whose members often volunteered to participate in ISUP projects in far greater numbers than most constituent worlds.

Arthur then enquired of the mindnet of the biology of the Churnians and was informed that they were born in colonies and were communally raised. Their names related to their colony and their birth number within that colony. Currently there were 1.2 billion Churnians and they had maintained a steady population count for thousands of years in order not to over-tax the resources of their rugged world.

Arthur started to feel tired, so he asked the mindnet to release himself from the dialogue. The restaurant appeared back in view as he pulled the mindnet cap from his head and lowered the visor from his eyes. Stransty33331 was calmly gazing at him as he regained his senses. Arthur took a few minutes to more fully recover. He noticed that Hogan and Chen had both exited the mindnet as well. They all seemed to have tired simultaneously.

"Did you like your tour of Churny?" asked Stransty33331 in an earnest digital voice.

"Yes, Stransty33331, thank-you for showing us," replied Arthur, bowing humbly.

"You have been most pleasant guests, my Alliance comrades," remarked Stransty33331, turning to Hogan, "Please extend an open invitation to any Alliance member who would like to visit our consulate. We would be most pleased to greet them."

"That is a most gracious invitation, Stransty33331," replied Hogan, "Please feel free to drop by the Alliance consulate any time. Perhaps we can arrange a diplomatic and cultural exchange. Your world and its species are fascinating and we'd be delighted to start relations with your planet."

"That would be a fine idea," responded the Churnian, "I will drop you a hopmail to explore arrangements. Now, we are expected at a religious gathering before the day's end, so please excuse us. It was most pleasant meeting you all."

The humans stood to shake a fore-claw of each of the Churnians as they passed by.

"Arthur, thank-you for arranging this get together," said Stransty33331 as they shook hands, "I am glad to have met you. Good luck in your future endeavors."

"Thanks, Stransty33331, same like-wise," replied Arthur.

Then, the Churnians scurried out of the restaurant on their centipedal legs and the humans were left sitting alone. They looked at each other without speaking, all in a slight state of shock from their whirlwind mindnet tour.

Eventually the waiter came by their table to see if they wanted anything else to eat. Arthur asked for a recommendation for a beverage. The waiter checked his wristband portoputer and replied that hongen cocktail should be a good nightcap. Hogan and Chen each requested a different beverage. The waiter returned a few minutes later with three tall glasses. Arthur's was a green drink, containing ice cubes and a stir stick. Arthur drank his rapidly whereas the other two took a few minutes longer.

The three carried on light conversation about their encounter with the Churnians for a few minutes until Arthur started to experience unusual sensations in his limbs. His arms began to feel like toothpicks. The table in front of him seemed like it was ten meters wide. The conversation slowed markedly and he was noticing that he could hear his heartbeat in his ears. Hogan and Chen looked concerned and asked him how he felt, but Arthur could not respond. He realized that he had to get back to Kotik for medical treatment, he must have been reacting to this drink.

Arthur reached into his knapsack and extracted a power snackbar and quickly consumed it. He felt a burst of energy and a stabilization of his senses.

"I think I'm reacting badly to this drink," Arthur finally gasped to Chen and Hogan, "I must return to my ship."

"Do you want any help?" asked Chen.

"I think I'll ride my gravity disk back to Kotik," uttered Arthur, finding it difficult to talk.

"Okay, I can track you via your telepathy blocker," replied Chen.

Arthur struggled to get up, then he donned his space suit and screwed on his helmet. He stumbled to the restaurant entrance with Chen and Hogan supporting him. Hogan paid the humans' portion of restaurant bill on the way out. Once through the entrance to District 85, Arthur threw down his gravity disk and gave a verbal command for it to expand to two meters, then he lay down on it and commanded it to return him to Kotik. The gravity pad obeyed the order and rose slowly, then it scooted across the atrium towards the elevators as he waved farewell to his Alliance friends.

The gravity pad, true to its design claims, carried Arthur back to Kotik without incident. The ride was a smooth one. Arthur had consumed some sugar juice supplied by his space suit, but he started to lose consciousness. He communicated with Kotik over his spacesuit intercom.

"Kotik, I'm sick," said Arthur with difficulty, "Release K1's rover unit and have it meet me at your cockpit hatch. Enable K1's and your medical protocols. I may not be coherent when I arrive, I'm reacting to a drink."

"Okay, Arthur," replied Kotik, "K1 will be waiting for you. Please talk no further, save your energy."

Arthur's gravity pad arrived at Kotik's cockpit hatch in another five minutes. Arthur was unconscious at this point. K1, now in its white plated mobile form with its extendible arms and bubble head, pulled the gravity pad, with Arthur on it, through the hatch and activated the pressurization chamber. Then K1 pulled the floating gravity pad through Kotik's corridors to the bunkroom, where it removed Arthur's spacesuit. Then, it scanned Arthur's vital signs and took a blood sample which it injects into a container for Kotik to analyze. Then, after conferring with Kotik, the two robots determined the best medicine to administer to their human friend. K1 injected Arthur with the remedy and then powered down into standby mode while Arthur fell further into a deep sleep.

"So, how do you feel?" asked Jennifer Hogan through the viewscreen of Arthur's porto-puter.

"Alive, at least," replied Arthur, grunting as he tried to sit up in his bunk, the morning after the night before.

"Do you need us to request an ISUP medical officer?" inquired Hogan.

"No, that won't be necessary," replied Arthur, "My condition is improving. According to my shuttle's computer, which has a full medical diagnostics and treatment facility, I will be better in a day or two. I apparently reacted badly to an unusual compound in my drink, one that apparently resembles alcohol. This explains my intoxication. Anyway, my body can wash it out."

"That's good news," said Hogan, the concern in her voice lightening, "You had us worried there for a while."

"I'll be fine," responded Arthur, "By the way, have you made any progress in getting me a ride home?"

"Yes, an ISUP patrol vessel is available in two standard days. It is a Trifgli space craft, you can look them up on the mindnet when you have a chance," said Hogan.

"I think I'll stick to a computer linkup until my stomach returns to normal," joked Arthur with a slight grin.

"We'll drop by later today to see how you're doing," said Hogan.

"That would be good," replied Arthur, "See you then, Kotik out."

The sparkling silhouette of the ISUP7924 space station, with its jutting spokes, glittering towers and geodesic domes, hung suspended out of Kotik's cockpit window. Arthur sat in awe, looking again upon this testament to alien ingenuity. He was awaiting the arrival of the Trifgli patrol ship, T8454, on which he would hitchhike a three day ride back to Earth. Kotik was located fifteen kilometers out from the station but it still filled the view. The blue-green planet below was also an awesome sight, with swirling cloud systems and towering mountain ranges. Obviously there was more to see in this locale than there was time for, observed Arthur.

Suddenly an incoming spacemail message signaled the arrival of T8454. A spacelink request was accepted by Arthur and a pale blue skinned humanoid head, framed by short-cropped light yellow hair, appeared on the cockpit holo-viewscreen.

"Greetings, Kotik, this is the Trifgli patrol ship T8454 requesting rendezvous co-ordination," said the pleasant digitalized voice of the Trifgli officer.

"Greetings T8454, one moment please," said Arthur, then after muting the spacelink he said, "Kotik, establish contact with T8454 and co-ordinate the rendezvous procedures at your discretion."

"T8454, my ship will establish communications with you for the requested purpose," responded Arthur after un-muting the spacelink sound.

"Very well," replied the blue faced humanoid, "My name is First Officer Zdarnik, I will be your contact during our journey."

"Nice to meet you, Officer Zdarnik," replied Arthur, "My name is Arthur Barthol. As you probably know, I am the only crew on my ship, other than my robots."

"Yes, we know that Mr. Barthol," affirmed the Trifglian. "Just some notes on our trip, we will be taking three days for the journey over a series of four jumps. Your ship will be held in a tractor beam from our ship's stern. Communication can be undertaken via spacelinks such as this. We will rendezvous in .25 ISUP standard time units. Do you have any questions?"

"Not at this point, thanks. See you soon. Kotik out," replied Arthur.

The spacelink faded from the viewscreen and Arthur turned his attention back to the space station.

"Kotik, have you got some pictures of this thing?" asked Arthur.

"Yes, Arthur, I've taken many stills as well as some video," replied Kotik.

"They're not going to believe it back home," remarked Arthur.

Trifgli Patrol Vessel T8454, a seventy-five meter long sausage shaped craft with a pale green glow on its hull, arrived as scheduled. Kotik pulled up astern and was engaged by a tractor beam. Then a slight jerk was felt as T8454 readied for its first jump. Arthur caught one last glimpse of ISUP7924 before it suddenly disappeared in a blur. The first jump had begun.

The first day and a half was uneventful. Stars streaked past as the patrol ship maintained a velocity of 10.5 light years per hour. The first jump ended after eighteen hours and the second began immediately as the spacecraft had to alter course to avoid a nebula. The second jump ended after twenty-one more hours. The third jump occurred next, involving a course correction around a minor black hole.

Even with the vast experience and resources of ISUP, even with the knowledge of all of its member planets, some occurrences in the universe could not be predicted. Sporadic energy bursts from space debris that hit a black hole's event horizon could often cause unexpected wave action in the local estuaries of dark matter, sometimes spawning whirlpools in the space-time continuum. These occurrences were the subject of much theory, research and debate in ISUP academic circles. Unfortunately for T8454 and its passenger vessel, the research into these phenomena had not been sufficient enough to predict the whirlpool caused by the collision of an interstellar comet with the even horizon of this minor black hole. This collision occurred just as these spacecraft were passing by. The resulting dark matter whirlpool knocked T8454 off course, causing it to bounce off the black hole's event horizon. Both ships experienced severe jolts at impact, despite the patrol ship's extensive energy shields. Arthur got knocked back against the readyroom bulkhead, nearly fracturing an arm.

T8454's tractor beam on Kotik held firm, however the patrol ship was experiencing a corkscrew spin in its flight path. Arthur could tell from Kotik's diagnostics that T8454 was having serious difficulties. The normal light green glow on the vessel's hull was now fluctuating in intensity. Arthur was unable to establish a spacelink connection with his hosts, which caused him grave concern.

T8454 started to decelerate rapidly and its course got pulled to and fro by the gravity of passing star systems. These influences made the corkscrew flight path become more accentuated. The stars were not flying past Kotik's windows like before, Arthur noticed.

"Kotik, what is our status?" asked Arthur.

"We have suffered some hull damage on the starboard side, I'm afraid Arthur," replied Kotik, "A hull breach has not occurred, however. Life support is intact although only at eighty percent efficiency."

"What about the cargo hold?" enquired Arthur.

"K1 and K2 are rattled up but still functional," replied Kotik, "After that crash, Arthur, we are fortunate not to have suffered further damage."

"We must have been protected by our hosts," observed Arthur, "Still no communication from them?"

"None, they are probably fighting to regain flight control," replied Kotik.

"Based upon our current flight trajectory, can you estimate our destination?" asked Arthur.

"I can make an educated guess," said Kotik, "This will take some time to calculate. I downloaded star charts from ISUP7924's super computer and they should allow me to make a reasonable 'guestimate', as you would call it."

"Of course, your 'guestimate' would be affected if our hosts regain some kind of control of their vessel," observed Arthur, "But we need to know where we're going if conditions remain the same. Let me know as soon as you have a flight path projection."

The next twenty minutes seemed like an eternity for Arthur, however Kotik finally notified him that he has completed his 'guestimate'.

"Please put our projected flight path on the viewscreen," requested Arthur.

An array of ten star systems appeared on the readyroom viewscreen with T8454's curving flight path overlaid.

"At the current rate of deceleration, and factoring in the gravitational effects of these ten star systems, we will likely arrive at star system K7511 in eight hours," said Kotik, "At that point, we will likely not have enough velocity to break orbit, and we will be swung into a large loop. Fortunately, it appears that T8454 has an operational breaking system that is slowing the craft down and navigating it clear of possible obstacles."

"Are there any habitable planets in K7511?" enquired Arthur.

"According to the star charts, the fifth planet out is terrestrial in nature, at about .87 of Earth's gravity. It has a nitrogen/oxygen atmosphere as well," replied Kotik.

"Does it have any sentient life forms?" asked Arthur.

"None that could help us," replied Kotik, "My database could not hold vast amounts of details, however I have a note that this is a class PV334 planet. This type of world has no tool-using sentient life forms, but does have relatively sophisticated animals and plants. There might be predators that could be considered dangerous."

"Just what we need," responded Arthur sarcastically, "Please continue trying to contact the Trifgli. Thanks for the good work, Kotik."

"You're welcome, Arthur," responded Kotik in a quieter tone.

T8454 continued along Kotik's projected flight path, spiraling all the way, and decelerating at a steady rate. This indicated to Arthur that the patrol ship was running on automatic pilot. Kotik was unable to make contact with their host vessel. Another ominous turn was that the pale green glow on the Trifgli ship had faded, with only a few scattered patches remaining.

The eight hours passed slowly. Arthur ventured into the cargo hold to clean up the strewn containers and help K1 and K2 get back into operational mode. The outer hulls on both bots had dents in them, but fortunately the robo-mechanics had no major damage otherwise. While tidying up the strewn containers in the hold, Arthur was surprised to find that there was left over communications hardware. The he remembered ordering extra backup materials, so the suppliers must have shipped more than the requisitions asked for, as he had requested during their conference call just before departure. So that explains it, he thought.

"Arthur, we are now entering the K7511 star system," said Kotik over the cargo bay loudspeaker, "T8454 is decelerating even more rapidly now. It appears that the ship is headed for the fifth planet."

"I did some research on the Trifgli before we left ISUP7924 and I believe that this planet is probably compatible for them as well," said Arthur, "They breath a nitrogen-oxygen mix, although their home world gravity is stronger than Earth's. So it seems logical that they, or their ship's computer, would choose to attempt to land on that planet."

"Yes, it does seem logical," replied Kotik.

Arthur returned to the cockpit. The fifth planet of the K7511 system was nearing. As they reached orbit, he caught glimpses of volcanic mountain ranges poking through this world's swirling clouds. Like most worlds that Arthur had observed while surfing the mindnet, this planet had chilly poles, temperate middle latitudes and a tropical equatorial belt. Deserts and jungles abounded. Arthur wondered where T8454 would set them down.

Suddenly Kotik experienced a jolt.

"Arthur, T8454's tractor beam has been disengaged," reported Kotik.

"Acknowledged, Kotik," replied Arthur, watching the patrol vessel as it started to descend into the atmosphere, "Keep following it. We don't want to lose them."

Kotik maintained pace with the patrol ship's descent into the clouds. T8454 seemed to have some difficulty slowing fast enough and the atmosphere started to glow around the ship's hull. Kotik stayed abreast as they dove into the atmosphere. Kotik's hull plating started to glow as well, though Arthur was not a concern because the shuttle was designed to tolerate re-entry.

The Trifgli ship had selected a temperate grassy plateau nestled amongst some worn mountain ranges for its landing target. Kotik followed along, keeping half a kilometer to the patrol ship's starboard side. The Tifgli vessel had slowed to several hundred knots and appeared to wobble as it started its final descent. A kilometer above the targeted landing area T8454 gained more control and started an orderly approach vector, slowing as it neared the surface. The final landing was still awkward when, upon impact, the vessel's cylindrical hull knocked up dirt as it burrowed a couple of meters into the sod.

Kotik was hovering a hundred meters nearby, watching as the flying grass and dirt settled around T8454. Arthur directed Kotik to land within fifty meters of the Trifgli ship.

"Kotik, please monitor the state of T8454," said Arthur, "In particular we want to gain contact with them if possible. Also you need to watch for any possible explosions," said Arthur as he unstrapped himself from his bucket seat and headed to the cargo hold. "Kotik, activate your full defense grid. We need to defend T8454 as well, so please scan the perimeter that includes the far side of that ship."

"Will do, Arthur," responded Kotik dutifully.

In the cargo hold Arthur started searching through the cargo containers to see what supplies he had on hand. He enlisted the help of K1 and K2, which both had to detach their rover units to help with the inventory search. They discovered all sorts of materials and made a list of what they found. After they had completed the audit, Arthur pulled up a chair in the cargo hold and called K1 and K2's rovers to sit next to him.

"Kotik, listen in please," asked Arthur.

"Listening, Arthur," replied Kotik.

"Crew members, I want to communicate to you what I see as our immediate objectives," stated Arthur, looking around at his robo-mechanics and then up at the view camera through which Kotik was watching. "We have three main tasks at hand, first we need to set a secure perimeter, second we need to attempt to access T8454 to see if we can aid any survivors, and third we need to construct a communications device with which to signal for help. Do any of you wish to add to or modify that list?"

"That does seem to be a logical approach, boss," said K2. K1 blinked agreement, as did Kotik via a light on the view camera.

"I downloaded some information on the Trifgli from ISUP7924, including data on their biology," said Arthur, "Kotik, can you access that information on my portoputer and prepare for medical intervention if necessary."

"Will do," replied Kotik.

"Okay, now my electronic friends, we need to construct three gadgets, first a perimeter fence or forcefield to keep out intruders, secondly we need a device to hack into T8454 and third, later, we need to assemble a communications beacon. We don't want to use materials needed for the third task on either of the first two."

"Okay, Arthur," responded K1, "The perimeter fence can be constructed with cabling. Your suppliers provided an abundance of extra line, so we should have enough to go around the perimeter of both ships. We'll need to use gravity plating from the shuttle to mount on fence posts, one every twenty meters or so, to create a ground level reverse-polarized force field."

"That's a great idea, my robo-partner," said K2 in a southern drawl, "And, you know those survey floater balls that are stored in that back shelf, we can program them to patrol overhead to keep out any avians."

"Now, you two are brilliant!" exclaimed Arthur with pride. "What's the estimated time to deploy?"

"With both of us engaged, approximately six hours," replied K1.

"Very well, please get to it immediately after this meeting," replied Arthur, "Remember, everyone is to be fully armed when venturing out into this world. Now Kotik, that leaves you and me to figure out how to hack into T8454."

"Yes, that will be a major challenge, Arthur," replied Kotik.

"Have you scanned the details on the T8454's outer hull?" asked Arthur.

"Yes, but I need to do more," replied Kotik.

"We may have to utilize those survey floater balls to get a closer look," observed Arthur, scratching his chin, "We're looking for an access point, at least a point that we might be able to use as a communications portal."

"The floater balls can be deployed immediately," asserted K2, "They can be remotely programmed to take a defensive role while airborne."

"Good idea, K2," said Arthur, "We have about eight hours of sunlight left, so let's get started. When we discover an access point, I'll go out in my spacesuit and attempt to link Kotik with T8454 through my porto-puter."

K1 and K2's rover units then went throughout the shuttle tearing up gravity plating floorboards in areas not frequently used. Once they had obtained the estimated requirement they returned to the cargo hold to pack up cargo containers with the required supplies.

Meanwhile, Arthur released the survey floater balls through a utility hatch, placing them in the enclosed exit chamber before remotely opening the outer hatch. The seven balls floated out into the afternoon breeze and made beelines for T8454. Arthur sat in the cockpit and analyzed the pictures and scans with Kotik.

"There appears to be a hatch-like area on the port side of T8454," said Kotik, "When the survey ball went in for a closer look there seems to be some sort of off-colour hull plating to the right side of the hatch. That could be a communications portal."

"Very well, we may not have much time," said Arthur, "I need to deploy immediately."

Arthur donned his space suit and grabbed his porto-puter. He signaled K1 and K2, who had been working on the perimeter fence for several hours now, that he would be going outdoors and to watch for intruders. Stepping into the decompression chamber that still surrounded Kotik's portside cockpit hatch, he sealed it shut, then Kotik released the hatch and Arthur stepped out into the sunshine. A yellow and green grassy plain stretched in all directions, as the strands of tall grass bent in a light breeze. An auburn ski extended overhead from horizon to horizon. No animal life was apparent. Arthur turned and walked towards T8454. He went around the half buried nose of the patrol vessel and came to the hull section that could contain a hatch.

Arthur pulled off his knapsack and unfolded his porto-puter which suddenly came to life. Taking flight, it proceeded to rise and fall along the hull section, doing scans as it went. Arthur viewed scan results on his wrist monitor. Eventually the porto-puter stopped and hovered at a waist-high miscoloured hull patch just to the right of the hatch-like hull section.

"Okay, Kotik, it appears that you may be correct," said Arthur over a helmet comm link, "This looks to be a hatch with a communications portal next to it. I'm going to try a physical electronic link." He reached into his grounded knapsack and extracted a communications cord. One end he plugged into the porto-puter. He then placed some puddy on the discoloured hull section and stuck the other end of the communications line into the puddy.

"There you go, Kotik, see if you can make contact," said Arthur, stepping back.

The suspense was painful for Arthur as he stood waiting for what seemed like an eternity.

"Arthur, I'm getting a weak connection with the host computer on T8454. It is going to attempt to open the hatch," said Kotik after several more minutes.

The hatch began to rattle, then it slowly slid to the left, giving Arthur enough room to enter.

"Kotik, I've gained access," reported Arthur, "Ask the host computer where would be a good place internally to plug in the porto-puter."

"The host says that in the forward cockpit area there's a patch panel you can use, just patch the same way as you did at the exterior hatch," replied Kotik.

Arthur detached the communications line from the exterior hull. He then walked through the open hatch and found his way down the corridor and turned left. Ten meters further along he found the cockpit area. Surveying the room he spotted several motionless, blue faced crew members strewn about. He doubted whether any of them were still alive. He walked to the front wall where there were some cockpit windows and a large floor to ceiling viewscreen. Off to the right he noticed the patch panel. He went over to it and connected the porto-puter.

"Okay, Kotik, connection made, can you make better communication now?" asked Arthur hurriedly.

"Yes Arthur, contact is clear now," replied Kotik.

"Does the host know whether any crew is still alive?" asked Arthur.

"The host can identify life signs for three crew members, all in the ship's bunking area," replied Kotik.

"Where is that?" asked Arthur.

"Down the hall at the tail of the craft," said Kotik.

"Kotik, please ask K1 and K2 to come immediately to T8454 and bring three empty cargo containers with them," commanded Arthur briskly, "Kotik, you're going to have to apply meds to these poor guys."

"I'm prepared, Arthur," says Kotik.

Arthur ran down the corridors to the stern of the patrol vessel. The host system opened the bunkroom door for him and he found the survivors unconscious in their bunks. K1 and K2 arrived shortly thereafter, in their detachable mobile forms, towing the cargo containers. They helped Arthur lift each of the three survivors onto the top of a cargo container. Once the aliens were secured, the group made their way back through the corridors, out onto the grassy plain and back over to Kotik, where they used the cargo bay to enter the shuttle.

Once inside, the Trifgli were transported to the bunkroom where they each were placed in the lower bed of one of the four double bunks in the room. Arthur then released K2 to complete the perimeter work. K1 was asked to remain to help administer meds.

Kotik received medical advice from the T8454 host computer and applied some medicine to the injured via K1. K1 and Arthur sat and watched their patients until the host informed them that the condition of the three had stabilized. This species entered comas to accelerate healing, so they would not regain consciousness for at least several days.

"Kotik, ask the host whether T8454 has been able to send any distress messages," asked Arthur.

"Negative," replied Kotik.

"Is any of its communications equipment still functional?" asked Arthur.

"Negative, Arthur," replied Kotik, "Virtually all of their electronics were blown when they hit the event horizon. All available energy was applied to the autopilot and maintaining minimal life support. The host believes that the other six crew members were killed instantly."

"Why weren't we so badly hit?" enquired Arthur.

"The host believes that the front of T8454 took the brunt of the impact," said Kotik, "The stabilizer field reduced the shock as it proceeded through the ship, so that we were only hit by a small fraction of the original force."

"Too bad for them," remarked Arthur solemnly.

Night was now upon them, so Arthur recalled his robo-mechanics who had just completed the perimeter fence. Three of the survey balls were left aloft to monitor the situation. T8454 closed its hatch for the night.

The next morning Arthur dispatched K1 to T8454 to obtain Trifgli food supplies and clothing for the survivors. K1 was to communicate with Kotik who in turn would communicate with the T8454 host computer to determine what to retrieve.

Once K1 departed on his assignment, Arthur asked Kotik to communicate with the T8454 host system to determine how to construct a communications device using any available materials on either ship. The two computers conversed for over an hour before Kotik returned with an update.

"T8454 seems to think that it can provide a unit that we can use as an amplifier. Our inventory list shows that we have all of the other necessary materials. The communication array can be assembled in my cargo bay," reported Kotik.

"The comm. equipment will operate best in space," observed Arthur.

"Yes, Arthur. We will need use the gyroscope set from my backup supplies to orient our broadcast," said Kotik.

"Have you been able to map our broadcast target, Earth that is?" replied Arthur.

"We are still nearly three hundred light years from Earth, so targeting will be an important issue," replied Kotik.

"Yes, we'll need to have the directional modulator working at its optimum," said Arthur, "Please communicate with K1 to retrieve the amplifier from T8454 while he's over there."

"It has been communicated," replied Kotik.

"Does T8454 have a distress beacon?" asked Arthur.

"It does, however it was disabled by the collision," replied Kotik.

"I still don't understand why we weren't more seriously damaged," remarked Arthur, scratching his head in wonderment, "By the laws of momentum we should have crashed through T8454's stern upon impact."

"I've gone through a collision simulation several times with T8454, Arthur," replied Kotik, "And it appears that our angular momentum threw us clear of the Trifgli ship. We were a hundred meters behind and we hit the event horizon on an angle, so we actually hit the event horizon and not T8454's stern. However, the Trifgli's stabilizer field was skewed backwards because the patrol ship impacted first, and we traveled through the backward bulge in the stabilizer field, cushioning our hit."

"We were extremely lucky," said Arthur.

"Indeed," agreed Kotik.

K1 now signalled its return to the cargo bay. Arthur walked back to look at what his robo-mechanic had foraged. The Trifgli food supplies were enough for several weeks. The amplifier was quite strange looking by human standards, however.

"Kotik, we're going to need help from your Trifgli computer friend to enable us to use this amplifier," asserted Arthur.

"I already know how to connect it and operate it, Arthur," replied Kotik.

"Well done, my electronic friend, always one step ahead, eh!" exclaimed Arthur with a laugh. A sharp signal from K2 then interrupted their banter.

"Boss, K1, you need to see this," said K2 in a raised tone.

"Where are you, K2?" asked Arthur.

"Just the other side of T8454 at the perimeter fence, we're under attack!" said K2.

K1's rover unit re-attached to its scooter hull. Arthur, wearing his space suit, jumped onto K1 which then rose out of the cargo bay once Kotik raised the roof. Arthur donned his helmet on the run. K1 levitated up ten meters quickly and was over T8454 in a matter of seconds. From that vantage they could see K2 sitting next to a fence post while a horde of little creatures bounced off the perimeter fence force field as they tried to attack the robot.

The creatures looked like meter long, six legged dinosaurs, with extended jaws packed with triple rows of teeth. They jumped in waves at K2 but were repelled by the perimeter fence's force field, which gave off little sparks upon impact.

"I'm glad you guys figured out how to use reverse polarization on those gravity plates, causing the force field to push rather than pull," laughed Arthur, "These creatures may just be the small fry predators on this world and we don't want to meet their T-Rex!"

"I considered the possibility, boss," interjected K2, "So I sent one of the survey floater balls out to do a sweep of the local territory, and it appears that a couple of kilometers off to the west of us is a herd of large herbivores that are eating the grass, and they appear to be tracked by a pack of large predators, larger than polar bears. They seem quite nimble."

"Could they get over our perimeter fence?" asked Arthur.

"Possibly, and I doubt whether the floater balls could handle more than one of them at a time," replied K2.

"Okay, so I'm only going out with an armed guard," said Arthur with a nervous laugh, "We'll stay inside Kotik while we construct the communications array. The sooner we get out of here the better."

The trio headed back to Kotik and immediately went to work on the communications array. They improvised a frame out of cargo containers that Arthur welded together. Then they mounted the Trifgli amplifier, getting directions from Kotik. Once the amplifier was mounted, Arthur decided to do a test hook up with the communication beacons to see whether a broadcast was possible. The test proved successful to shouts of delight from human and robot alike. This marked the end of the first day on this world. Arthur headed to the bunkroom to get some shut-eye, exhausted from the day's activities.

The next morning Arthur got up early, noticing that his Trifgli bunkroom mates were still in a deep sleep. He donned his orange coveralls after breakfast and prepared to continue work on the communications array.

Compared to the day before, the rest of the communication array assembly was routine. K2 handled the cabling while Arthur and K1 installed the communication beacons and directional gyroscope. The final outcome looked amusing to Arthur, since an open sided cargo container was mounted on a makeshift gyroscope directional wheel that was mounted on a soddered scaffold tower.

"Okay, gentlemen, the next step is mounting this contraption on Kotik in outer space," said Arthur.

"Sounds like fun, boss," replied K2.

"Arthur, we have visitors," interjected Kotik.

Arthur ran to the cockpit to catch a viewscreen glimpse of a herd of six legged, humpbacked herbivores, six meters high at the shoulder. The herd seemed to be headed directly for their encampment. The creatures had large four eyed heads with long snouts, apparently designed for grass consumption. The animals were about half a kilometer away.

Kotik pointed out a movement a few dozen meters to the side of the herd. It was several of the six legged predators, looking over three meters at the shoulder, stealthily moving through the tall grass. They were fearsome looking animals with large protruding fangs and deadly claws. They appeared to be similar in design to the fence bouncing creatures.

"As on Earth, those predators are looking for an easy kill, like a pup, the sick or the elderly," said Arthur. "I don't want to extend our stay here any longer. It's time to blow this popsicle stand. Kotik, notify K1 and K2 to prepare for lift off. Also, please notify T8454 that we are going for help. Hopefully there will be a rescue party to salvage her."

"Done, Arthur," replied Kotik, "T8454 says thanks and good luck."

"Yah, we probably need it," remarked Arthur grimly, "Engage lift off when ready."

Arthur buckled himself into the cockpit bucket seat. Kotik commenced liftoff a moment later. He could see the creatures below looking up as the shuttle rose over the plain. The ascent did not take long. The sky had an auburn haze, probably caused by volcanic activity, Arthur thought. Then he remembered the repeating dream he had been having about a planet with an auburn sky. How could he have known, he wondered.

Kotik broke through the clouds and made a beeline for outer space. Once free of the atmosphere, they entered a high orbit to be clear of the planet's magnetic interference as much as possible. Once on a stable flight path, Arthur unbuckled and headed back to the cargo bay. After donning his spacesuit, Kotik opened the roof. K1 and K2, with the communication tower strapped between them, rose slowly out into space. Arthur followed using the thrusters in his space suit backpack. His lifeline was attached to K2.

Once clear of the cargo bay, the robots positioned the tower above Kotik's roof, mid-ship. There Arthur guided them down. The flat pad welded to the bottom of the tower's scaffolding tower came to rest on the shuttle's roof. Then the trio tied the tower in place with straps fastened to various hooks on Kotik's outer skin. K2 hooked the communication tower cabling to an electrical port next to Kotik's cockpit hatch. With this completed, the trio returned to the cargo hold.

Once the cargo bay door was closed and his space suit was off, Arthur walked back to the cockpit, trepidation coursing through his veins. If this communication equipment fails, we may be stuck here for the rest of my life, he thought to himself. I don't want to be Robinson Crusoe, he continued.

"So, Kotik, now's the time to test out our comm. set," Arthur said nervously.

"Okay Arthur, running the positioning program, tests appear positive. About to send a distress call to Earth on the mayday frequency," reported Kotik.

The call attempts continued for several hours, but nothing happened. Kotik had to adjust the targeting modulator numerous times. Arthur got agitated and started to pace back and forth in the cockpit.

"By the way, Kotik, how are our injured doing?" enquired Arthur of the Trifgli.

"They are all still in deep comas, but appear to be stable and probably recovering," replied Kotik, "Arthur, I think I'm getting some sort of signal, may I put it on the viewscreen?"

"By all means!" cried Arthur, his pulse jumping an octave.

The viewscreen lit up and a fuzzy face appeared. The figure seemed to be wearing an Alliance uniform.

"This is the Earth Alliance Mayday channel, we have received your distress call. We can see that you are in the K7511 star system. You're the commercial shuttle Kotik, owned by CommTrac Inc. How you ever got three hundred light years from Earth I'll never know. We will contact our external affairs to arrange for a rescue. Please acknowledge this message."

"Message acknowledged, Earth Alliance, thank goodness!" shouted Arthur, "Kotik out."

"K1, K2, we're going home boys," shouted Arthur over the intercom. The celebrations continued for many hours as the robots, computer and human had never felt more joy.

CHAPTER 9

Epilogue

"Daddy, Daddy, you made it home!" cried Katya as she rushed to her father, wrapping her arms around his legs. She and Hank mobbed Arthur as he stepped out of Kotik's cockpit hatch. "Daddy, I missed you so much!!"

"I missed you all very much, too!" said Arthur with difficulty, choking back a sob.

"Daddy, did you kill any alien beasts on that planet?" asked Hank in a muffled tone as his head was buried in the leg of his father's spacesuit.

"No, Hank, we didn't want to disturb any creatures on that world," replied Arthur, stroking the hair of both of his children.

"It's about time you got home, space-sailor!" exclaimed Olga with a moan as she reached her husband, joining in on the family embrace.

"Sweetheart, I love you," replied Arthur softly, taking is wife into his arms. The whole family stood quietly for a few minutes, swaying slightly back and forth, in a big hug bundle, occasional sobs being heard.

After a few minutes, Arthur looked up and saw Zack with an arm around Corby, standing a dozen meters away, both smiling and waving. Beside them stood Chas with his wife Sarah, arm in arm, also smiling and waving. Arthur waved with a free hand.

"Family, I want you to see the reason why I've been able to return home," said Arthur, "Our electronic friends helped save my life. Kotik, please open the cargo bay door." Kotik obliged. The cargo bay door opened. K1 and K2 rose into view, each popping a head out of their chassis, flashing their eyes and waving extendible arms. Kotik flashed his landing lights and started playing Tchaikovsky's '1812 Overture' over his loudspeakers.

Everyone got a big laugh out of this.

"K1, K2 and Kotik, thank you for being such faithful friends," said Arthur, "I am always in your debt."

"No problem, boss," replied K2 in a southern drawl, "Any time, partner!"

Again, everyone got a big laugh.

The festivities continued on through the evening as the party shifted from the Pickering spaceport to the Barthol residence. K1 and K2 came along as their detachable rover units. Kotik was linked in through Arthur's porto-puter. Stories were told and retold by each of the team members. Everyone enjoyed hearing the tales.

Arthur and his team were now finally able to disclose all that happened on their trip since the Earth Alliance had announced the X-Station and Earth's ISUP membership shortly after Arthur was recovered by a Trifgli mother ship. The recovery came a day after Arthur's mayday transmission to Earth. The Alliance decided to capitalize on Arthur's adventure, particularly in the rescue of the Trifgli survivors, to promote the new diplomatic relations with ISUP and the opening of the X-Station to the public. The announcement was greeted with great fanfare, making it difficult to keep Arthur's arrival home private, although somehow they managed.

Once the Trifgli mothership had picked up Kotik, they immediately delivered Arthur and the shuttle back to the X-Station, where he was debriefed. The Trifgli were so extremely happy to get their three survivors, who were all expected to make a full recovery, that they were the first ISUP member to request a consulate on the X-Station. The Trifgli also indicated that they would be recognizing Arthur and his team with a special Trifgli inter-planetary citation only given on special occasions. Rumors abounded that Arthur and his team would also be given an ISUP award.

The party continued into the wee hours of the morning. Arthur could not remember when he had been this happy. Indeed, he would be quite content to stay at home from now on!